Two Suitcases
1929 - 1934

Red Vienna

A Novel

In the dark times,
Will there also be singing?
Bertolt Brecht

Eve Neuhaus

WingSpan Press

Published in the United States and the United Kingdom
by WingSpan Press, Livermore, CA

The WingSpan name, logo and colophon are the trademarks of
WingSpan Publishing.

ISBN 978-1-63683-058-2 (pbk.)
ISBN 978-1-63683-494-8 (hardover)
ISBN 978-1-63683-954-7 (ebook)

Printed in the United States of America

www.wingspanpress.com

Acknowledgements

While the other children in my suburban Philadelphia neighborhood spent their weekends at the pool or Little League, I was frequently the only child at a gathering of Viennese refugees, my parents' social circle, in a Brooklyn or Manhattan apartment. I would set up my dolls on the bookshelves and disappear into their world while lively discussions went on around me in German.

Though German was their first language, my parents didn't speak it at home and I wasn't encouraged to learn it. I was a shy child who didn't ask many questions, so I missed the opportunity to hear the stories that they and their friends might have told about the war years in Europe firsthand. Since my mother and father preferred looking forward to back, I grew up happily unaware of their bravery, creativity, and resilience in the face of unspeakable horrors.

Some thirty years later, while wandering through the library book sale in Ithaca, New York, I found a book by one of the regulars at the Brooklyn gatherings, Ernst Papanek. *Out of the Fire* is a memoir that focuses on Papanek's work getting children out of Austria during the war. As I read it, snippets of conversations I'd overheard as a child began to come back to me. Things began to fall into place. I began the research that informs *Two Suitcases*. It would be another thirty years before I started to write it.

So, first, I have to thank my parents, my aunt, and their circle of friends, for the inspiration and the stories they did tell me that form the basis of the novels. My father's younger cousin, Alice Gingold, who was still alive when I began the project, was a goldmine.

A handful of other children were born into my parents' circle, and I'm grateful to those whose stories I could add into the mix, in particular to Elisabeth Weiss, who gave me invaluable support and advice at the beginning of *Red Vienna*, and especially with the translation of Josef Luitpold's poetry. The stories shared by the others will be woven into later volumes.

To learn about the period in general, I used several published sources consistently: archived articles written at the time by foreign correspondent George Gedye, as well as his book, *Betrayal in Central Europe*, which I inherited from my parents' shelves long ago and read many years later, as well Ernst Papanek's and Bruno Kreisky's memoirs, and Helmut Gruber's more recent non-fiction analysis of the period, also called *Red Vienna*.

Most of all, I'm grateful to my husband, Tom, our children, and to all the dear friends, especially Judy Brown, who read my story in bits and commented on it over the years and years I've taken to get it done, to Yoeke Nagel for her invaluable support and assistance, to Lucy Ackroyd, who painstakingly copyedited the final version, and to my writing group in Cordes-sur-Ciel, France, where Tom and I now live, without whose encouragement I would have given up long ago.

Introduction

R*ed Vienna* is the first of a three volume series, *Two Suitcases*, based on stories my parents told me about their youth in the urban utopia of Vienna between the wars, the period now called Red Vienna, and their subsequent years in France before coming to the United States in 1942. The first volume takes place between 1929 and 1934 when the main characters meet in the Socialist Youth Movement. The second and third volumes cover their flight to Paris in 1938 and then to the south of France in 1940. Though some of the details are true and some of the characters real, *Two Suitcases* is a work of fiction.

Perhaps the greatest relevance of the story of *Red Vienna* lies in the dream of what could have been—a peaceful, egalitarian society built over generations from the ruins of the first world war and decades of poverty caused by early urban industrialization. Instead, fascism crushed the dream of a generation of idealistic young people and their visionary leaders. My parents and their friends who survived the holocaust that followed the fall of Vienna held onto their ideals for the rest of their lives. For most of the world, the experiment is just another piece of lost history. Yet, as the world slowly comes to realize the damage that unbridled capitalism is causing, there's much to be learned from the rise and fall of the brief utopia.

The first book begins when the couple meets in Vienna in 1929 at the height of Red Vienna. Eleven years have passed since the Social Democratic party (SDAP) took power in Austria following the loss of the Austro-Hungarian Empire

1

in the Great War. Without its empire, Austria was left a tiny, land-locked country cut off from its former resources. Vienna, so recently the grand imperial capital of all of central Europe, was impoverished and inundated with refugees looking for work. Workers were needed in the factories, but the living and working conditions were terrible: the squalid tenements couldn't hold all the families, there wasn't enough food to go around, and tuberculosis was everywhere. To ameliorate the housing shortage and near starvation of so many of Vienna's working people, the Social Democratic government embarked on a massive housing program. Much of *Red Vienna* takes place in two of the new municipal housing complexes, Austerlitz-hof, renamed Rabenhof after the war, and Karl-Marx-Hof, still considered the greatest accomplishment of the movement by many.

Utopia is on the horizon: I go two steps, she moves two steps away. I walk ten steps, and the horizon runs ten steps ahead. No matter how much I walk, I'll never reach her. What good is Utopia? That's what: it's good for walking.

Eduardo Galeano

A note about German pronunciation:

A *G* before an *i* is not softened. It is pronounced like the
G in geese.
I is pronounced *ee*.
S is often pronounced like a z in English.

E is at the beginning of words is pronounced like the *A* in
ape, or *ae*,
E at the end of words is pronounced *eh*.
J is pronounced like *Y* in English.

Hence, among the main characters you will find:
Gisi (short for Giselle) - "Geezy"
Emil - "Ae-mil."

Secondary characters include:
Seppe - "Sehpeh"
Helene - "Hell-ane-eh"
Edith - "Ae-dit"
Johannes - "Yohannes"
and Josef - "Yosef"

PART I

The Workers of Vienna

lyrics by Josef Luitpold to the melody of an old folk song

We are the builders of the coming world,
We are the sowers, seed, and field.
We are the reapers of the next reaping.
We are the future and the deed!

So fly, you flaming Red Flag,
Lead and we will follow.
We're the faithful fighters for the future,
We are the workers of Vienna.

Lords of factories, Masters of the world,
Your old dominion soon will end.
We're the army of a new creation
Blasting through your iron shackles.

So fly, you flaming Red Flag.
Lead and we will follow.
We're the faithful fighters for the future,
We are the workers of Vienna.

Though lies will mock and slander circle us
Our spirit will always rise again
Its power smashes through all lies and chains
As we plan the final battle.

So fly, you flaming Red Flag,
Lead and we will follow.

We're the faithful fighters for the future,
We are the workers of Vienna.

CHAPTER 1

THE BIG MEETING

April 9, 1929, 7 pm
Austerlitz-Hof
Vienna 3, Austria

The meeting is about to begin. Though the day is warm enough for the lilacs to have released their rich fragrance, Gisi's hands are freezing. She stands framed in one of the iconic Gothic arches of Austerlitz-hof, the newest of the social housing in complexes in Vienna, and shivers a little. Then, catching the heady scent of the lilac, she breathes it in deeply and smiles.

Spread out in front of her, along tree-lined streets, open plazas, terraced gardens, busy shops, theaters, and schools, in the eclectic architecture so elegantly melding public and private space, lies the future of urban society.

Remembering the time, Gisi sets out again, hurrying along the broad curving street that winds through the complex. She passes under two more grand arches before she reaches the huge doors of the lecture hall where the city-wide Socialist Youth Party, the SAJ, is meeting. She hesitates again, not quite ready to enter the hall, and rubs her hands together to warm them. Her fingers feel so skinny—she must have lost weight again.

Squinting to scan the rapidly-filling room as she steps

into the lecture hall, she sees that a seat near the front is free. She apologizes diffidently to the young people already seated in the row, slides into the empty chair, and tucks her school bag under it. After a few moments, she stands up to look around again, trying her best to seem like she's expecting someone. Could it be that she's the only sixteen-year-old at the meeting? Everyone else looks years older than she, university students or seasoned apprentices, people already earning a living, young adults, not *Gymnasium* students with a whole year to go before taking the *Matura* exam, like her. And so many of them are dressed in brand new blue shirts with red ties, the uniform of the SAJ. She looks down on her own wrinkled and dusty school shirt and skirt and shakes her head at herself. What on earth gave her the idea that she should come to this meeting?

Then she smiles again, remembering. It was Papanek, the man about to address the group. Gisi recalls with pleasure the inspiring talk he gave about the upcoming Second International Socialist Youth Congress at her Red Falcon meeting in March. How thrilling it was! On the other hand, that was just a neighborhood group where she'd known most of the members since they'd joined as seven-year-olds. This is different. Now she's facing the consequence of being so taken in by Papanek's rhetoric that she'd—utterly unnecessarily—volunteered to represent her Red Falcon troop at this enormous meeting.

The overhead lights flash a few times, and Papanek, small and elegant, walks onto the stage. Turning, he casts his sparkling eyes and twinkling smile over the enthusiastic crowd. Everyone in the room smiles back. Papanek raises both his arms, returning the adulation to his audience, taps the microphone, and clears this throat. Gisi begins to forget that she is alone.

"Welcome future leaders! Welcome world-changers! Welcome peace-makers!" the youth leader calls out.

The crowd responds, "Welcome Doctor Papanek!"

"No titles, comrades! Remember, it's time to leave the old cultural hierarchy behind!" The audience stamps their feet enthusiastically. "But none of that now," he continues. "Let's move directly to the business at hand.

"I'm very happy to share with you that well over 50,000 young people will be joining us for our big event in July! How exciting to exchange experiences and ideas with youths from all over the world—in particular around this congress's powerful central theme: THE NEED TO END ALL WAR FOREVER!"

The room thunders with stamping feet. A chant starts: "NO MORE WAR! NO MORE WAR! NO MORE WAR!" Gisi joins in, at first softly, her spirits and voice rising along with the crowd's. "NO MORE WAR! NO MORE WAR!"

As she chants, her eyes travel along the row of wooden seats in front of hers. Suddenly the words stop in her throat. A boy with black curly hair and glasses is looking right at her, trying to meet her eye. She looks down quickly, hoping he hadn't seen her looking back.

When she dares to look up again, the young man—who looks like he's at least seventeen—is still there. He winks at her before turning his attention back to the speaker. Gisi can't repress a small smile.

After a passionate speech about the ever-increasing need for pacifism, Papanek begins to delegate tasks for the upcoming event. "Everyone interested in working for the Cultural Branch, the *Kunststelle*, follow Luitpold to the left, those concerned with housing, go to the meeting room on the right, the tenants group is at the back, and junior union leaders go down the hall." The list is long and the auditorium empties slowly. After few moments' thought, Gisi decides to join the *Kunststelle*.

She follows Luitpold and his group across a spacious courtyard. The circle of four-story apartment houses opening onto the gardens and lawns are hives of activity, alive with color and humanity. Children are everywhere, dashing in and out of the buildings, running along the paths to the playground, calling out to one another other, shrieking with joy as they come down the big slide. Women lean from the windows chatting and laughing. Others work together taking down laundry from a military array of washing lines, some joining in with the children to sing a song Gisi knows from her Red Falcon group. She hums along quietly as she follows the others.

Austerlitz-Hof is the largest and most ambitious of the new municipal housing projects in Vienna, covering more than four city blocks, incorporating several existing city streets and many of the older buildings. Twelve more complexes like it have already been built in Vienna, and many more are rising, each a city within a city. Home to nearly seven thousand people, Austerlitz-hof provides social care, education, and a rich cultural life to its residents. It's Red Vienna's greatest accomplishment, the realization of its utopian socialist dream.

As she passes it, Gisi's eyes travel to the laundry building where she sees a group of women working at washtubs and pulling sheets through wringers. Warm steam billows out of the room and fills the courtyard with the smell of soap. At the workers' complexes, women don't have to do their own laundry. The city pays other women to do the heavy work. It's a good system, providing a much-needed paycheck for the washerwomen's families as well as a great deal of relief for other working women and mothers.

The thought of laundry brings Gisi back to her own world. Laundry is a burden for her mother, Helene, who works full-time as a seamstress as well as doing most of the housework. Gisi tries to help with the laundry but no matter how hard she tries, she can never fold the clothing to her mother's satisfaction. It's a constant source of tension, and in the end, her mother always insists that school is more important anyway, and tells Gisi she should go back to her homework instead of wasting time folding clothes that will only have to be refolded. Yet Helene isn't willing to apply for a place in one of the new housing complexes, despite the fact that her application would be given priority because she's a widow with a daughter and an elderly father to support. She insists that all the complexes are too far away from their neighborhood, at least half an hour by foot and tram, a fact Gisi knows isn't true.

Her mother is so set in her ways; Gisi just can't understand her. Imagine not even considering moving to a place where you could look out of your windows onto park-like gardens instead of a dirty street, where there are at least thirty shops and small businesses right in the complex, as well as beautiful communal kitchens and workshops, kindergartens, doctors' and business offices, and libraries. And lecture halls! Cinemas and theaters! All right in the complex—really, what more could one ask? The housing projects are truly people's palaces. The words of one of party leaders come back to Gisi: the new complexes are "proletarian oases in which sun and light, space and color set the tone of a new form of decent and dignified living." She sighs.

Entering the smaller meeting room, Gisi feels the sunlight pouring through the tall windows and sees it bouncing off the warm colors of the walls. She's glad she came after all.

As she settles into a chair, Josef Luitpold, house poet of the party, steps up onto the dais. Gisi adores his work: epic, passionate poetry, often put to music and sung by choral groups at larger Social Democratic Party (SDAP) meetings.

His anti-war poems, which were written while he was a soldier in the Great War, galvanized the peace movement. Gisi savors the honor of being so close to such a great man as Luitpold; one of the many benefits of being a member of the Social Democratic Youth, she thinks.

As the sonorous voice of the great poet flows over her, she breathes a sigh of satisfaction.

"As the example that surrounds us aptly demonstrates, Socialism has come into its prime," says Luitpold. "Now you, the next generation, must move it forward. The time has come to move beyond discussing ideology! It is time to move beyond analyzing the role of class struggle and philosophizing. Now is the time for real work in the real world. Now, deep and broad cultural change is called for: new kinds of education, new kinds of entertainment, new ways of sharing, of living, and working together. The time has come for us all to step into the great Socialist future we believe in so passionately—the future in which you, the young people sitting before me in this beautiful sun-filled room, will be our leaders!"

When the applause, back-slapping, and foot-stamping stop, Gisi returns her attention to the front of the room and focuses resolutely on Luitpold, who moves on to more practical topics concerning the July event.

Groups for planning the cultural portions of the upcoming gathering are being formed. Though she isn't musical herself, everyone in Gisi's family loves music, so she decides to join the group helping organize the musical interludes. She stands up and makes her way to the round table where the music group is gathering.

On the other side of the room, the curly-haired young man with glasses is sitting next to a tall, dark-haired woman. Surely he noticed her when she stood up.

Chapter 2

Max and Anna

April 9, 1929, 8:00 pm
Austerlitz-Hof

The curly-haired young man, Max Baum, had indeed been watching the girl sitting in the row behind him. When the large group breaks up after Papanek's speech and he knows for certain which direction she is taking, Max turns to his sister Anna and announces that he too will be joining the *Kunststelle*.

"The cultural branch? You?" Anna answers with the disdain that colors most of her communication with her younger brother.

"Maybe I could help choose the art for the exhibits, or I might join the committee organizing the music," he says.

His sister opens her eyes wide. "So you're an art expert now? You know something about music suddenly?" She looks around at their friends sitting nearby. "I'd think you'd be more interested in building the dais or moving chairs around. Why not join the carpentry group? Or the Mr. Fixits, over there?" She points a long finger in the direction of the Buildings and Grounds group.

It's true that Max is not particularly musical, nor is he qualified to judge art of any kind, but he does consider himself creative, and he knows what he wants.

Standing taller, he says, "I did say music, yes. I'm sure I could find a way to be useful there."

Anna raises her eyebrows and says, "What next?" to their group of friends. Then, turning to her best friend Klara, she grimaces. "You can't imagine the crackpot schemes he comes up with. Something new every week. Every day." Klara laughs. She knows the stories.

Most recently, Max has been working hard to convince Anna and their father Seppe that he would rather build furniture than continue the family business of making security gates for windows and doors. Though it happened years earlier, when he was only thirteen, Max hasn't forgiven Seppe for investing the money from the sale of their grandfather's forge in a machine that makes modern folding gates. Max loved his grandfather's powerful forge and the ornate pieces he created. He loved watching the iron rods being bent and curled into unique, beautiful, and useful objects. In his mind, the sale of the forge was a tragedy almost on par with his mother's death.

Max never learned to like the new machine. In addition to being noisy and ugly, it makes the same boring steel curtains over and over. All Seppe and Max have to do is measure the window or door the curtain will protect, cut the steel to the right size, feed it into the machine so the fasteners can be attached, and then install identical gates on one storefront after another. The iron gates Max's grandfather made were both beautiful and consistently the most profitable part of his business—a good gate is a necessary addition to any new building—but to make the same gate over and over? And only gates? Where was the beauty in that? When Max lets his mind wander, he can think of dozens of useful and salable articles he could have made had his father not sold the forge.

But now, at the end of the 1920's, the truth is that making and selling gates, even modern folding gates, hasn't been profitable for years. Money in the city is scarcer than ever, and other than the new municipal housing projects, barely any new buildings are going up. No one needs Seppe and Max's gates. Shop-owners can't afford replace older gates, even though the new steel curtains are far more secure. To make the situation even worse, Seppe doesn't seem to mind the lack of work—he prefers spending his days at the coffee house reading the papers and arguing politics with his friends. Max is often left minding the shop, waiting for almost non-existent customers to come in to ask for estimates that never came to anything. It hadn't taken him long to figure out that he could leave the shop for hours at a time and no one would even notice. A few afternoons each week, he hangs a sign on the door saying "Back in ten minutes" and spends the rest of the day in a coffee house—not his father's—playing chess with his friends.

In the hours when he's in the shop with nothing to do, though, Max spends most of his time thinking of creative ways to revive the dying enterprise. A few weeks earlier he had come up with a new idea he thinks is his best yet.

Since he can't replace the forge—and to be honest, steel does look less old-fashioned than iron—he'll do something different with the new machine. Using the offcuts from jobs he and Seppe did in the past, Max designed and built a chair that can be made out of the steel and hardware used for the gates. It's a modern chair, inspired by the spare and elegant style of the Wiener Werkstatte.

Unfortunately, Max's first prototype doesn't represent his true vision. The steel curtain machine would have to be retooled to do what exactly what he wants it to do, an expensive proposition, but even so, he feels his chair is handsome and distinctive enough to sell well. Unfortunately, Max hasn't been able to convince Seppe of its worth yet, and his sister Anna has barely given it a glance.

Red Vienna

Anna, at nineteen, has little tolerance for her brother's fantastic ideas. Since their mother died six years ago, she's been running the household in addition to continuing her studies at *Gymnasium* and now at University. Anna began caring for her brother and doing most of the housework when she was ten and their mother first fell ill. The situation never pleased her, but she accepted it when she was younger. Always a serious girl, she worked hard and did well at school. Miraculously, Seppe hadn't objected when she announced that she wanted to continue her studies.

"No suitable prospects for marriage in sight?" he'd asked. Anna rolled her eyes. "Well then, you might as well go on to university and make something of yourself." Anna, with all firsts on her *Matura*, applied and was admitted to the psychology program at the University of Vienna, an impressive accomplishment.

She can never understand why Max hadn't made the same choice. He isn't any less clever than she. In fact, when they were in primary school he was always considered the bright one in the family, something she deeply resented at the time. But Max had chosen to leave school to work in the family business when he was twelve, a few years after their mother died. It worked out nicely at first. Seppe was pleased with his son's choice and Max was enthusiastic about being part of the metalworks.

It didn't last, though. The fewer orders came in, the more the two fought. The more they fought, the more Seppe drank. Now both Max and Seppe are spending far too many hours at their respective coffee houses, and Anna is considerably less forgiving. She often complains to her girlfriends that she's given her best years to the useless men in her family.

At the meeting that evening, Anna doesn't have to think about what committee to join. She's been a member of the SAJ for nearly three years and is beginning to take some leadership roles. Though the idea of following and continuing to harass her brother is compelling, she'll join the poetry group as usual—she'd recently become aware that one of her friends in the group has a very interesting older brother. If he turns out to be sufficiently so, she might be convinced to switch to whatever group he's in.

"See you outside when we're done," she calls to Max as she turns and strides away, her long legs showing through the slit at the back of her black, fitted skirt.

⊷⊷⊶⊷⊶⊷

More and more prospective members of the music committee are trying to seat themselves at the round table at the back of the hall. Extra chairs are brought from somewhere, but there still isn't enough space at the table for everyone who wants to join.

"Why don't we go outside?" someone calls out, and the music committee moves into the courtyard where several young men push two big tables together. Max's small wiry body makes it easy for him to slip through the crowd and maneuver himself into the seat on Gisi's right. While she stiffens nervously in her chair, he, the epitome of relaxed confidence, leans forward and folds his arms on the table in front of him. Gisi glances sideways cautiously. He smiles at her and cocks his head once, just enough to make his curls bounce.

Chapter 3

Emil

April 16, 4 pm
a week later
Vienna, First District

In a crowded lecture hall at the University of Vienna, *Herr*Doctor Professor Philipp Furtwangler completes his lecture on number theory. He turns from the blackboard to the students and smiles broadly. Chalk dust glistens in the sun that slants through the high windows, open at the top, letting in the delicate scents of early spring. The students stamp their feet and pound their fists on their desks loudly in appreciation of his lecture.

"Tomorrow, cubic forms," the professor calls out as the noise subsides momentarily. "Read the text and work out the equations." He packs his books into his bag, buttons his houndstooth tweed jacket, and shuffles out of the hall.

Emil Bloch, his best student, extracts his legs one by one from beneath the ancient, built-in wooden desk where he'd been sitting cramped for the last two hours. In an unusually graceful movement for a nineteen-year-old of his height, he stands, flips up the wooden seat behind him with the backs of his knees, and swings his rucksack onto his back.

"Brilliant!" he remarks to his friend Johannes.

"Elegant! So very concise!" says his companion.

"Beautiful!" they say in unison, laughing. He gives his blond companion a friendly slap on the back, and says, "Tomorrow!"

"Same place, same time," Johannes answers as he moves slowly toward the end of the long row of seats with the other students.

Emil, taking advantage of his long legs again, steps over the backs of the row of attached seats in front of him and heads straight for the door. He's the first out. Glancing at his watch, he hurries down the hall toward the main door of the building. Though the lecture ran late, there's still time for him to catch the streetcar he usually takes home. He doesn't like to miss it.

As he bounds down the marble steps of the stately mathematics building toward the tram stop on the Ringstrasse, he fails to see the surly boy sitting near the bottom of the broad staircase with his booted foot ready to shoot out and trip an unwary passerby. The foot shoots out, Emil tips forward and flies toward the marble plaza below.

"Filthy Jew!" snarls the owner of the foot. "People like you don't belong in places like this. Get the hell out of here!"

"*Scheisse!*" cries Emil, just catching himself. Only his natural grace saves him from falling flat on his face on the cold tile. Instead, the trip turns into long leap, and then a run.

"Next time, Christ-killer!" the boy on the stairs calls after him.

Shaken, Emil reaches the streetcar stop just in time to catch the right car. Who was that fellow? Did they know each other from somewhere? Was he in one of Emil's classes? And even if the guy did know him, "Emil" isn't a Jewish name. "Bloch," on the other hand, is a fairly common one. But how would a low-life like that know his name?

Anti-Semitism isn't the official policy of the government

of Vienna or of Austria, but it isn't discouraged either. The tram after the one Emil usually catches stops at a factory as it changes shifts, and even though he doesn't look Jewish, Emil prefers not to deal with the rough workers. The reality is that it's getting harder to be a Jew at the University. Austro-Fascism and Nazism are quickly gaining proponents among the students. For the first time in his life, he's beginning to prefer to be at home or in his own neighborhood in the second district, an area where wealthy assimilated Jews are accepted as part of the fabric.

Once safely seated on the wooden bench at the back of the tram car, Emil allows himself to relax a little and let his mind wander to a more pleasant subject. He's looking forward to his studies tonight. He reviews the details of the day's math lecture with a great deal of pleasure. Furtwangler's theories are fascinating! What I love most about mathematics, he thinks, running a hand through his loose red curls, is the beauty of it.

Then he recalls the tall, dark-haired young woman who was sitting near him as he ate his morning pastry at the coffee house across from the university between lectures that morning. Emil wonders if it was him or the sweet, yeasty bun that induced her to look at him like that. He remembers her dark eyes in particular.

Assuming that she was interested in him rather than the bun he was eating, he had taken the liberty of introducing himself. Her name is Anna Baum, she told him in return, and she is a student of psychology. A striking young woman with a high forehead and prominent cheekbones, she was friendly and intelligent. By the time they parted for their next lectures, he'd agreed to meet her at Austerlitz-Hof that evening for a meeting of the SAJ, the Social Democratic Youth. He could probably finish the work for Furtwangler and his other classes in time to go out, now that there's a reason to.

The Social Democratic Youth, he thinks. He knows relatively little about the group, but why not give it a try?

Emil has never been interested in politics, but almost all the young people of Vienna are members of one youth group or another. He'd left the Jewish Boy Scouts a few years earlier when the leader of his troop became very taken with Zionism. Zionism, the new movement to create a Jewish homeland in Palestine, seems like a cult to him. Only the most conservative and paranoid of his friends are sold on the idea of all the Jews leaving Europe, even though one has to admit that their persecution is increasing everywhere. Nonetheless, leaving a civilized and sophisticated European city like Vienna for the barren North African desert strikes him as a totally absurd idea. However, he hadn't found another youth organization to tempt him since leaving the Scouts.

But maybe, he thinks, if this beautiful Anna is part of the Social Democratic Youth, it will be a good fit for him, too.

CHAPTER 4

GISI AT HOME

April 16, 4 pm
at about the same time
Alsergrund, Vienna, 9th District

Gisi climbs the four flights of stairs to her grandparents' apartment where she and her mother have lived for as long as she can remember. The steps are narrow, steep and dark, and her schoolbag is heavy, but she doesn't care. She takes the stairs two at a time, eager to share the results of her practice exams with her mother and grandfather. She received four firsts, in German, History, Latin, and Chemistry, and a second in Mathematics. Not bad at all!

Gisi's grandmother, her Oma, would have loved hearing those results. It was Oma's relentless push toward excellence that encouraged Gisi to prepare for and apply to *Gymnasium*, the high school for university-bound students, in the first place. Sadly, her grandmother died of tuberculosis the summer before Gisi's first term ended. Gisi misses her Oma's old-fashioned sense of how things were meant to be done, or not done, her clever fingers, and her sense of style right up to the end of her life—as well as her commitment to homework supervision. At the same time, she is thrilled that she and her mother were finally able to move into the tiny bedroom that her grandparents had always shared.

Her grandfather now sleeps on the narrow bed in the living room where her mother used to sleep, and for the first time in Gisi's life, no one at all is sleeping on the settee.

She bursts through the door of the long, narrow apartment and calls out, "Mutti? Opa? I'm home!" Dropping her schoolbag on the floor, she slips off her light jacket, hangs it on a hook in the hallway, and peers through the open arched doorway into the front room. Lately she'd become a little near-sighted, but she hasn't shared this with anyone. She takes off her damp shoes and sets them to dry on the old newspaper laid out in the hallway for that purpose, and hangs her hat over her coat. She can smell something simmering on the stove in the tiny kitchen—it smells like cabbage and potatoes with a tiny piece of beef, not her favorite, but it fails to temper her ebullience.

"I'm in here!" calls her mother from her seat at the sewing machine near the open window. The lengthening days of spring give Helene more time to work, so there's a little bit of extra money. That's why there is any meat at all in the goulash this afternoon. "How did you do?"

Gisi is the pearl produced by her little family's hard work and suffering. She couldn't remember her father, who left for the Great War in 1914 when she was not quite three, and never returned. In his picture on the mantle above the tiled stove he is straight and handsome in his soldier's uniform, yet no one talks about him, and Gisi never knew his family. It's almost as if he never existed. Since her grandfather lost his job as a machinist because he was getting older and slower, Gisi's mother has been supporting the family by making dresses from designers' drawings and then creating patterns so they could be reproduced. It's skilled work and she's very good at it, but women's work isn't well paid.

"I did well!" says Gisi. "Where's Opa? I want him to hear, too."

"Your grandfather thought, since I'm working late tonight, that he should spend some of my hard-earned schillings in the *Gasthaus*. We can only hope it's too early in the day for cards," her mother answers with the trace of acid that always comes into her tone when her father is out with his friends.

"Oh," says Gisi, disappointed. She loves her grandfather and forgives him everything. "Well, I got firsts in four subjects!"

"And what about Mathematics?" asks her mother. "How did you do in Mathematics?"

Gisi hides her dismay. If her grandfather or grandmother were here, they would both appreciate how well she did in the other four subjects. Only her mother would focus on the one area in which she didn't excel—although her grades, second only to Jakob Epstein and David Hertzl, two brilliant Jewish boys in her class, would impress most parents. Gisi knows she is the strongest girl student in her class. Why isn't that enough for her mother?

"A second in mathematics," she says, hiding her feelings. "Only Epstein and Hertzl got firsts." As usual.

"Next time you will surpass them," says her mother, her lips tight.

"I'll try," Gisi says, sighing. Turning away, she continues, "I'm going to start my homework. Call me when the meal is ready or when Opa gets back."

"That will be when the meal is ready, I promise you," replies her mother, carefully feeding the fabric into the sewing machine.

Deflated, Gisi runs one hand along the delicate stripe of paint that divides the darker paint from the lighter in the long hall to the bedroom. The whole family worked together to paint that hall. The color shifts from the blue of early evening at the bottom of the wall to the blazing white of bright sunshine on the ceiling. It took them weeks and many pots of paint to create the delicate gradation that made the narrow dark hallway seem to open to the sky. Gisi was too young to paint then, but she carried the paint pots and helped wash the brushes. She still thinks it is the most beautiful hallway she has ever seen.

"The SAJ meeting is tonight," she calls back to her mother. "If I finish my work now, I'll go straight there after school."

"That's fine," answers her mother. "Just be sure you spend enough time on your math."

Why is it, thought Gisi, that Oma could say the very same thing to me and I would just do it, but when Mutti says it, I feel like tearing up my book and throwing it at her? From the top of the dresser, her Oma's picture—in which she is young and dressed in an intricately detailed fin-de-siecle gown with perfect pin tucks going down the sleeves and front, a sash around her tiny waist held closed with an embroidered broach and a lace mantilla hanging over her shoulders—smiles at her gently.

CHAPTER 5

MAX AND ANNA

April 16, 1929, 5 pm
the same day
Brigittenau, Vienna

Max carries his old bicycle on one shoulder as he steps out of his father's metal shop and closes the heavy wooden door behind him. Leaning the bike against the building next door, he pulls the steel curtains—the first set his father made using the new equipment—over the small window and the door of the shop, slips the padlock in place and locks it. Keys in his rucksack, rucksack on his back, he climbs onto his bike and rides along Würtemberggasse to the canal and then along the canal to Cafe Josef Weiss, where he presumes he will, as usual, find his father.

A few people are sitting at tables in the tentative spring sunlight outside the coffee house, but a quick look inside assures Max that Seppe is relaxing with his usual friends at their *Stammtisch*, their regular table. Max sighs and locks his bike to a lamppost. When he has a son of his own, he vows, he'll work beside him until the work is done and never disappear to the coffee house at the first possible opportunity.

Though the mingled smell of coffee, beer, and tobacco in the dark room is inviting, Max has no intention of sitting down. He has plans of his own, and he doesn't like his father's coffee house. The furniture is dark and heavy, and the round tables are never really clean. The walls, yellow with smoke from years of exposure to pipes, cigars, and cigarettes, are hung with small, conventional and therefore uninteresting paintings of well-known Viennese buildings. Each one has a grimy price tag below it, but as far as Max knows, none has ever sold.

Three of Seppe's friends are seated at his father's table that afternoon. Jakob, who can repair anything, and Dolf, whose fishmonger's shop he'd left in the capable hands of his own son, are reading the newspapers they'd slipped off the wooden rods at the front of the cafe.

When Max comes in, Fredl, an out-of-work cabinetmaker, is saying to Seppe,

"So, I have a new joke. Graf Bobby visits the home of Graf Rudi and begs to borrow a few *groschen.*"

"I've already heard that one," says Dolf from behind his paper.

"And so he shouldn't tell it?" asks Jakob.

"*Ach*, let him tell it," Seppe says. Dolf grunts his grudging consent.

Fredl continues, "So, says Graf Bobby to Graf Rudi, 'Rudi, your indulgence please! My wife is sick again and cannot work,'"—here Fredl sniffs sadly and wipes his eye elaborately—"'my sons are only two and four years old so they cannot work either'"—a second sniff—"'and I, as you can see, am on crutches because a horse kicked me just there.'" Fredl points to his leg and looks up at his audience. "Of course Bobby has a great many more reasons for needing the loan but I won't bother you with them now."

"Thank you," says Dolf drily.

Fredl then assumes Graf Rudi's upright posture. "In the end, Rudi lends Bobby twenty-five *groschen*. 'That's a lot of money! Use it wisely!' says Graf Rudi to Graf Bobby.

"The very same day, Rudi passes by a restaurant and sees Bobby sitting inside eating salmon mayonnaise. 'What!' he says to Bobby. "This is how you use my money? You borrow money from me and then go out and order salmon mayonnaise for yourself?'

"'I really don't understand you,' Bobby grumbles as he puts a hefty piece of salmon into his mouth. 'If I don't have any money, then I *can't* eat salmon mayonnaise, and if I have some money, I *mustn't* eat salmon mayonnaise. Tell me then, Graf Rudi, when *am* I to eat salmon mayonnaise?'"

Everyone at the table laughs, even Dolf.

"Okay," he admits, "I haven't heard it before. But you should change it to roast veal in mushroom sauce."

Seppe objects. "The salmon mayonnaise is fine!"

"Papa," Max interrupts. "Anna says dinner is ready. I'm sure it's neither roast veal nor salmon mayonnaise, but it's ready now." Muttering, Seppe gets up and follows his son to the door.

"Wait!" Seppe turns back to his friends just before the door closes behind them. "One more! Graf Bobby and Graf Rudi take a walk along the Danube. 'Bobby,' says Rudi, 'Didn't you notice that you're wearing one brown shoe and one black shoe?'

'Of course I did!' says Bobby. "They're my favorite! In fact, I have another pair exactly like them at home!'"

Almost all the men in the coffee house laugh.

"That's an old one but a good one!" says Dolf. "Do you know the one that goes..." but Max pulls the door closed firmly, and father and son ride home together along the cobbled street.

at about the same time
Klosterneuberger Strasse 10,
Brigittenau, Vienna

Anna is not feeling happy at all as she cooks supper in the apartment she shares with her father and brother. Though her second year at university is going well, and she has new boys asking her out daily, or perhaps not quite daily, but certainly frequently, somehow the right one hasn't shown up yet. She's nearly twenty, for heaven's sake! All her friends, even Klara, who hasn't a *groschen* to her name and works without pay at her family's nearly-empty grocery, are already engaged—or if they aren't, at least they all know who they'll soon be engaged to. The problem is that she is so tall—the pool of tall-enough young men is limited. Anna tries not to think about it.

As she slices the potatoes for the thick soup, she imagines that she's forming perfect little semolina dumplings and dropping them into clear, fragrant beef broth. Sadly, semolina dumplings require eggs, and even eggs are too expensive to buy more than once in a while.

Then she recalls the elegant young man she met at the bakery that morning, Emil Bloch. She liked his gracious demeanor and handsome face, but it was his head of disheveled red curls that won her over. Perhaps he'll take her up on her invitation and come to the SAJ meeting. One can always hope, she tells herself, though it doesn't make sense to have unrealistic expectations. Anyway, she isn't sure if he is tall enough, and then there is the class issue. Emil obviously comes from another world: he has money for pastry at mid-morning and his clothes looked practically new. No, there isn't any chance of it. He would never come to the meeting, and why should he? He and his ilk are part of the problem the Social Democratic party is trying to solve. The SDAP is the party of the working class, not the bourgeoisie.

Chapter 6

Gisi at the Second Meeting

April 16, 1929, 7 pm
the same day
Austerlitz-Hof, Vienna 3

As she almost always does, Gisi pauses by the door before going into the *Kunststelle* meeting at Austerlitz-Hof. She sets her bag on the floor and bends over to adjust the strap on her shoe. The shoe is fine, though old and a little tight in the toes like all halfway fashionable shoes, but she wants to stop for a minute to see who is already at the meeting. She's early; she likes to be able to see what was happening in a new situation before committing to anything, like where or where not to sit, or whether to take a notebook and pencil from her bag. It doesn't look like there is anyone she knows in the room yet, though she finds it hard to see the people on the other side of the room clearly. She stands up and walks into the smoke-filled room, trying to seem more confident than she feels.

A lively, dark-haired woman in a red dress carrying a camera bag greets her immediately. "Welcome! I'm Edith, and you are? I don't think you've been here before, have you?"

The woman's rapid approach and speedy speech catches Gisi off-guard and she stutters a little. "No, I ... I haven't been here before, but, but I went to the big meeting last week, and *Herr* Doctor..."

"No titles!" says Edith. "We are all the same here, no class differences, no professional differences, so we all go by first names. I'm Edith and you are?"

"I'm Gisi. But I don't think I know the first name of the man who invited me here, just his surname, Papanek."

"And this time, that will do! We all call him Papanek, though surely he does have a first name. Still, he's the exception." She laughs and Gisi finds herself liking the older woman a little more. Edith goes on, smiling, "Why does the exception to the rule show up first? Well, that's the way it is this time! And you are?"

"Gisi, and you are Edith!" Gisi relaxes and smiles too. "Shall I call my mother by her first name?"

"There, you've found the second exception already! Young, but very bright! No, no, we don't use first names for our parents and grandparents. They wouldn't understand, would they? But with everyone else, we are equals." At that moment, Edith spots someone else to greet and leaves Gisi standing alone and a little disappointed at the edge of the rapidly filling room.

❦

Outside the door, Max and Anna are trying to finish their argument before joining the meeting. She's wearing a dark green dress she recently remade, lowering the neckline and bringing the line of the skirt in to curve around her hips before it flares just below the knee. Sewing is not her strength, but it's a necessary skill—she worked hard on the dress and is pleased with the way it turned out.

"What I don't get," she says to her brother between

clenched teeth, "is why you think you have anything to say at all about the way I dress."

"Because I have eyes to see!" Max hisses, keeping his voice low enough that the people passing them won't hear. "You don't see yourself!"

"And you know nothing about fashion!"

"I know what's appropriate!"

"You're such a prude!"

"I am not! You've lost track of what's reasonable!"

"And who wants to be reasonable?" asks a young man with a comical smile and mop of frizzy, reddish blond hair. It is their friend, Hugo Schneider. "Why don't we go in," Hugo suggests. "It's almost time for the meeting to start. Have either of you seen Gert yet?"

"I haven't, no," says Max.

"We're just arriving ourselves," Anna adds. She scans the room for Emil Bloch but he doesn't seem to be there. Max looks across the room, too, hoping to spot Gisi, whom he does see. She's standing near the front of the room, about to sit down.

Without saying goodbye to Anna or Hugo, Max darts across the room and slides into the seat next to Gisi.

She can't help but notice. "You again?" she asks, trying to suppress the smile tugging at her lips.

"*Ja*, it's me again," says he. "I wondered if you'd notice!"

"I think everyone in the room saw you dash across like that. You looked like a little boy, a silly little boy!"

"And that," says Max, looking serious, "is something you should know about me from the start. I am still a little boy at heart, a silly one, and I hope I will never be anything else."

Gisi laughs, charmed. "I hope you aren't looking for a mother to take care of you!" she counters.

Max looks down. "Perhaps I am," he admits. "Since

our mother died, my sister thinks she's my mother and it doesn't always work so well."

His honesty surprises Gisi. "Oh, I'm sure that's not easy. How old is your sister?"

"Two years older than me. She's here." He stands and looks for Anna. "Stand up and you can see her there, the tall one on the other side of the room, with hair and a nose like mine but without glasses. She's talking to a fellow with a big head of light red hair." Gisi stands and looks in the right direction, but can't pick out the couple Max means.

"I can't see them," she says.

"Well, I'll introduce you later and you can decide for yourself if she's a suitable mother for me." They both laugh.

"We'll see," she says. "I'll be the first to tell you if I think she's less than suitable."

Max's lightheartedness reflects the mood of the group now filling the room to capacity. The talk around the couple is suffused with excitement, laughter, and optimism.

A few rows ahead of Max and Gisi, two young men in blue shirts and red ties are sharing their dream of making a film of Bertolt Brecht and Kurt Weill's new work, "*The Three Penny Opera*," which they had gone to Berlin to see recently. They hope to bring the film to cinemas in Vienna.

"We would charge three pennies to see it, of course!"

"Yes! Do that!" responds a boy in a worker's cap, and several of his friends agree. "Cinema should be accessible to everyone!"

"Brecht and Weill's new opera is a fine critique of capitalism. Everybody should see it," says the first young man.

His friend adds, "It's both obvious and very subtle, and the music is magnificent—how it pulls at the heart! I especially liked the songs 'Mack the Knife' and 'Pirate Jenny'!"

"And there's so much truth in it. Real wisdom!"

"Yes, one of my favorite lines is 'First comes a full stomach, and then come ethics'—that's so true! Isn't it Mackie who says that in the second act?" the first boy remembers.

"What? What's that you're saying?" asks the boy in the cap. "Are you saying we should set aside our ethics? Our sense of good and bad? Of right and wrong? I think ethics always should come first!"

"No, no," the first boy said. "You don't understand. Brecht is saying we have to fill people's stomachs before we can expect them to be ethical. Hunger makes people do and say things they would never consider doing if they weren't hungry. So, it's our responsibility to share what we have."

"Well," the boy in the cap says, "I, for one, haven't got enough of anything to give away."

"Then it's me who should share what I have with you," the first boy responds. "Here," he pulls a half-eaten chocolate bar from his pocket, unwraps it, and hands it to the boy in the cap.

"Thanks!" the recipient cries, taking a bite. All the boys around him immediately put their hands out.

"Can I have some?"

"You're giving away chocolate?"

"Mine is gone!" the boy in the blue shirt laughs. "Is your stomach full now?" he asks the boy he gave the chocolate to.

"Not exactly," comes the reply. "I've given most of the chocolate away." He breaks what remains of it into tiny pieces and hands it out.

"There, you see? Even the tiniest piece of chocolate fills the stomach enough to promote generosity!"

Anna and Hugo are sitting together near the door, he still hoping Gert Wald would show up, and she, not expecting Emil to come anymore—it's too late—but watching the door all the same. There was a time when she would have flirted with Hugo under such circumstances, but now he's too enamored of Gert for it to be of any use.

❦

Edith stations herself at the side of the room, opens her camera bag, pulls out the folding tripod and sets it up. She chooses a lens, clicks it onto the camera, and looks through the viewfinder to adjust the lens roughly. When the camera is properly attached to the tripod, she makes a series of further adjustments to focus on Luitpold, who is standing at the front of the room about to call the meeting to order. He signals for everyone to sit down.

"Shh!" people in the audience say to those around them still chatting.

The poet begins with a quick reminder to the group about the need to house the many thousands of socialist youths and their leaders who would be arriving for the *Internationale* in July. There's more, but Gisi is having a hard time concentrating because Max is continually stealing glances at her. She straightens her skirt, adjusts a curl falling over her forehead, and fixes her eyes on the speaker. Luitpold has a kind face, she thinks. She likes these people; she feels at home among them.

The meeting continues with a report on the wildly successful International Women's Day March which was held the previous Sunday.

"Fellow citizens!" Luitpold calls out. "May I now introduce Rosa Jochmann: Rosa!"

The audience stamps their feet loudly as a woman

about ten years older than Gisi walks up to the podium. Once the room is quiet, she smiles and says, "Comrades! I am very happy to announce that last Sunday, April 14, well over 100,000 Austrian women and children took to the streets to demonstrate in favor of birth control!" The audience stamps their feet enthusiastically. Many of the young women at the meeting were organizers of the parades and almost all of them had marched.

When she could be heard again, Rosa goes on. "Nearly a dozen parades, each one led by a brass band, took place all over the city. At the front of every parade, just behind the brass bands, women carried banners declaring our support for women and children, and specifically, our opposition to Paragraph 144."

Anna grins and turns to Hugo. "Paragraph 144 is the law that makes it illegal for doctors to perform operations on expectant mothers if the operation threatens the life of an unborn child. Klara and I were there! We marched together arm in arm. It was a wonderful experience—all of Brigittenau must have been out in the streets watching—or I should say, all of the men of Brigittenau were watching, because all of the women were marching!"

Hugo snorts. "Huh! You think I didn't march? I was there too, marching with my sisters, and Gert, and even Gert's mother!"

Rosa continues, "As we all know, it's high time for Paragraph 144 to go. It's an old law, and one based on an even older church law."

"Separate the state and the church now!" someone calls out to a clamor of support.

"Not so fast!" replies a deep-voiced man in the back. "The power of the SDAP in Austria's national government is entirely dependent on our coalition with the Christian Democrats. Don't scare them off with your atheist rhetoric!"

"It's not about the church!" a woman cries. "It's about women and birth control!"

"But it's the church and its outdated beliefs that are oppressing women!" another one answers.

"Wait! Let's save this discussion for later," Rosa calls out above the other voices. "Now let's have a round of applause for the wonderful members, young and old, of the SAJ and the SDAP, who worked so hard to make this stupendous event happen!" The audience roars with appreciation.

Gisi wishes she could have gone to the march, but her studies kept her at home on Sunday. It takes a lot of studying to stay so close to the top of her class. And anyway, whom would she have gone with? Her cousins Litzi and Theresa were much too conservative for such activities, and her best friend Frieda was studying as hard as she was that Sunday afternoon. It's inspiring, though, to be sitting among so many of the young women who did march.

The meeting ends with everyone standing and singing the *Internationale*.

"I love that song," Gisi says at the end.

"Me, too! There you are: we have something else in common," Max points out happily as he leads her across the room to meet his sister and their friends.

Gisi feels very shy and very young as he introduces her to Anna, who is a good head taller than she, has a sharp eye, and probably a sharp tongue to go with it. Hugo, with his funny smile and bright blue eyes, she likes immediately, and the two brothers whom Max grew up with in Brigittenau, Leo and Felix, seem warm and gentle. The group walks out of the social housing complex together, parting only when the streetcars to their different neighborhoods arrive.

Red Vienna

'To friendship!" they call out to one another as they board.

No one notices Emil, who arrived halfway through the meeting and sat at the back, as he boards the car to the Second District.

CHAPTER 7

SLUKA

April 22, 1929
The University of Vienna, Ringstrasse

Anna is relieved that her afternoon class, Dr. Charlotte Buhler's lecture on Child Development, was over a few minutes early as she hurries down the steps of the Psychology Building. The main courtyard of the University is still relatively empty when she arrives. After experimenting with three different benches, she chooses the second of them and sits down, her book bag on her lap.

Once settled, she looks first to the right, and then to the left, and then to the right again. She intends to keep an eye on the door of the building that Emil is most likely to emerge from, while simultaneously watching the route he's likely to take to the Konditorei where they'd first met, in case she misses him coming out.

She doesn't have to wait long. Emil's mop of wild hair is obvious above the group of students pouring out of the Mathematics building. Apparently he *is* tall enough for her! She can see that he's walking with someone and gesturing animatedly. What next? Should she stand up and go over to him? Or hope that he notices her there on the bench? That's unlikely. By now, the courtyard is crowded and noisy with students leaving their classes.

Anna decides she shouldn't chance sitting, so she stands and makes her way toward Emil and his friend across the current of chattering students, for once glad of her own height. Should she call out to him? She could miss him if she doesn't. She raises her arm, ready to wave, ready to call out his name, when he turns, spots her, and grins. He says something to his companion and makes his own way, cross-current, to where she is.

"Hello!" he says, genuinely glad to see her. "I was hoping we'd run into each other again!"

"I was hoping the same!" she says, pleased. He's very handsome despite the pockmarks on his face. She hadn't noticed them before, but it isn't an uncommon sight. Lots of children get smallpox and most of them die. Emil is lucky to have survived, she thinks. Money and good doctors are always a help.

"Join me for an afternoon snack, will you? I'm going to Sluka for *Jause* today."

"I'd love to," says Anna, letting herself be drawn into the outward flow of the crowd with Emil at her side. She loves going out for *Jause*, the Viennese custom of having coffee and something sweet in the late afternoon, especially when a good-looking guy invites her out. Then it hits her. Sluka! Not at the little bakery across from the University where they'd met! What have I done, she thinks in horror. What kind of a fool am I to have accepted an invitation to go to a place like Sluka?

Konditorei Sluka is one of the best bakeries in the city. It is elegant, luxurious, and outrageously expensive, a place inhabited by tourists, the wealthy, the very wealthy, and even the very, very wealthy. The Empress Elisabeth was a regular customer there. Anna knows where it is, of course—everybody does—but she has never been inside. As a child she'd looked through the window with longing, but more recently she looks in with disdain. Sluka represents everything she's dedicated her life to fighting against: a society starkly divided into rich and poor. Frantically, she searches her mind for a reason to back out now, to decline Emil's offer politely, to walk away and never see him again. It's blatantly obvious that they have nothing in common; they'd never get past their class differences. She's poor. He's rich. That's that.

Before she can come up with an inoffensive excuse, Emil turns to her and asks how she likes her coffee. With cream? One teaspoon of sugar or two? His smile is so endearing that she can't help responding.

By the time they reach the *Konditorei*, Emil and Anna have discussed their mutual enjoyment of good coffee, sweets, and the cinema, as well as establishing the comforting fact that they are both Jewish.

Once they are in the bakery, however, Anna's problems begin. Not only does she feel she's betraying her values by being at Sluka, but she has no money with her, not a *groschen*. She feels terribly uncomfortable. But it smells so wonderful in the bakery! She breathes in the smell of baking and good coffee deeply. Well. Maybe she could allow Emil to pay for a small cup of coffee. But that'll be it. It would be hypocritical of her to let him buy her a luxurious pastry—even though they look so delicious. But really, it's hypocritical for her to be in such a place at all!

A man all in white brings a tray stacked with beautiful rolls from the kitchen. Oh, the smell of it! But she needs to say something to Emil and to go home.

"What would you like?" he asks.

Anna hears her voice saying, "I don't know..." instead of what she meant to say.

"I'll show you your choices. It's my treat."

"No, no, you mustn't," she says. In addition to everything else, it is much too early in their relationship for her to let him buy her anything. He takes her coat and hangs it up next to his on a graceful standing coat tree.

Anna sighs and looks around. A wall of ceiling-high windows draped in diaphanous curtains fills the lavish cafe with light. Glistening chandeliers hang above and matching lamps extend outward from the walls all around. The walls are a deep yellow with gold trim interspersed with panels of pale green framed in rich brown. Ladies in silk and satin and dapper gentlemen sit at marble-topped round tables. The chairs have graceful bent wood backs and legs so delicate that Anna wonders how people dare to sit on them.

Emil takes her arm and leads her to the pastry case. The polished wood and glass case radiates golden light. The ornately decorated pastries and cakes satisfy every sense: moist cream fillings; bright fruit slices shimmering in fruity glazes atop voluminous cakes; crispy puff pastry layers surrounding vanilla scented creams; soft nut tortes, unctuous coffee-colored butter creams topped with crunchy crushed coffee beans.

"So," asks Emil, "What will it be today? Perhaps the *Schillerlocken*, so creamy and crispy—such an excellent contrast? Or the *Indianer* with its opposing flavors, chocolate and vanilla?" He moves slowly along the curved glass case, holding her by the arm with one hand, pointing with the other. "Personally, I love the *Haselnusstorte* because it's so light and creamy. Ah, and there at the back is the notorious *Punschkrapfen*, delectable pastry soaked in our lovely Austrian rum." He wanders on, describing one elaborately decorated pastry after another. "Huh. Personally, I always have a hard time deciding between the *Mohnstrudl*—oh, that delicious filling of ground poppyseed mixed with red plum jam and raisins—and the *Topfengolatsche*, with its wonderfully sour *Topfen* cheese filling. But in the end," he says, arriving at the far end of the case, "I'm usually my boring old self, and I order a *Buchteln*."

Emil's lengthy and enticing ode to pastry gives Anna a moment to think about how she'll handle the situation.

"Emil," she begins, having decided to be straightforward and perfectly honest in her explanation. "Emil," she begins a second time, though she isn't ordinarily a person who loses confidence in what she is saying and needs to begin again. "Emil," she says a third time, "Let me be forthright with you..."

The comfortably round woman behind the counter interrupts her.

"*Gruss Gott, Herr* Bloch, it's good to see you again! I kept these two *Buchteln*, the lightest ones again, especially for you," she says to Emil. "May I wrap them up for you as usual?"

Emil puts a soft hand on Anna's arm to indicate that he will listen to her in a moment, and answers, "Thank you, that's very kind of you, *Frau* Charlotte, but the lady and I will be taking a table today. I'm just recommending my favorites to *Fräulein* Anna."

"Would *Herr* Bloch and the lady like to take that table near the window? We're very crowded at this time of the day and you're fortunate one is free there."

"Certainly, *Frau* Charlotte. The table next to the window would be most excellent."

"Thank you, *Herr* Bloch. It is our pleasure."

Emil smiles at her. "And I thank you too, *Frau* Charlotte. You're most kind. See you the next time!"

He takes Anna by the elbow again and guides her through the maze of silk, satin, and fine wool, past masterpieces in cream, butter, and golden pastry, through fragrant clouds of the scents of coffee and of baking. Forks and spoons clink softly; the conversation is just loud enough to be heard at the tables.

Anna can't help comparing her father's choice of venue for afternoon coffee with Emil's. At least one can be heard here. Nobody is shouting across the room. No one is arguing politics. She'll tell Emil she isn't willing to accept his offer to pay for her pastry when they sit down.

Their table is one of the best in the house. It's at the center of the front window, where the sheer curtains are swept back, and one can watch the people walking by on the *Rathausplatz*. Emil holds Anna's chair out for her.

As she lifts her skirt to seat herself, Anna remembers what she's wearing: a dress so often updated and remade that no one could mistake it for anything else. Everybody in the room will know exactly which social class she belongs to the moment they look at her. Most of them already do.

Well, she thinks, so what. Here's an opportunity to prove that class doesn't matter. She straightens her back and holds her head high. But wait, class does matter! She'll give him a piece of her mind.

"Emil, listen," she begins. "I haven't got any money at all with me. In fact, I have no money. My family has no money. And a pastry would be too rich for me. I can't afford it and I don't feel comfortable letting you pay. I'll have a small cup of coffee, please, and that's all." It wasn't everything she'd meant to say. She'd intended to tell him how much she hates bourgeois places like Sluka and everything they represent.

He cocks his head a little and says, "What? You'll let this excellent opportunity go to waste? You're so often offered your choice of such exceptional pastries?"

"It's not that. Of course not. It's just that we don't know each other at all!" She's ready to tell him how hypocritical she feels in such a setting, and then to point out in some detail the stark contrast between the way her family lives and way Sluka's customers live—but his smile disarms her. "But I do know you," he says, tilting his head a little. "I know that you like your coffee with cream and just a little sugar. And that you enjoy funny films."

A waitress in a crisp black dress and a frilly white apron is already standing next to their table.

"Good afternoon, *Herr* Bloch. Are you ready to order?"

"Indeed I am, *Fräulein* Inge," Emil answers. "For me, the *Buchteln* as usual and a *Verlängerter*, and for the lady, a *Melange*, and the *Schillerlocken*."

"No, no! Just an ordinary coffee for me, please!" Anna objects.

"Be so kind as to bring the *Schillerlocken* as well, *Fräulein* Inge, and do make it the *Melange* for the lady," he says to the waitress. "And that will be all for now."

As the waitress moves on to another table, he lowers his voice and says to Anna, "I'll eat it if you won't. But I certainly hope you won't be so silly."

A few minutes later the voluptuous dessert is sitting in front of Anna. She looks at the roll of delicate, flaky pastry with its dusting of powdered sugar and sprinkling of chopped walnuts, its filling of lightly sweetened whipped cream spilling onto the plate. With a sigh, she picks up her dessert fork. Emil is sipping his coffee and looking across the room.

Tentatively, she presses the long edge of her fork into the pastry. The consequences of cutting into the crispy roll are immediately apparent: the whipped cream will spurt out and spill over the gold rim of the bone china plate and the paper doily below it. She turns the fork and scoops up a little of the cream, and puts it in her mouth. Oh my.

"Good?" he asks.

The cream is such a luxury and she is so hungry for

something sweet, for something special, that she almost has no words. Between bites she manages, "It's wonderful! It reminds me something my grandfather once brought me for my birthday when I was very small."

"In my opinion, it's the best in Vienna. But you've only eaten the cream. You must try the pastry."

By then, Anna had eaten most of the cream and every little bit of walnut from around the crispy roll. Now there is no option but to attack the roll itself. With vigor borne of the pleasure she found in eating the cream, Anna strikes the crisp pastry with her fork.

The result is worse than she anticipated. The remaining cream spews out, flying over the edge of the plate, over the edge of the table, and onto her dress.

Without speaking, Emil hands her his still-perfectly-folded cloth napkin.

Furtively, Anna wipes the errant cream from her dress. "How clumsy I am!" she says, looking down.

Emil is surveying the room again. "I didn't see a thing," he says. "I should have told you to use your fingers." Then he turns back to her and continues more softly, "Do you see that gentleman near the pastry case with the short black beard and pince-nez?"

Anna gives up on her dress and glances in the direction Emil is indicating with his eyes, a quirk of his mouth, and his eyebrows. If she wasn't so embarrassed, she might have found the gesture endearing. She sees the man with the beard.

"That's Viktor von Ephrussi, the banker," Emil says so quietly she can barely hear him. "I can't see who is with him."

Anna's eyes widen. What one earth am I doing here, she wonders. Viktor *von* Ephrussi.

"*Von* Ephrussi, is that what you said? You aren't aware that aristocratic titles like that haven't been used since

1918?" She shakes her head in disbelief. "I'm afraid you aren't much of a candidate for membership in the SAJ."

Emil blushes deeply, one of the difficulties that comes with having red hair.

"You're right, of course," he says. "It slipped off my tongue. It's what my parents call him, you see. As for myself, I never think of the man, but there he is, and he's a great hero in my family."

Anna decides to discontinue her acquaintance with Emil as soon as possible.

The pastry, almost all of its cream gone, is more compliant throughout the rest of their visit to Sluka. Anna carefully refrains from saying anything disparaging about the very, very rich and their role in the woes of society. Emil doesn't point out the identity of any of the other customers. Instead, they speak of films.

As they walk back to the University, they laugh as they share their favorite scenes from Charlie Chaplin's movies: the boxing scene in *City Lights*, the barber scene in *The Barber Shop*, the fight scene in *The Kid*. When they part, Anna hears herself agreeing to meet Emil for a simple coffee in an ordinary cafe in two days' time.

Chapter 8

Arts and Crafts

April 29, 1929
Alsergrund, Vienna

It's late afternoon, and Max and Gisi are sitting outside at a small cafe on Währinger Strasse, not far from Gisi's family apartment. Nearly everyone around them is enjoying a beer, but Max, in reaction to his father's habits, neither smokes nor drinks. The balmy air and the aroma of the blooming chestnut trees and lilac is intoxicating enough. It is already their third meeting. Max doesn't like to waste time once his mind is made up and he hasn't wasted any. Gisi is the girl for him.

She sips her coffee slowly as Max talks about his plan to make Bauhaus-style chairs.

"The chairs I want to make are based on a design by Marcel Breuer. You're familiar with Breuer's work? Are you aware that bicycle handlebars inspired his tubular steel furniture? His work is so clean and spare; in my favorite chair, the frame is all one piece!" He draws the S-shape of a Breuer chair with his hand. His hands looke strong, but they are delicately formed. "It's genius!"

Gisi agrees. "There is so much creativity emerging from the Bauhaus and the Wiener Werkstatte now! I think combining the crafts and the fine arts is the way of the future!"

"These movements are even more than that," says Max. "They apply the values and learnings of the fine arts— aesthetics, appreciation of beauty for its own sake—to *all* of the applied arts, not just the traditional crafts. For example, my chairs, and Breuer's for that matter, aren't made by hand using techniques passed through the generations, but they're entirely in the spirit of the Wiener Werkstatte."

"I'm sure that's true. I'd like to see them. And you're right: using the words 'applied arts' is better than saying craft. *Kraft* is a word like *Volk*." Gisi's face turns serious. "The far right, especially in Germany, claims to own such words now, as well as the traditional customs they're associated with, and they're using them to promote nationalism. It's frightening to see how proudly some men wear *Lederhosen* and other traditional clothing."

"Worse is when they sing songs to the German homeland when they're very drunk on beer," says Max.

Gisi objects. "That's not the same thing at all. I'm talking about the danger of populism; you know, when politicians falsely identify with the common people against the elite— to which they actually belong!"

"And stir up the people's feelings of disenfranchisement..."

"...in order to divide us rather than to bring us together," she finishes his sentence.

Max sips his coffee and smiles at her. "And thus gain power. You're right, of course. Populism and propaganda are excellent tools for promoting authoritarianism and fascism."

"They go hand in hand, don't they? The fascists are sickeningly adept at using propaganda. It's so clever," she says.

'Right, they always begin with something you can't deny—the times are hard, people are oppressed—before they launch into whatever it is they want you to believe."

"And they target people who already feel aggrieved—

for good reason—with carefully designed lies and hand-picked facts meant push them into focusing their anger on a particular group."

"Like the Jews," Max mutters, pushing away a wave of fear.

Gisi doesn't pause. "And people who aren't like them: foreigners, gypsies, homosexuals."

He recovers. "Sadly, it's regular folks, the people, the proletariat, who're most often susceptible to that kind of manipulation."

"Because they're undereducated!" Gisi exclaims. "They were peasants under feudal lords and now they're workers under capitalist bosses. They've been brought up to obey, not to think critically or ask questions."

Max likes her thinking and her fire. He says, "It pays to court the common people, of course. There are many more of them than the very few who hold all the power."

"I hate it when populist politicians pretend to be regular people. They adopt folksy manners and accents even when they come from the richest families and they've been to the best schools. It's disgusting." "They try to find a real working class person to represent their party whenever they can. "

"I know," she says. "Have you noticed there are always a couple of workers—in caps, with dirty faces—standing behind the right-wing politicians when they give speeches?"

Max shakes his head. "How did things turn around like that? We Democratic Socialists, who truly represent the working people, are accused of elitism by the rightist conservatives, who *are* the elite."

Gisi looks thoughtful. "That's true, and it's disturbing. But there's another angle too, maybe an older story. The right has always valued tradition over improvement, right?"

They both laugh. The conversation suits them both; they're comfortable with each other.

He says, "Which makes sense, in a way. The right is conservative, so they want to keep things as they always have been."

And she goes on, "Exactly. We Social Democrats are progressive, so we value creating something new more highly."

She has more to say but Max interrupts. "In any case, I've always hated traditional leather shorts. I would be happy never to wear them again." He likes laughing with her very much.

"Don't be so quick!" she responds, eyes flashing. "Leather shorts are very good for long hikes. The best, in fact. And you never have to wash them! And what's more, to be perfectly honest with you, I think *Dirndls* are very pretty."

"Pretty! Well, there's the problem in a nutshell! Perhaps they are pretty, but are they beautiful?"

"Tell me more about your chairs instead," Gisi says. Max is happy to do that.

"My chairs are made of metal tubing like Breuer's, but while he bends steel tubes into the frames of chairs and tables, I work with the cast-off parts of my father's security gates. Breuer's tubes are round, and mine are flattened." He forms the shape of the round tube and the flattened one with his thumb and forefinger, and peered through each shape at Gisi. He winks at her through the flattened form. "Using the equipment at my father's shop, I can make chairs similar in design to Breuer's, but I can't bend the tubes with the machinery as it is now, so the frame of my chair isn't one piece. Instead, I join the pieces of tubing with the hardware we use in making the security gates."

"Very ingenious!"

"So my chairs have the same essential shape, but they

have square corners," he demonstrates with his hand again, "instead of having Breuer's fluid, rounded corners. But I wouldn't want to make exact copies anyway. My chairs will have my own stamp to them. Inspired by Breuer, but not copied. I'd be happy to take you to the shop to see them sometime."

"I'd like that very much," says Gisi.

"But now, I believe it's time for us to become less formal with one another," Max says with only the slightest question in his tone. Gisi is ready.

"*Prost!*" they say, clinking their coffee cups. Looking into each others' eyes, they intertwine their arms, and each drinks from the other's cup. And then they kiss lightly, laughing.

Chapter 9

The Bummel

June 10, 1929
University of Vienna, Ringstrasse

Anna agrees to meet Emil early Saturday morning on Molker Bastei at what had become their regular coffee place, a cafe neither too shabby for Emil nor too posh for Anna. They hope to get through the courtyard of the University to their lecture halls before the procession of political parties and interest groups who marche through the Main Arcade each Saturday, the *Bummel,* begins in earnest.

Seated at an outdoor table under an awning, Emil takes a long drink of his coffee and says, "As for me, I can't imagine ever wanting to take part in a *Bummel.* The idea simply doesn't move me. It's absurd to put so much time and energy into all that ceremonial claptrap: caps with ribbons, flags, scarves, and big banners, just to march through the arcade every week. I don't think anybody's mind is changed by the slogans on the banners or the fancy uniforms." He puts down his cup, brushes back his curls, and fixes the sardonic twinkle in his eye on Anna. "Why take politics that seriously? And why are politics so very important to you? Tell me, I want to understand. As for myself, I find it hard to agree with any party all the time. My view of how the world works changes daily."

"Your view changes daily? So that's how it is?" Anna is suddenly incensed. "No wonder you have no real understanding of what social democracy means! How shallow can you be?"

Her fury has no effect on him at all. "Who says I am shallow?" he asks.

"You don't understand how a *Bummel* works. It isn't about convincing anybody to join the groups. It's about solidarity. Gathering everyone together and walking down the Arcade builds unity within each group, and it also reminds all the groups that they're part of a larger organization, in this case, the University."

"I don't think I'm shallow," Emil continues his own train of thought. "Each time I change my mind about how the world works, I build a more complex understanding. Or so I like to believe." He lifts his cup to his mouth and sips his coffee.

She cools a bit. "Stop trying to distract me. Of course politics matters. Democracy is built on citizenship. Austria is a Democratic Republic. If we don't take our citizenship seriously and participate in politics, we give up whatever power we have. Being part of a group matters, too. We're always strongest together."

"But you know as well as I do that the *Bummel* is more dangerous every week. It's getting bad just to walk nearby. Those idiot Zionists are actively aggressive toward the Pan-German groups, and particularly toward the Austrian Nazis. They're asking for trouble. It's nuts. I hope your group won't be marching today." Draining the last drop of his coffee, he adds, "We should go."

"My group is marching," she says, standing up taller. "They have to march, Emil. The SDAP still holds Vienna even though the conservatives have taken over the rest of Austria. Imagine how it would look if the youth branch of one of the ruling parties didn't show up because they were afraid?"

"Your people are brave, I have to say that," says Emil as they hurry along. "Or crazy."

"Pacifists don't cause trouble."

"Most of the workers in the SDAP aren't pacifists. You must know that."

Anna does know. "We're working on it," she says.

As they round the corner onto Schreyvogelgasse, the imposing facade of University comes into view. Built in the 1870's in High Renaissance Italian style, the main University building has wide steps, now quickly filling with students, which lead to three massive, ornately carved, arched doorways. The arches lead to the open arcade where the Bummel is held.

Anna and Emil cross the Ringstrasse with care; there are more and more automobiles on the broad roadway. They pause on the median strip to let a tram go by, and Emil takes Anna's arm as they step down and continue.

When they are safe on the plaza in front of the massive University building, Anna glances up at the statue of the golden angel on top of a column near the entrance. She looks at that angel whenever she's there, and when no one is around she sometimes talks to it. They have a relationship, Anna and the golden angel. It is the Angel of Peace.

The crowd moving through the building and out into the Arcade Court is getting denser. Students in uniform with brightly colored ribbons and sashes are everywhere. As he and Anna leave the entrance and are about to cross the interior courtyard, Emil looks down the main Arcade. The *Bummel* will be there in less than an hour, but now the low morning sun is lighting up the long line of busts and statues of scientists, artists, poets, and professors along the terracotta colored walls, and bouncing off the yellow-gold arched ceiling. The blue, white and dark red geometry of the shiny, tiled marble floor adds to the vibrancy of the students' multicolored uniforms, sashes, and ribbons now gathering.

"What a circus!"Emil says to Anna as more and more brightly colored flags and uniformed students fill the space.

"Well, I think it's beautiful!" she answers, catching the defensiveness in her tone as the words leave her lips.

He doesn't seem to notice. "I wonder what all those old men lining the walls think of the *Bummel*," he says.

Anna smiles. Emil often makes her smile, she realizes. "They've been watching it every Saturday for a long time. If they objected, don't you think they would have jumped off their plinths and left the Arcade by now?"

They both laugh then, imagining the noble heads and torsos bouncing and wobbling out of the Arcade.

"We still have a little time before class," Emil says. "Shall we sit by the big fountain?"

A heavy scent of the still-blooming lilac follows them as they pass the tall bushes bursting with flowers and rows of perfectly pruned trees of the formal garden.

As they circle the fountain looking for a place to sit, he asks her, "Did you know that air is drawn into the heating system for the lecture halls of the University through this fountain? It adds just a little moisture to the heated air, making the rooms much more comfortable."

Anna has never considered the heating system, so Emil describes it to her in some detail.

Now, the courtyard is filling rapidly. "We really should go to lecture now if we want to avoid the *Bummel*," she says, though neither of them is ready to part. Next time we should meet earlier, she thinks.

As they wind their way through the groups of uniformed students assembled at every column waiting to hear the signal to fall into line, she looks for the blue shirts and red ties of the SAJ. There they are, already in formation, just beyond the stairs to the library. I should be there, she thinks. Why am I letting this man drag me away from what I know is more important?

At that moment, she notices Hugo's reddish-blond frizz sticking out from under his cap. He, on the other hand, shouldn't be here. Hugo is a student at the Polytechnic and participation in this *Bummel* is restricted to University students. Well, she thinks, who will know?

Between the library and the dividing of the sidewalk where she and Emil pause to say goodbye, some members of the Jewish fraternity Unitas are finishing their final preparations. Skill at fencing and owning a sword is prerequisite to membership in the group, but since swords aren't permitted at the *Bummel*, they're adjusting their sashes and the ribbons on their hats. A few members of the group wear traditional long side-curls and skull caps, but most of the Unitas members dress like ordinary students, except that, for the *Bummel*, they are wearing Unitas ribbons on bowler hats, because Jews are forbidden to wear caps.

Emil is asking Anna, "Will I see you after lecture today?" when someone behind him cries out, "Stop that!"

They turn to see a student with a swastika on his cap, indicating his membership in the far-right *Hakenkreuzler* group, hitting one of the the Unitas boys with a walking stick. The Unitas boy defends himself with his arms but his attacker is fierce.

"Foreigner! Dirty pig!" the *Hakenkreuzler* boy shouts, hitting the Zionist student so hard that he falls. "Get your stinking, hairy, monkey body out of here!" Then he turns and whacks the head of a boy in side curls who's bending over trying to help his fallen friend. He, too, falls to the ground. Two more boys wearing swastikas join in, hitting the Jewish boys with their sticks as they try to get up from the sidewalk. Blood is streaming from the head of the boy with side curls.

A cry rises up from the crowd, "Jews out! All Jews out!" and suddenly the arcade is a madhouse. Dozens of anti-Semitic students rush toward the Jewish group with sticks and then whips in hand. Those trying to intervene for the Jewish students are easily subdued by the growing numbers of students with weapons.

"Police! Help!" people cry, but no police seem to be around. Whips crack, wooden sticks hit bone, and the rhythmic shouting of "ALL JEWS OUT!" grows louder.

An older man, a professor in a tweed jacket, tries to pull one of the attackers off, but he can't stop the boy from grabbing the hair of a shrieking Unitas member and banging his head on the pavement. Another swastika-wearing boy yanks the professor backwards by the collar of his jacket and punches him in the face. Blood is everywhere. Those who want to help are so outnumbered by the attackers that few are brave enough to step forward to defend the victims. The screams are terrifying. Hundreds of students are involved, and the victims are no longer limited to the Unitas group. All Jews are under attack.

Emil and Anna back up against a column, his arm wrapped around her protectively, fervently hoping that no one around them knows they're Jews, when a boy in a blue SAJ shirt runs past them and throws himself into the fray. They see him grab a swinging stick out of the air and break it in two over his knee. Before he can throw the weapon out of harm's way, though, its owner grabs part of it back and goes after the blue-shirted boy.

"Leo!" Anna screams, realizing who the boy is. She pulls herself out of Emil's embrace and rushes forward to save her friend.

"Anna!" cries Emil. "Are you nuts? Get back here!" He sees

her kneeling beside Leo, who is struggling to get up after a sharp blow to the head with the broken stick. The owner of the stick towers above them, about to deliver another blow. Emil plunges forward, grabs him by the arm, pulls the stick out of his hand, and throws it as far as he can above the watching crowd. Then he gives the attacker a good shove with his knee, sending him sprawling onto the grass. Pulling both Anna and Leo to their feet, Emil hustles them out of the riot.

"What on earth were you thinking?" he asks the two of them as they huddle next to the wall. "Look how outnumbered the Jews are! Have you no sense of what is reasonable or safe? Are you both out of your minds?"

Anna dabs the blood from Leo's thick thatch of dark hair. "I can't see the wound," she says. "You have too much hair. But I think we should get you to a doctor. I can't seem to stop the blood from flowing. Look." She holds out her bloody handkerchief.

"Head wounds always bleed a lot," says Emil, handing her his own handkerchief, "But I think you're right. Maybe a stitch or two is needed. Let's go over to the University clinic now, before the line is so long you bleed to death waiting."

Leo doesn't appreciate the dark humor. "I can't go there, anyway. They won't take me. I'm not a student here."

"Then what in God's name are you doing here?"

"Solidarity," answers Leo, touching the warm blood on his hair tentatively. "A few of us from the Polytechnic come over every week to support our comrades here."

Anna bends close to Emil to speak softly. "You yourself said it's not safe for Jews to march, and a large number of SAJ members are Jews—in fact, most of us. You're right that it's dangerous to take part in the *Bummel*, and it's dangerous for us to be here now. Let's see if we can get Leo out safely."

The eyes of the Angel of Peace are sad as she watches them make their way out of the University.

CHAPTER 10

ANNA AND EMIL

July 3, 1929
Molker Bastei, Vienna

Anna doesn't complete her term at University that spring. After the riot, equal numbers of victims and perpetrators are arrested by the suspiciously late-appearing police, and in the end, the Jews receive the harshest punishments. It's enough to convince Anna that she's better off in a kindergarten teacher training program where Jewish women are welcomed. Her professors in the psychology department, especially Dr. Bueller, are sad to see another promising student leave the University, but everyone understands.

"I'm not sure how much longer I'll last here either," says Emil as they sit indoors at their cafe while a gentle rain washes the city outside. "But what else can I do?" He breaks a piece off the *Buchteln* they're sharing and looks up at Anna. "I suppose I could join my father's bank, and naturally that's what he'd like me to do, but I'm damned if I've worked this hard at theoretical mathematics to become an accountant." He frowns with distaste softened by humor.

"That's good to hear, I suppose," answers Anna. "Banks are the enemy."

"Oh, come on, don't be ridiculous!" he says. "The Nazis

are the enemy! Banks have their purpose. Do you want to go back to bartering?"

Anna glares at him. "Of course the Nazis are the enemy, but that's not what I meant and you know it." She puts down her piece of the pastry without biting into it. "Surely you agree that the banks take from the poor and give to the rich—it's obvious enough that the people are starving while the bankers are living in luxury." Her spoon clinks a little too hard against the side of the cup as she stirs her coffee. "The banks hold the power and wealth once held by the monarchy."

"That's my family you're talking about, my dear. Be careful. And, as usual," says Emil, "you're oversimplifying things." He sighs. "There has always been a gap between rich and poor. Of course one wants to decrease it, and that's why banks lend money." He licks the sugar off the top of his piece of the *Buchteln* and then bites slowly into the plum puree-filled pastry, saying "Ah, *Powidl*, how I love you!" After swirling the puree on his tongue for a moment, he swallows it with a satisfied smile.

Anna is simmering. "But such a wide gap between rich and poor isn't moral or necessary!" she goes on. "The SDAP is already proving that we can create a new society in which wealth and power are fairly distributed. Unfortunately, it apparently takes more imagination than you have and more commitment than you are willing to give to understand that." Dark eyes flashing, Anna turns from Emil to her own piece of pastry and attacks it. Between bites, she continues, "Our social housing plan alone puts other cities to shame. In these most difficult of times, when the very existence of the city is threatened, when unemployment has never been higher, and when all private capital was consumed by the last war, the SDAP is building communities in which everyone is supported in every way possible, where a truly new kind of society is being born—and it's all being paid for by taxing the rich."

He considers. "The housing program is impressive. Monumental, in fact. I can't say much for the aesthetic though. Enormous, clumsy blocks going up all over the city. I think German municipal housing is more modern and beautiful."

"But German municipal housing is just housing. Viennese municipal housing is social housing, a complete society providing education, gardening space, medical services, sports and other clubs, and even entertainment— everything that's needed to raise a new generation of well-fed, healthy, thoughtful citizens."

"I'm not so sure the Germans would agree with your glib assessment of their housing program, but I have to admit, the concept of creating an environment to engender a new culture is intriguing. But you know, the Nazis have a similar goal—they also want to to create a race of super-men."

"Yes, I know, a pure race. But their concept, methods, and goals couldn't be more different than ours: they want to create an ideal elite; we want to create an ideal world for everybody." She eats the last of her pastry and wipes her mouth with her napkin. Emil watches her. For a tall woman, she has lovely, small, even teeth. He enjoys making her laugh so that he can see them. Raising one eyebrow, he says,

"I should like to create my own utopia sometime. In my perfect world, everything would be orderly. Life would be like a beautifully choreographed dance. Classic mathematical proportions would govern everything from architecture to the curves of the streets. People would never hurry; they would flow gracefully from one activity to another."

Anna laughs. "It sounds like they would all be ghosts! Or angels. It would certainly be beautiful. You value beauty highly, I see."

"I do," he says. "And you are a very beautiful woman!" He leans across the narrow table and kisses her gently. She laughs again.

"The International Youth Congress is in two weeks, you know. You really should come. There's room for your perspective, and I think you'll find lots that's impressive about the socialist movement."

CHAPTER 11

THE YOUTH CONGRESS BEGINS

July 12, 1929
Vienna

Gisi looks into the old mirror inside the door of the armoire and straightens her red tie for the fifth time. Her new blue shirt looks reasonably good—she'd spent a long time ironing it—but the tie won't hang right. It's always been important to her that everything be just so. After a few more adjustments, the tie is very close to good enough, so she leaves it. Moments later, she's hurrying down the stairs to catch the streetcar to the Heldenplatz for the opening ceremony of the Second International Socialist Youth Congress.

The sight that meets her as she steps out of the tram car is astounding. She's early of course—but the huge plaza in front of the Hofburg Palace is already filling with many thousands of young people. Troops of Red Falcon children, aged seven and up, line up behind their leaders, and throngs of young adults pour in from every direction, each small group following or clustering around a red flag.

The deep red of the all the flags symbolizes International Socialism. At each of the entrances to the courtyard and on the steps of the palace, tall narrow flags flutter from very high poles. Similar tall flags are scattered across the plaza, but the great majority of the thousands and thousands of flags—every participant is carrying one—are simple rectangles of that beautiful red. Each group carries at least one larger flag too, these in varying shapes and sizes with added symbols to identify the particular groups. Whatever the size or shape of the flag, though, whatever the added symbol, every single one of the flags is the same deep red. Gisi finds it so inspiring! As she winds her way through the sea of color and eager young faces, the excited energy of the crowd fills her.

"Hi! You!" she calls out, waving her arm at Leo and Felix when she spots them waving their flags on the steps to the Federal Chancellery where their group planned to gather. The brothers woke at four that morning in order to be in time to stake a claim on that fine spot.

"How amazing!" says Gisi, pulling her own flag out of her backpack. "You chose a place with a perfect view! And it's even better from up here!" she continues, climbing up a few more steps to survey the plaza. Furtively, she slips on her new spectacles.

She looks around, astounded. Never before had such a group gathered.

"You won't be able to stay up there," Leo calls up the stairs to her. "Those steps are reserved for functionaries more important than our little group of event coordinators."

"This is truly remarkable!" says Felix, his eyes never leaving the gathering attendees. "It's like an enormous symphony orchestra!"

Max and Anna arrive next, their flags on their shoulders.

"We just came from the train station," says Max. "So many young people were arriving, and what an amazing welcome we gave them. There was a good-sized brass band and they were playing plenty loud, but our welcoming group was even louder. As the train pulled in, we formed a long, broad wall of young people along the sides of the tracks, and we waved our flags and chanted 'Friendship! Friendship!' You should have seen the eyes of our comrades on the train!"

Next Hugo and Gert come, she, showing off the new spring coat she made for herself out of offcuts from the dressmaker's shop where she works.

"It's beautiful!" exclaims Gisi, seeing the coat for the first time. "You're so creative with so little!" She hopes no one saw her putting her glasses away as she came back down the steps.

"Now, that is truly a compliment!" Gert replies. "Your mother is the queen of creative reuse, Gisi! And you're no slouch yourself."

Gisi smiles and turns a little to model her grey skirt, until recently an old coat, swinging it outward gently to let the red trim show.

"Thanks! I'll never be as good a seamstress as my mother, though," she says. "I can't compete. That's why I worked so hard to get into *Gymnasium*."

"*Ach*, that's not true. You're so smart! You'd be bored being an apprentice like me."

"I don't think I'd mind if I could work for someone in a big shop at the center of the city like you do. But if I wanted to be a seamstress, I'd have to work at home for my mother. I don't think I would be able to stand it!"

"I like your mother very much, but I can understand that perfectly!" Gert laughs.

The group talks animatedly as a large group of musicians files in and seats themselves on the balcony above the palace entrance. Then Anna looks up in surprise.

"Emil!" she cries out. "You came!"

"Would it be okay if I joined you?" asks Emil, as he makes his way up the steps.

"You aren't part of our group," says Hugo. "You really shouldn't..."

"Why not?" Anna's voice cuts sharply across Hugo's. "Everyone, let me introduce my friend from the University, Emil Bloch. Emil, these are my friends in the events coordination group that I told you about. Hugo Schneider, the rude one right there," she glares at Hugo, "and Gert Wald, Leo and Felix Goldfarb, my brother Max whom of course you've already met, and this is Max's girlfriend, Gisi."

Emil subdues his inclination to flinch at her boldness, and nods and smiles at one after another of Anna's friends. "Glad to meet you," he repeats to each of them. Only Gisi notices his discomfort with the way Anna spoke over Hugo; she feels the same way herself.

The orchestra begins with Richard Strauss's *Festival Procession*. By the time they finish and the chorus joins in for *Wake Up* from Wagner's *Meistersinger,* every heart in the massive plaza is joined to every other.

The hope of a new world is gathered. 50,000 young hearts beat as one.

Otto Felix Kanitz, founder of the Red Falcon scouts and head of the progressive Kinderfreunde school, opens the Congress.

"I bow to the Future of Socialism, standing spread before me!" he calls out, and bows.

Karl Seitz, Vienna's mayor since its Socialist experiment began in 1918, speaks next. He begins,

"Youth of the world, I am honored to welcome you all to Red Vienna, the living proof that a City of the People, For the People, is possible!"

Red Vienna

The Dutchman Koos Vorrink, representing the International Socialist Youth Movement, is next. "I am filled with joy to announce that Internationalism, the greatest vision of what humanity can be that has ever been conceived, Internationalism, is alive and flourishing in Vienna today!" he announces.

The orchestra starts to play again but is immediately drowned out by the enormous cheer that rises from the crowd as the beautiful red flag of International Socialism is carried through the crowd and up onto the dais.

❦❧

In the afternoon, most of the young people go into the city in small groups, enjoying guided tours of the social housing complexes as well as of Saint Stephen's Cathedral, the Opera House, and other sights. The event coordination group splits up to do what's necessary to prepare for the twenty-five concerts, readings, celebrations, and performances that will be offered all over the city that evening.

Anna volunteered for a position of considerable responsibility—she's the chairwoman of the group preparing for Josef Luitpold's poetry reading in one of the large meeting rooms at Austerlitz-Hof at eight that evening. It's her intention to be there well before six, but how can she refuse when a group of her friends say they're going to a cafe for a drink and a bite to eat?

One of the young men in the group links arms with Anna and pulls her along. Sensing her hesitation, he turns back and calls out to Emil,

"Hey, red, you can come too!"

Emil is very entertaining on a couple of beers—Anna already knows that. An hour passes in laughter as comical imitations of the morning's speakers are interspersed with a deep appreciation of how the Youth Congress is going so far. The sheer numbers of young people! So many nationalities! The power of the music and the language: "A City of the People, For the People." And how tightly organized it all is—several members of the group around the table take a certain amount of pride in this aspect of the gathering.

But then, oh my! Anna suddenly remembers that she is supposed to be getting ready to set up the room for Luitpold's poetry reading. Hundreds of people will be coming to hear the great poet. She should have left for Austerlitz-Hof at least ten minutes ago.

"I'll find something for you to do, Emil," she calls over her shoulder as she hurries down the street. "But you really should have decided to come when I first invited you. We would have found a good job for you. There are so many things you could have done!" He catches up with her. For a few moments, their long strides match exactly.

"I'm usually good at making myself useful wherever I am. What still needs to be done before the bard declaims?" he asks.

"Just tag along and I'll see when we get there."

They step onto the tram together.

CHAPTER 12

THE SKATERS' WALTZ

July 12, 1929
Austerlitz-Hof, Vienna

G isi arrives at Austerlitz-Hof on foot, even though it took her over half an hour to get there, walking as fast as she could. She heads straight to the large meeting room. The room is unlocked, but no one is there. She walks over and looks up at the clock. It seems that she's more than half an hour early. All the way over, she worried that she'd be late.

The high-ceilinged room is lovely in the late summer afternoon. All the windows are wide open, letting in a pleasant, fresh breeze. The summer sun, still high in the sky, bounces off the shiny wooden floor and fills every corner of the room. At the front, the podium is already set up on the dais. Red banners hang on all the walls. Hundreds of folding chairs are neatly stacked on wheeled carts lined up along the back wall.

The center of the room is gloriously open.

As quietly as possible, almost on tiptoe, Gisi crosses the huge space. She hangs her bag on the back of one of the folding chairs, squints to take in the whole room, and checks the clock one more time, though it's hard to see it.

Then, humming the Skaters Waltz to herself very softly, she begins to glide around the perimeter of the room, sliding on the highly polished floor as if she were skating. After the first few bars of the melody, she realizes how much more smoothly she could glide if she weren't wearing shoes, so she pauses, unbuckles her sandals and slips them off. Looking at the clock one last time, she leaves her shoes near her bag, and begins the waltz again. Her thin stockings slide beautifully.

This time she sings out the familiar melody: dah, dah, dah, dah! Soon she leaves the edge of the room and glides across the center. For the next few minutes, she skates around happily, making big swoops, figure eights, and graceful curves, singing all the time.

Anna and Emil arrive at Austerlitz-Hof together.

"Go ahead of me, Emil, and see if we need to turn on the lights in the large meeting room," says Anna. "I want to stop in at the office first. There's some paperwork I need to take care of."

Emil finds the large meeting room filled with light, and it seems there is a fairy, some lithe little thing in a blue blouse, a pretty skirt, and stocking feet, gliding around the room alone, accompanying herself with a slightly wobbly version of the Skater's Waltz.

He is instantly enchanted. Should he announce his presence? Surely she will see him on one of her turns. In the meantime, he relaxes, leaning against one side of the wide doorway, and takes in the sweetness of this young girl dancing by herself so beautifully.

"Dah, dah, dah, dah!" Gisi sings as she makes a wide turn at the end of the room. Then she sees him. Oh, no! A man is standing in the doorway watching her! Her heart pounds and blood rushes to her face. Someone has seen her being so childish!

Without retrieving her shoes, she heads toward the door to see who it is. When she realizes it's Anna's friend Emil, she's even more upset. He must be at least Anna's age—what, twenty?—and he'd stood there watching her make a fool of herself. When had he come? How long had he stood there watching her, not saying a word? Suddenly she is angry. How extraordinarily rude of him!

Breathing heavily, she marches across the room to where Emil is leaning in the doorway. How dare he look so calm, so nonchalant? His long limbs remind her of a grasshopper.

"What are *you* doing here?" she asks bluntly. She is standing firmly in front of him, hands on her hips, looking up. He is a head and a half taller than she. "Didn't Anna tell you the poetry reading doesn't start for another hour and a half?"

"Anna sent me up here to turn the lights on for that very event," says Emil calmly. "It seems it isn't necessary. At least not yet." He smiles at the fire in her eyes.

Footsteps echo from down the hall.

"Ah, here comes the great leader herself," he says, turning to look down the hall and calling out, "Anna, Gisi is already here!"

"Gisi! Well, good, then there are three of us. That's helpful. Let's start getting the chairs set up," Anna says entering, brisk and businesslike, apparently not noticing Gisi's stocking feet. "There are a lot of them. Emil, you unfold them and set them up and Gisi and I will arrange them."

Gisi gets right to work, grabbing her sandals as discreetly as possible as she passes by the windows and scrambling to put them on while Emil and Anna are talking to each other.

It isn't too long before the rest of Anna's group arrives,

all of the three hundred chairs are set up in neat rows, and coffee is brewing in several enormous samovars.

⊷⊱⊰⊹⊱⊰⊷

Josef Luitpold is reading his work. The poetry is mythic, thrilling, larger than life. It speaks equally to the glory and to the utter humility of humanity. It extolls peace and condemns militarism.

The Red Litany

Work and strength toward a new society, oh humankind!
Knowledge and art as guide of all community!
Life and light for the short years of earthly breath!
Dance and music for the sweet hours of leisure!
Peace and joy to the young, old, men and women!
Freedom and bread to all workers on this green earth!
Life and light and freedom and joy and beauty!
Freedom and bread and love, wisdom and work!
Freedom and bread!

The crowd cheers.

Emil wonders if he is the only one in the room who considers much of the poetry bombastic and grandiose. But he is no fan of Wagner's operas, either.

CHAPTER 13

SOCIAL DEMOCRACY

July 13, 1929
Vienna

It's Papenek's talk on the benefits of International Socialism on the second morning of the Youth Congress that finally wins Emil over to the cause. At Max's invitation, he sits with some of the young men from Max's neighborhood in Brigittenau: Hugo, Leo, Felix, and a fellow called Franz; and listens to Papanek for most of the morning. Not only does the speaker make Democratic Socialism seem reasonable, caring, expedient and attainable—all important values to Emil—but it turns out that Papanek, unlike Josef Luitpold, is not a pacifist, at least not such a pure one. It isn't that he promotes or even approves of militarism, but he does believe in facing up to the dark forces that oppose the dream of a unified socialist world. It makes sense to Emil.

At lunchtime, Gisi, Toni, and Gert join the men at a nearby cafe to share their own experiences of the morning. Edith shows up a little late. She'd been at the tent camps taking photographs.

"Eighteen thousand kids in three thousand tents! You really must find the time to go over to see them," she urges as she pushes her bulky camera bag under her chair and sits down. "Vienna is housing a total of twenty-two thousand

74

young guests for these three days—and they're all having a the time of their lives, from what I can see."

An enthusiastic discussion follows, but Emil is itching to bring up Papanek's stand on fighting. At last he finds an entry point.

"The ideas I'm hearing are all tremendous, but I wonder if you aren't being somewhat naive. Even Papanek believes that the children may not be safe in today's world. We shouldn't imagine that by not thinking about it, we can make the Nazis and their hatred disappear. We may need to fight to protect the children."

"Papanek wouldn't say that! You've completely misunderstood him," Edith responds. She tends to get shrill about such issues. "He abhors war."

"Ah, I think it's you who misunderstand," Emil answers. "He was quite clear. He doesn't rule out the necessity of war under extreme conditions. Were you there at his talk this morning?"

"But the conditions leading up to war need to be mitigated before war becomes necessary," says Hugo.

"That hasn't happened yet," Emil says. "I doubt if it ever will." He pauses and then asks the group, "So, why do you think we have wars?"

"Because we're ruled by an elite group of sociopaths who own the banks that fund both sides of war for profit!" says Edith, slamming her fist on the table.

"The current coalition government isn't in control? I thought we were celebrating the success of Democratic Socialism here," Emil says, one eyebrow raised.

"We are." Edith lets out a breath so derisive it's almost a snort. "But sorry to say, socialism hasn't overcome the forces of capitalistic militarism yet. War is far too profitable for the banks to give up financing it easily. The capitalists just waiting for the right moment to launch a new war."

Emil is about to begin his standard defense of capitalism and banking when Anna preempts him.

"That's why the work we're doing here is so important," she says. "Until now, young people have been raised to think war is inevitable, even romantic, and will always be part of our lives. The generation being raised in the socialist paradigm will know better."

"And they'll refuse to be sacrificed like pawns in a game of chess," says Gert.

"I don't think it's that easy," replies Emil. "Boys like to fight. You can't overcome instinct. Ask Dr. Freud."

"And that's exactly why this afternoon is dedicated to games and sport!" Toni says, hoping to end the discussion. "Are any of you playing in the games?"

"We're both on the all-Vienna football team," Leo replies for himself and his brother. "We're playing against the Czech team at four o'clock. Are you all coming to watch?"

"Of course!" come responses from all around.

The early afternoon is great fun. Not only are games and athletic exhibitions held at every social housing complex and park, but all the municipal swimming pools are open and free of cost. At four o'clock, everyone will be gathering for an enormous stadium on Hohe Warte for the final and biggest of the games and contests. The Brigittenau group plans to meet halfway up the south-facing slope of the stadium in time to watch Leo and Felix play.

3:15 pm

Emil suggests that he and Anna walk through Heiligenstädter Park instead of going directly to the stadium. They'd gone back to Austerlitz-Hof, where Anna is just finishing up some office work.

"We have over three-quarters of an hour to get to the

stadium. We can easily go the long way through the park," he says. "I prefer being out in nature to watching sports anyway. Playing, of course, is another matter."

They walk along the curving paths of the old park, and through the beautifully tended woods and up a gradual slope until a sparkling green vista opens in front of them.

"Look at the sun pouring through the branches of that wonderful old weeping willow," says Emil, pointing. "Weeping willows have always been my favorite tree. They're so graceful. Don't you think that the contrast between the deep green of the leaves and the glistening sunlight at this time of day is extraordinary? What could be more beautiful?"

"What about those flowers in the meadow it's standing in?" asks Anna, sighing with pleasure at the cloud of blue and yellow flowers dancing in the light breeze. "I've always loved this park."

He laughs. "Even though that anti-Semitic, Christian Social mayor, Karl Lueger, built it? Really, Anna, you're unfaithful to your cause."

Anna scoffs. "Huh. There's very little I credit that man with. He pandered to all the worst in people: hatred, anger, and envy."

"Ah, but he got so much done. You really can't deny that he's father of modern Vienna. So many schools, hospitals and parks were built when he was mayor. He brought water the quality of mineral water to the taps in our homes! An extraordinary accomplishment! Before Lueger, Vienna was nothing more than a stuffy, stuck-in-the-past backwater."

Anna stares at him in disbelief. "Lueger was a vulgar, wicked man, Emil. He purposely fostered social discontent and brought out the worst in people. The terrible form of anti-Semitism that's so popular among the lower middle classes today can be traced directly to him."

"But surely he wasn't all bad, Anna. After all, he built the tram system, which, I believe, serves the poor very well."

"The poorest are still walking, believe me, and there are more of them than ever," she counters. She picks up her pace and is soon looking back at him over her shoulder to speak.

Emil is saying, "In addition, it was *Der schöne Karl*, handsome Karl, who brought electricity to the city. Surely you can't deny that that has changed our lives for the better."

"Right, and electricity allowed the factories to stay open later so the workers, already badly underpaid and hungry, could be exploited even further. The owners benefited, not the workers. That's why getting the eight-hour workday into law was one of the first things the Party did when we came into power after the Great War."

He catches up with her. "In fact," he continues, "I would even go so far as to say that the SDAP's pride and joy, the municipal housing system, is completely dependent on Lueger's infrastructure improvements. He put in the gas, for example, and the streetlights. The streets are safe because of him."

But Anna is on a roll. "Emil, stop, for heaven's sake. Lueger wanted to turn the University into a religious institution! He was the worst kind of Catholic. Come on, you must know all this: when he didn't get his way with the University, he limited the number of Jews who could go to there, or even go to *Gymnasium* to prepare. He didn't give the Social Democrats or any Jews jobs in his administration. Only his own narrow-minded Christian Socials."

Emil acts as if he hadn't heard her. "A huge portion of the infrastructure of the city—including this lovely park—and most of the organizations and institutions responsible for the high standard of living we have today were created during Lueger's term in office." He indicates the long row of ornate benches they are passing.

"The high standard of living of the bourgeoisie, you mean. Not the working classes or the poor. And he financed his whole program through borrowing, Emil. He did it all through debt financing. The rich got richer and the poor got poorer." Anna barely notices her surroundings.

"Lueger oversaw the city when most of the big ideas your movement embraces were hatched—and during the incredible blossoming of the arts at the turn of the century: Gustav Klimt, Oskar Kokoschka, and Egon Schiele. The fathers of the modernist design movement of which your dear brother, Max, is so fond: Otto Wagner, Adolf Loos, and Josef Hoffmann."

It's too much for Anna. She's incensed. This man doesn't listen, she thinks angrily. "Emil! You're praising a man who got elected by spreading hatred! And what on earth does the Modernist Movement have to do with Lueger? That burst of creativity at the turn of the century happened in spite of him. It rose *in reaction* to his small-minded rhetoric and style."

"And how about the music? A breath of fresh air—Gustav Mahler, Arnold Schönberg, Alban Berg, Anton Webern..."

"Oh, for god's sake, stop being absurd. I love the arts from that period as much as you do, but that creative energy and innovation had absolutely nothing to do with Lueger's exclusionary, capitalistic politics."

"You could at least credit him with inspiring the revolt that spawned the creativity."

"I don't want to argue anymore," Anna says, her mouth in a firm line. "You're just trying to provoke me again. I get tired of it."

He thinks for a moment. "But you must admit, it's an interesting theory that Lueger's small-mindedness may have caused the modernist movement in a backhand way."

"Leave it, Emil. Forget the past." Anna tries to shake off

her irritation. They are in the middle of the event that she'd been looking forward to for months, and she is letting this painfully bourgeois, ignorant man spoil it for her.

She slows her pace and takes a deep breath. "Let's talk about what's happening this weekend instead of having an argument. Our city is filled with young people from all over the world and it's looking so beautiful. We take all this beauty around us for granted—I won't mention the social services—but imagine how glorious it must seem to young kids coming from other places."

"You're right," he says simply. "We really do have something to be proud of here in Red Vienna."

His turn-around takes her by surprise. She turns and looks at him. Emil confuses her, Emil makes her angry, Emil's politics, or lack of politics to be more precise, can be genuinely horrifying, but still, but still, she thinks she might be beginning to fall in love with him.

The exuberant energy of the crowd watching the games overtakes them as they climb the hill and find their friends.

"Our match is on in fifteen minutes," calls out Hugo as he moves over on the blanket to give them a place to sit down.

CHAPTER 14

THE TORCHLIGHT PROCESSION

the same day, 6pm
Brigittenau

In the early evening, Max hurries up Brigittenauer Lände as Gisi runs along Alserbachstrasse. They'd both gone home for supper, but they plan to meet in the middle of the new Friedensbrücke, the Peace Bridge, which crosses the Donaukanal to connect their two neighborhoods, and then to take the tram back to the Hohe Warte where the torchlight procession will be starting at dusk.

"Oh my, I'm so glad to see you!" Gisi says to Max as they stand at the center of the bridge and watch a coal barge pass slowly beneath it. "My mother isn't happy at all that I'm taking part on the torchlight parade. But I'm sixteen years old! She knows she shouldn't, but she really doesn't want me out after dark. It's so annoying. She worries about everything."

"Which is worse? A family that cares too much or one that cares too little?"

"Is it yours you're talking about?" She pauses, waiting for him to say more. When he doesn't, she goes on. "Too little is worse. Of course." She looks at him sympathetically for a moment. "All the same, my mother's constant concern is hard to take. It's overwhelming. She smothers me. Sometimes it makes me wish I could pack up and move somewhere far away, maybe to another country. To France. To America. Just to get her off my back." Gisi looks out over the canal. "I really shouldn't complain, though. She didn't stop me from coming."

"And that's a very good thing," says Max. He'd been making most of his own decisions about coming and going from home or the business for as long as he can remember. Anna tries to supervise him, but she's out of the apartment herself as much as she can manage. He turns to Gisi. "You know, there's something I've been thinking about and meaning to ask you. Your family, they don't mind you getting so involved with a Jew?"

"Are you kidding me?" she answers, a look of surprise on her face. "My family is completely secular. They have been for generations. I'm not sure if I was ever baptized, so I don't think I'm even on the books as a Catholic. And to be honest, I think the only thing my mother would like better than my dating a Jew would be for me to date a Jewish medical student."

Max laughs softly. "If she were alive, I'm sure my mother would like the same for my sister. But I'm afraid I'll never be a medical student. You'd better tell your mother that. I'm pretty good at fixing things, but not good at all at fixing people."

"And that's perfectly fine with me!"

As they watch the barge make its way down the canal, he takes her hand.

She looks up at him and says, "Isn't this perfect? You and I, from different backgrounds and opposite neighborhoods, standing at the center of the Peace Bridge, the bridge named for the highest value of our movement: Peace!"

"Ooh, very magical," he answers, "I think it's an omen," and they kiss.

An hour later everyone is gathered and the torchlight procession along the canal is beginning. The Brigittenau group lines up in formation, Franz at the front carrying the torch, the others in neat rows behind him.

Gisi chose to march with Max and his group on the east bank of the canal instead of with her old Red Falcon troop from Alsergrund on the west. She feels much older and more sophisticated than her neighborhood friends now that she's so involved with the SAJ, meeting young people from all over the city—and now during the Internationale, from all over the world.

Her heart swells as the brass band begins to play. All around her voices rise up singing the new song, *The Workers of Vienna*. Set to an old folk tune, Luitpold's new lyrics are easy to learn.

She joins her group singing,

> *We are the builders of the coming world!*
> *We are the sowers, seed and field.*

The flames of thousands of torches lap the darkening sky.

Hugo and Leo sing till their lungs almost burst. No one cares that they're off-key.

Streaming along both sides of the canal, 50,000 young people from all over the world joyously commit to creating a kinder, more thoughtful, more equitable world. Hearts in unison, they take responsibility for the future.

Max raises his torch high as the procession moves along the same path he uses every evening to bring his father home from the cafe.

Red Vienna

We are the reapers of the next reaping.

Leo and Felix march arm-in-arm with Gert and Toni, strong, young bodies entwined, strong, young voices harmonizing.

Anna's alto blends perfectly with Emil's bass. Their faces are glowing.

Together they sing,

We are the future and the deed!

Tears are streaming down Gisi's cheeks.

So fly, you flaming Red Flag
Lead and we will follow.
We're the faithful fighters for the future,
We are the workers of Vienna.

Up and down the canal, brass bands play and tens of thousands of young people, torches blazing, sing their hearts out.

Lords of factories, Masters of the world,
Your old dominion soon will end.
We're the army of a new creation
Blasting through your iron shackles.

The two streams of fire coursing along the banks of the Danube canal join into a great river when the young people parading on the east side cross a bridge to join the group on the west and flow together onto the Ringstrasse.

So fly, you flaming Red Flag
Lead and we will follow.

We're the faithful fighters for the future,
We are the workers of Vienna.

Gisi has never felt more complete. Max is filled with fire.

Though lies will mock and slander circle us
Our spirit will always rise again
Its power smashes through all lies and chains
As we plan the final battle.

From one of the bridges, Emil watches the two endless lines of torches flowing along the canal. The sound of the joyful singing washes over him. Surely the whole city can hear the sound of those voices! For the first time in his life, he feels genuine awe.

So fly, you flaming Red Flag
Lead and we will follow.
We're the faithful fighters for the future,
We are the workers of Vienna.

Toni looks over at Leo and Felix, and Hugo and Gert, and knows deep in her heart that they will all be friends forever in a shining and just new world.

So fly, you flaming Red Flag
Lead and we will follow.
We're the faithful fighters for the future,
We are the workers of Vienna.

The Brigittenau group marches on, minds, hearts, and arms entwined.

Anna glances at the University as they pass and thinks of the angel on the pedestal. "See?" she says to it. "Our dream is coming true!"

Red Vienna

Marching twelve across on both sides of the Ringstrasse the crowd is chanting:

"NO MORE WAR!"

"NO MORE WAR!"

"NO MORE WAR!"

Then, as they turn into the plaza, a giant fairy castle, light pouring from every window, rises up in front of them. It's the *Rathaus*, Vienna's City Hall, proud bastion of Democratic Socialism in Europe.

Emil pushes his way through the crowds. He climbs up onto a wall and he sees it too. For the second time that night, his chest swells with awe.

Wave upon wave, young people flood into the massive courtyard. Bands all around strike up the *Internationale*, and 50,000 voices join together to sing:

Arise ye pris'ners of starvation
Arise ye wretched of the earth
For justice thunders condemnation
A better world's in birth!
No more tradition's chains shall bind us
Arise, ye slaves, no more in thrall;
The earth shall rise on new foundations
We have been naught we shall be all.

Refrain:
'Tis the final conflict
Let each stand in his place

The International Union
Shall be the human race.

We want no condescending saviors
To rule us from their judgement hall
We workers ask not for their favors
Let us consult for all.
To make the thief disgorge his booty
To free the spirit from its cell
We must ourselves decide our duty
We must decide and do it well.

The law oppresses us and tricks us,
The wage slave system drains our blood;
The rich are free from obligation,
The laws the poor delude.
Too long we've languished in subjection,
Equality has other laws;
"No rights", says she "without their duties,
No claims on equals without cause."

Behold them seated in their glory
The kings of mine and rail and soil!
What have you read in all their story,
But how they plundered toil?
Fruits of the workers' toil are buried
In strongholds of the idle few
In working for their restitution
The men will only claim their due.

We toilers from all fields united
Join hand in hand with all who work;
The earth belongs to us, the workers,
No room here for the shirk.

Red Vienna

How many on our flesh have fattened!
But if the noisome birds of prey
Shall vanish from the sky some morning
The blessed sunlight then will stay.

(Adaptation of Charles H. Kerr translation from the original, for The
IWW Songbook (34th Edition).

"Max and I are both completely in love with the ideals of
the *Internationale!*" exults Gisi, as she, Gert, and Toni board
the tram half an hour later. She smiles broadly and hugs
herself. "Who would have thought one could love an idea so
passionately!"

"An idea, huh!" says Gert, and she and Toni break into
rich laughter.

CHAPTER 15

A LENS THROUGH WHICH TO SEE LIFE

July 14, 1929
a cafe in Vienna
the following morning

"Socialism is more than a political conviction," says Hugo. "It's a lens through which you see all of life, a complete worldview. In brief, instead of focusing on the individual, it focuses on the whole of society." He takes off his glasses and holds them to the light, scrutinizing the lenses.

Leo laughs. "Everything is a lens to you since you began learning to grind them, Hugo!" It's Sunday morning and the Brigittenau group has come together for coffee before going to the final rally of the Youth Congress at the *Rathaus*platz.

"Don't make fun of him," says Toni. "Grinding lenses is a very good skill."

"And it'll certainly keep dinner on the table more reliably than being an artist would," adds Anna. "Though your caricatures are so good, Hugo, you might be able to make a living as a political cartoonist."

"They don't make any money either," Gert says. "No artists do."

"That's true today," Hugo says, "but it won't be true in the New World we're creating. Another generation and the starving artist will be an anachronism." With a satisfied smile, he takes a long drink from his cup.

"To return to the idea of socialism as a complete worldview," say Max, still thinking about Hugo's comment earlier. "From that perspective, one could argue that socialism is more like a religion than a political ideal."

Hugo considers the idea. "Yes, I would say so. Like a religion, it answers all of mankind's big questions."

Gisi says, "I see socialism as fully holistic perspective: philosophical, practical, and even emotional."

"I like to think of it as a moral conviction that binds us through obligation to the community," adds Anna.

"I like that!" says Gisi. "You mean that we feel more connected to the others in our group because we all want to work to make the world a better place, Anna?"

"Yes, we feel connected to our group, to the community we live in, and to the whole world. And it's everyone's responsibility to take care of each other."

Max picks up the thread. "Once we recognize that we are *all* suffering, some more, some less, the importance of the individual naturally diminishes," he says. "When you feel safe because you know your basic needs will be taken care of, then you're free to work for the greater good, for the good of the whole."

""First a full belly, then ethics!'" Leo quotes.

"I love the feeling that we're all part of a grand whole!" exults Toni.

Minutes later the small group merges into the enormous crowd at the Rathausplatz for the closing ceremony. Once again, every speech is uplifting.

Shivers run down tens of thousands of young backs as Otto Bauer, founder of the SDP, concludes with the words,

"You, our youth, are heir to all the struggles for freedom

throughout the ages. You will be the generation to finish what others have started! You will reach the goal, and you will see the Perfection of Humanity's Cultural Heritage: to be intrinsically One People. Let the memory of this day give meaning and purpose and dignity to your life! Human freedom and human dignity are given into your hands. It is you who will preserve them for all future generations!"

As they walk in the kilometer-long procession to the main avenue of the Prater and watch the flags and the young people carrying them, now full of color—for they'd all switched to carrying flags representing the home of their group, and many of the marchers had changed into traditional costume—Anna says to Emil,

"What a remarkable experience! The spirit of the *Internationale* was truly a reality for three days. Aren't you glad you came?"

"Indeed I am," he says, smiling.

PART II

Dear, Darkening Ground
Rainer Maria Rilke, Book of Hours, I 16

Du dunkelnder Grund

Du dunkelnder Grund, geduldig erträgst du die Mauern.
Und vielleicht erlaubst du noch eine Stunde den Städten zu dauern
und gewährst noch zwei Stunden den Kirchen und einsamen Klöstern
und lässest fünf Stunden noch Mühsal allen Erlöstern
und siehst noch sieben Stunden das Tagwerk des Bauern -:

Eh du wieder Wald wirst und Wasser und wachsende Wildnis
in der Stunde der unerfasslichen Angst,
da du dein unvollendetes Bildnis
von allen Dingen zurückverlangst.

Gieb mir noch eine kleine Weile Zeit: ich will die Dinge so wie keiner lieben
bis sie dir alle würdig sind und weit.
Ich will nur sieben Tage, sieben
auf die sich keiner noch geschrieben,
sieben Seiten Einsamkeit.

Wem du das Buch giebst, welches die umfasst,
der wird gebückt über den Blättern bleiben.
Es sei denn, dass du ihn in Händen hast,
um selbst zu schreiben.

Dear Darkening Ground

Listen
Dear darkening ground,
you've endured so patiently the walls we've built,
     perhaps you'll give the cities one more hour
     and grant the churches and cloisters two.

Red Vienna

And those that labor—let their work
grip them another five hours, or seven,
before you become forest again, and water, and widening wilderness
in that hour of inconceivable terror
when you take back your name
from all things.
Just give me a little more time!
I want to love the things
as no one has thought to love them,
until they're worthy of you and real.

CHAPTER 16

THE GRANDFATHER CLOCK

December 4, 1929
Alsergrund,Vienna

Josef Berger, Gisi's grandfather, carefully lays down his fork and knife. Sunday dinner is officially over.

"Thank you so much for having me, *Herr* Berger and *Frau* Reyer," says Max. "It was delicious! I rarely have such a satisfying home-cooked meal."

"Yes, thank you, Mutti and Opa. *Serviettenknödel* with wild mushroom ragout has always been my favorite." She turns to Max. "But your sister is an excellent cook, Max! A good meal isn't such a rare thing for you."

"Still, your family has really gone out of the way to make it special this afternoon, Gisi. *Herr* Berger and *Frau* Reyer, I hope you'll let me repay you."

Gisi's mother and grandfather both shake their heads.

"Of course not," says Gisi.

"No, no!" says Helene. "*Serviettenknödel* is made from stale bread, and we're lucky that it was so warm that it rained this week and good mushrooms were available at the market. It isn't so special that you have to repay us!"

"All the same, I'd like to. I was thinking I could do something useful around the house."

"Well, well! That kind of repayment would be most

welcome!" says *Herr* Berger before Helene can object. There are an increasing number of jobs around the apartment that he no longer feels like doing. "How about starting by putting some oil on the treadle of Helene's sewing machine?"

"Papa! I can do that myself. If the sound bothers you, you should tell me and I'll take care of it. Max doesn't have to do that."

Max smiles. "I was thinking I could work on the big clock, the one that chimes at the wrong time."

"I don't know about that," Gisi's grandfather says. "I'm accustomed to it the way it is. I like it that way—it has character. When it chimes, I know it's eight minutes past the hour."

"Character? You call that character, Papa?" says Helene.

"I do," her father answers firmly.

"This week it's eight minutes, but last week it was only seven," points out Gisi. "As soon as we get used to it being eight minutes past, it'll be nine."

"I'm almost certain I could fix it so that it chimes at the right time. I repaired my father's alarm clock once."

Herr Berger looks skeptical. "His alarm clock, eh?"

"Let him do it, Mutti, Opa! I'm nearly late for school so often!"

Her mother raises her eyebrows. "Really? You? Late?"

Max laughs. "I'd really like to try my hand at it, *Frau* Reyer."

"Papa?" says Helene, tapping her father's shoulder half an hour later. The old man is leaning over Max, who's sitting on a stool in front of the enormous clock writing numbers on a piece of paper. The glass door on the front of the old clock is open and Max is experimenting with adjusting the weights on the pendulum. "Papa," Helene repeats. "I think we should leave Max in peace and go on our regular Sunday walk. I'm sure I couldn't work with you peering over my shoulder like that."

"Huh," grunts *Herr* Berger, but he gets up and takes his hat and coat off the hook in the hall.

Once all three family members are outside the apartment on their way down the stairs, *Herr* Berger says, "I don't know if I can trust this young fellow, Helene."

"You think he'll rob us blind when we are out?" Gisi's mother asks, pausing and turning back to look at her father.

"We all know there's nothing there worth stealing!" Gisi calls back as she continues going down ahead of them.

"Of course I don't think he'll steal from us. He's a good young man. That's not the problem."

Gisi is relieved, "I'm glad to hear you say that!" she says as she reaches the front door and opens it.

Helene hasn't started down the steps again. "Then what are you suddenly so concerned about, Papa? Shall we go back up?"

"No, no. Let's go. We'll take our walk as usual. It doesn't matter." They start down again. Even more relieved, Gisi holds the heavy door open as they pass through.

It's a radiantly beautiful early winter day, and the little family heads for the Liechtenstein Park, as they often do. On the corner of Wiesergasse and Fechtergasse, Helene catches up with her father, who is walking faster than usual.

"Something is still worrying you, Papa," she says.

"I told you it's nothing, Helene."

"But obviously it isn't nothing. I can tell."

Finally he gives in. "It's this, you see. I worry that he may take the whole damn clock apart and never be able to put it back together. I should have stayed there to watch him."

"Ah. That's it. But it's too late now," Helene says. "Let's try to enjoy the day."

Josef sighs.

When they return an hour later, Max has the table filled with small pieces of paper. Each piece is covered with carefully written notes and diagrams including many arrows, and a single piece of the clock.

"Don't touch that!" he cries out as Gisi tries to pick up one of the shiny gears. "Those gears are set out in a very precise pattern!"

"Oh," says Gisi, backing away from the table quickly.

Max's initial hypothesis about why the clock is losing time had not yielded positive results. He lengthened and shortened the weights scientifically, measuring, observing, taking notes, comparing; but in the end, it made no difference.

"I'll put it back together in a minute," he apologizes. "I'm sure you want your table back for your evening meal."

"Huh," says Josef again. He pulls out his pocket watch. It keeps very good time. "I see I still have an hour for a quick stop at the coffee house. Send Gisi for me when you're ready, Helene."

CHAPTER 17

THE CLOCK MUSEUM

February 10, 1930
Brigittenau

By the time a few months pass the clock has been disassembled and reassembled many times, but it still doesn't work. The pendulum stubbornly refuses to swing or the gears won't turn. The two or three times Max had managed to get it to work, the original problem with the chimes going off at the wrong time was worse than ever.

The tall clock towers silently over everything and everybody in the tiny apartment.

Obsessed with the problem but frustrated and embarrassed, Max decides to take yet another afternoon off from work to tackle the problem. After all, his father isn't working either. It's the middle of winter. Nobody is buying steel curtains or the handful of chairs he's made.

Instead of going to Gisi's family apartment where he finds it difficult to work under *Herr* Berger's constant gaze, he bundles up and sets off for Platz Am Hof in the first district, the neighborhood in which the watchmakers guild is based. With any luck, he'll find someone, maybe an apprentice like himself, with some useful advice.

The expansive square with its massive white church spreads out in front of Max as he steps off the tram. The watchmaker in his own neighborhood had given him an idea of which direction to take, so he sets out confidently, leaving the open square for the maze of narrow streets surrounding it.

He goes down two cobbled streets just wide enough for a horse and carriage before he sees the first watchmaker's sign hanging on an even narrower street to his left. The shop is closed, but a little farther along he sees another watchmaker's sign. This time he is more fortunate. An old man sits behind a desk with a strong lamp lighting up the pieces of a pocket watch in front of him.

"I can't help you," he tells Max after hearing the story of the clock in pieces, the grandfather, and the beautiful young lady. "Unless, of course, you can pay me for my help, which, from the look of you, is not in the realm of possibility. Unfortunately, you're likely to find it's the same with all of us in this quarter. There's no longer enough business to go around—none of us can put food on the table."

The watchmaker returns to his work, adjusting the light and his magnifying glass before carefully picking up a tiny gear with tweezers and gently putting it in its place. He then chooses another tool, moves the lamp slightly, and uses the delicate tool to turn the gear very slowly. Max wonders if he's done speaking and begins to say thank you and good-bye when the old watchmaker looks up again.

"But now it occurs to me," he remarks, "that you might try *Herr* Kaftan at his clock museum on Schulhof. He used to teach at the *Gymnasium*, but now he does nothing all day but wind all those clocks and demonstrate to people how they work. If he's not busy, it could be that he would be willing to give you some free advice.

"I wish you the best of luck," he goes on, eyes twinkling. "I wouldn't want to be in your shoes—that grandfather will never let his granddaughter marry you unless you get the clock to work again."

Max finds the clock museum easily. The four-story stone building, once part of the Palais Obizzi, sits slightly angled on a small plaza. The front windows are filled with clocks and a sign reading *Uhrenmuseum der Stadt Wien*, City of Vienna Clock Museum. Max's breath catches as he pushes the door open to reveal an elaborate and busy display of clocks of all sizes. The sound of so many of them ticking at once is instantly mesmerizing. On one wall dozens of regulator clocks hang side by side, their massive pendulums swinging rhythmically; another is dense with cuckoo clocks. To his right a room opens up where he can see rows and rows of elaborately ornate standing clocks displayed on long tables, some topped with spinning golden ballerinas, birds, or couples bowing to each other.

At the center of the main room is the most extraordinary thing of all: the interior workings of the clock that was in the great cathedral, Stefansdom, in the seventeenth century. An open iron framework, standing perhaps three meters high, three wide, and two deep, decorated with oversized leaves and vines, surrounds a series of massive gears that can be adjusted with ropes. Max is captivated. He reaches in to touch one of the heavy ropes, not daring to pull it, but wanting to feel like part of the long line of men who had pulled those ropes. With his eye, he follows the path of motion the gears would take if he were to pull on one of the ropes. It's as if *Herr* Berger's clock has been enlarged many, many times, so he can study the physics of how it must work.

In order to imagine the turning gears more accurately, he puts his hand on one of the gears, runs his finger along it until it meets the next, and then lets his finger follow that gear's turn. His system works until one of the gears turns two more instead of one, one of them much larger than the other. He can't follow both gears at the same time with one finger, so he is reaching into the clockworks with his second hand when a voice behind him comments,

"It's tricky, isn't it?" Startled, Max turns to see an older man with a handsome white beard standing behind him. "Here," the man says, "I'll show you how it works."

"Oh! Are you Doctor Kaftan? I'm so sorry I touched your clock!" Max says, terribly embarrassed.

"That is indeed who I am, and there is no need to apologize. I had this piece put here so people could touch it and see how it works."

A hour-long guided tour of the museum follows. Doctor Kaftan would gladly have gone on longer—there had only been one other guest that day—but a recurring image of Seppe sitting at the cafe while Anna fumes at home reminds Max that he should be going. He apologizes again and thanks the good doctor heartily. Even though he never did ask directly about *Herr* Berger's clock, having seen for himself the delicate balance of the workings of so many clocks, Max now knows for certain that he will never be able to fix it himself.

He feels terrible. How could he ever repay the Bergers for breaking something that had been in their family for so long, something that played such a central part in the comings and goings of their lives?

It's almost dark when Max leaves the museum, and the weather has changed. Heavy dark clouds hang low over the city portending snow and an icy wind gusts down the narrow streets. He pulls his coat and hat tighter and bows his head into the oncoming breeze.

Something will have to be done to make up for the broken clock, but what? There's no way he can replace it. He'd brought his alarm clock over to the Bergers' place the day after he'd taken the big clock apart and left it there, but that was meant to be temporary. Now it might be permanent.

By the time he reaches the tram stop, Max has rejected every idea he can come up with to make up the loss to Gisi's family. Offering his help to fix things is out of the question. Giving the family one of his chairs isn't a good idea because the little apartment is already too crowded with furniture. Buying them another broken standing clock and repairing that one wouldn't work either. He'd seen enough of the complexity and delicacy of the interior workings of clocks to know that repairing them is a job that requires skills he doesn't have. Anyway, Gisi's mother and grandfather have already objected to his saving up and spending money on a replacement.

"We're old," *Herr* Berger said several weeks ago. Helene looked up from her sewing in surprise. She wasn't old. Without realizing that he'd insulted his daughter, the grandfather continued, "We don't need another big old clock, Max. That clock was part of our family for generations. It served its purpose, and in any case, it was always too big for this place. It dominated the whole apartment. It's not a bad thing to let go of it. I'll sell it. We can use the space it's taking."

"Right! Who needs so much heavy old stuff?" Gisi added. "Opa is right. Old things like that clock take up much too much room in our little place. All of this old furniture should go! It's a new world!" She smiled. "Maybe we can replace the clock with a modern one from the Wiener Werkstatte."

"I'm not so sure about that, my dear," said *Herr* Berger. "This is my family's furniture, your inheritance, Gisi. Don't be so quick to get rid of it."

Regaining her composure, Helene agreed, "We really don't need another clock. We can bring the small one from the bedroom and set it on the bookshelf right here." She moved a vase to clear a space for the smaller clock.

At the time, Max was still sure he could fix the clock, so he hadn't paid much attention. Anyway, working on the clock gives him a reason to be at Gisi's family's place every moment he's free.

Now the clock in the bedroom will have to be brought out, he thinks gloomily. They can put his alarm clock in the bedroom instead. Max will tell them he can't repair the old clock tomorrow. They should have moved the other clock out the bedroom weeks ago.

When the tram finally arrives, he climbs on quickly. Choosing a seat that's somewhat sheltered from the wind in the nearly empty car, he relaxes a little bit. At least he won't have to obsess over fixing the clock. He'd put so much of his energy into it! He thought about it day and night for weeks at a time. At least that will be over. Maybe now he'll be able to find the time for a chess game with one of his friends. Or to go out with Gisi for a coffee.

The snow starts, first a few flakes floating lightly through the air, catching on his clothes or the windows of the tram briefly, and then in great flurries swirling and glistening under the street lamps. The afternoon hadn't been a waste of time, Max thinks. He knows what he has to do next, even though he isn't looking forward to it. He'd toured the fascinating clock museum and he'd made the acquaintance of the delightful Doctor Kaftan.

Then another idea comes to him. He can save his money to buy a beautiful watch for Gisi. And he'll bring her to the clock museum, to the room he knew she would love the most—the one with all the clockwork figurines, the maiden milking the cow, the boy drawing the bucket from the well, the tiny carousel, the mice running in circles—to present it to her. It wouldn't make up for the broken grandfather clock, but it would help.

CHAPTER 18

MEETINGS WITH FRIENDS

October 30, 1930
University of Vienna

Emil returns to his studies that fall with mixed feelings. The scene at the *Bummel* haunts him every time he crosses the main courtyard. In fact, military parades of any kind—and there seem to be more and more—depress him, so he skips class on the days they're scheduled.

On Wednesday afternoons after his last lecture, he meets Anna at the cafe near the university.

"*Wie geht's*? How's it going?" he asks as they settle in, coffee and *Buchteln* on the table between them. A steady rain is falling outdoors washing away the fallen leaves. Inside, with the smell of coffee and tobacco and the gentle murmur of voices surrounding them, it's pleasantly cozy.

Anna smiles. "I'm enjoying my classes this term. Child psychology is fascinating! Do you know about reverse psychology?"

"No, but it sounds very interesting. Tell me about it." He picks up the tongs and drops two lumps of sugar into his coffee.

"Well, children naturally want to assert their independence, so a child will often do just the opposite of what you ask, just to prove to you and to himself that he's a separate person. So, if you ask the opposite of what you want, he'll do what you want." Anna doesn't take any sugar in her coffee. They can rarely afford it at home, so she's accustomed to bitter coffee.

"How very useful! Do you think it works with adults?" He picks up a lump of sugar with the tongs and holds it over Anna's cup. "Sugar?" he asks, raising an eyebrow in the way women usually find so endearing.

She shakes her head and puts her hand over her cup, refusing the sugar. "Not unless they're very childish. I wish I'd known about it when Max and I were younger. He was—he is—so stubborn!"

"You should try it."

"What? I should tell him to do something I don't want him to do? I think that could be dangerous."

"No, you should try the sugar," he says, eyes twinkling.

"I can do without sugar," she says curtly. Emil looks away so she doesn't see him rolling his eyes. Anna is very beautiful but sometimes she drives him crazy. Why can't she let herself enjoy life once a while?

"What is it you want your brother to do?"

"He should stop imagining being a famous furniture designer and try to sell some security gates for a change. What did he leave school for? To dream?"

Emil decides to walk home instead of taking the tram. The rain is letting up, and anyway, he has an umbrella, a new one with a handsome carved wooden handle. He thinks about Max the dreamer and his charming girlfriend, Gisi. He finds the young couple compelling. They're so idealistic, so committed to the new world they see themselves as part of. So innocent. And, he thinks, so naive.

⊗⊹3⊹✳⊹E⊹⊗

Red Vienna

November 21, 1930
Brigittenau

The Brigittenau group gathers at Cafe Rüdigerhof, where they'd recently established their *Stammtisch*. Originally a lively cabaret, the cafe is shabby by then, despite its elegant art deco exterior. It suits the members of the group well.

Edith is spreading her latest photographs out on the table: unemployed men, union marches, children in rags, slum housing. Her images are emotive, beautifully lit, and eloquent. The powerful black and white pictures are gaining an audience beyond Vienna now, so she won't have to go back to teaching Montessori kindergarten either in Vienna or in England, where she trained and taught for a few years.

Toni is staring at a picture of a young girl holding out her cup at a soup kitchen.

"She's so beautiful, this child, but you can see the hunger in her eyes," she comments.

"How do you get them to pose like that?" asks Leo, holding up one of an unemployed family, the father watching a small child playing in a wooden fruit crate.

"It's just who they are in their own setting. You have to make friends with the people and let them know you empathize with them," Edith answers. "They need to understand that you really do get it, and that you're going to use the pictures to help other people to understand their situation. Then they're happy to pose."

Gisi says, "The children break my heart. It must be so hard for you to go to these places."

"Your heart has to break if you want to make a real difference. These people and places are everywhere. You just have to open your eyes."

"None of us has to look very far," Hugo adds. "It's a matter of seeing it or not seeing it."

"That's true. The tenement in this picture actually looks very much like our apartment building," says Max, pointing. "It's probably about the same size and just as dark. I'm sure there's no hot water there either. In fact, our wallpaper might be even uglier than this." He indicates a dark, greasy wall in the kitchen of one of Edith's photos. "And would you believe it, our landlord wants to raise the rent."

"I think that sounds like the perfect opportunity to get your father to apply for social housing," Gisi says. "He ought to qualify."

"He won't do it, won't even talk about the possibility. We'd probably have to move to some other district, maybe to one of the suburbs. My father is rooted in Brigittenau like a tree, the business is here, and most important, his coffee house is here."

"My mother is the same," she says with a grimace. "Blind to opportunity. Impossible to move."

A gust of wind disturbs the pictures on the table as the cafe door opens and Emil and Anna walk in. Anna doesn't go to Cafe Rüdigerhof often, and Emil has never been there before.

"What are these?" asks Anna, coming over to their table and looking at the photographs. Emil remains standing near the door looking over the cafe. The geometric patterns on the walls are faded and dirty, and the once-elegant chairs sorely need reupholstering. The chandelier is filthy, and the clientele looks as down at the heels as the setting.

"Evidence of what we're working on changing in Vienna," says Leo. "Do you know Edith Suschitzky, Anna? Her father owns the Social Democratic bookstore? Or maybe you know her younger brother, Wolf?" Wolf, at the other end of the table, nods at Anna. Edith shakes her hand.

"Yes, of course we've met," says Anna. She's been less involved in the party over the past year, but she remembers

Edith, who is a couple years older than she, bright, vivacious, and very witty. Anna can never decide whether she likes Edith or not.

"Edith's pictures are making a real difference to the movement. The rich, who'd never dare set foot in the slums, can see for themselves the conditions their taxes are helping to change," Hugo said.

Emil wanders closer and looks at the photos over Anna's shoulder. "If you ask me, this isn't at all what the rich want to see. Quite the opposite. Show them pictures of happy families in sparkling clean municipal housing if you want to convince them that their taxes are doing something good."

"We do that, too, of course," replies Hugo. "But their eyes need to be opened to the reality outside their comfortable existence. Edith's pictures reveal the truth of income inequality. Everybody should see them."

Toni adds, "Images like this nudge the conscience. They make you want to change the situation for the better."

"I'm sorry to inform you," Emil says, looking down at the group seated at the table, "that a good number of the people that you're seeking to influence have no conscience to nudge. They're perfectly capable of seeing pictures like these and thinking, thank god I don't live like this, and going back to their coffee and pastry."

"Which is why Papanek's approach is so important! We need to be working with the next generation! Children can be taught to share and to behave compassionately," Gisi answers.

Emil looks at her. Such intelligent eyes, he thinks. "I only hope you're right," he says.

"Max, it's time to go. You're getting as bad as our father," says Anna.

CHAPTER 19

COLLAPSE

May 12, 1931
Leopoldstadt, Vienna

"What do you mean you didn't know? How can you not have known?" shrieks Ottilie Bloch, Emil's mother. Usually perfectly composed and artfully put together, she's still in her old housecoat and slippers, bobby pins holding her reddish blond hair in tight pin curls. She hasn't applied a stroke of lipstick, although it's already ten in the morning. She's standing in her husband Richard's library—a room she rarely enters out of deference to Richard, who works long hours at the bank and needs some peace and quiet at home—shaking a copy of the *Österreichische Volkswirt* at him. Richard is bent over his desk, an account book lying open in front of him.

"You can't expect me to believe that you read about the collapse of the bank in the paper this morning, just like me, just like any *nudnik* in Vienna!"

Richard looks up and shakes his head sadly. "But it's true, my dear. I didn't know, but there it is in this morning's paper."

"Bankruptcy!" she wails. "The Creditanstalt has declared bankruptcy!"

"I know, my dear. You don't have to tell me—I read it,

111

too." He shifts his large frame uncomfortably in his desk chair. "Please put down the newspaper, Ottilie." She slams the paper onto the enormous desk. The pages of the account book flutter.

"As you can imagine," he continues, "I'm just as distressed as you are, though I don't find it necessary to announce it quite as loudly. Surely the servants are lined up at the door listening."

Whether or not this was true at the time, they'd scattered when Emil bursts into the room.

"Mutter! Vater!" he cries. "What on earth is the matter?" Ottilie grabs the paper from the desk, pushes it into her son's hands, points at the huge headline, and continues addressing his father.

"What does it matter what the servants hear!" her voice a little less loud but still shrill, "They don't have jobs anymore! You don't have a job anymore! My family's money is lost!"

Emil looks at the headline and begins to read the article below it. His father puts both elbows on the account book and his head in his hands.

"Your mother is right, my son," he says without looking up. "It would seem we are ruined."

In the afternoon, Emil takes a long walk to digest the news. He left his mother lying on the settee, a damp cloth on her forehead. She cried all morning and skipped lunch. His father is still at his desk going over and over and over the accounts.

"Hey! Emil!" calls a voice from a cafe as he passes. It's Johannes, Emil's classmate from Furtwängler's class. "Come! Join us for a drink!" Johannes and a companion are sitting at an outdoor table having a beer.

Emil takes a deep breath. He isn't sure he's ready for company. He likes Johannes though; they'd had some good times together. "Alright," he says, squeezing between the tables and taking a seat. Johannes raises his hand to call the server, and soon the three were enjoying reminiscing about classes and professors they've shared. Johannes's friend Walter is also a student of mathematics, though his main area of study is chemical engineering.

"By the way," Johannes says as a third round of beers is set before them, "Doesn't your father work for the Creditanstalt, Emil?"

A wave of dread washes over Emil. He'd forgotten that Johannes knew what his father did. He takes a long drink of his beer and lights a cigarette before answering.

"He did," he says, taking a drag on the cigarette. "Until this morning. Or yesterday, you could say. I'm not sure what will happen next."

"I read in the paper that the Creditanstalt's problems go back a couple years," comments Walter. "To when they merged with that other bank, the Bodencreditanstalt."

Johannes adds, "I read that, too. They had no idea how heavily in debt the Bodencreditanstalt was until now, when it pulled them both under."

"That's what they say," says Emil. He suddenly remembers a long conversation he'd overheard while waiting for his father in his office about a year ago. It all makes sense now. Creditanstalt knew how heavily in debt the other bank was when they took it over. His father knew. They'd been borrowing money for years to recover that debt. But it didn't work, and now it's too late. He stares into his beer.

"I'd better get going," he says, draining his glass. "My mother is a wreck, as you can imagine. I should be there with her."

"Sorry, buddy," says Johannes as Emil leaves.

"Good to meet you. Let's do this again," calls out Walter.

Emil can feel the beer as he boards the tram that would take him from Leopoldstadt to Brigittenau. Sitting down heavily on a seat near the back, he closes his eyes to try to forget the way his world is crashing alongside the Creditanstalt. He can't think ahead, he can't bear to think back, and he has no desire at all to go home, regardless of how his mother is feeling. He wants to be with Anna, to feel her long legs curl around his, to smell her eau-de-cologne, to taste her lips, to lay his head on the soft curve of her breasts. It's four in the afternoon on a Tuesday. Where would she be?

Not yet back from her afternoon as a practice teacher at the kindergarten, he decides. For half an hour, he'll sit at the cafe near the school and wait. Maybe have another beer. He gets off the tram a block from the cafe, only the slightest bit unsteady, and takes his time walking down the street. There's no hurry. He already missed both his lectures at the University and he doesn't care at all.

When the dark green awning of the cafe comes into sight, he walks more quickly. It looks like Anna is already there. Surely those are her glossy black curls bouncing as she gestures to someone. And that's her laugh, carried back to him on the breeze. But who is that with her?

Emil slows down. He doesn't want to share Anna with anyone, especially that day. He moves closer to the storefront he is passing and tries to get a better look at her companion without being seen. Like a spy, he inches along the buildings, ducking into doorways, until he finds the perfect place for observing the cafe unseen.

It's Hugo, the fellow from the SAJ group, the artist. From his vantage point, Emil can almost hear what they're saying. He can certainly get the tone of it. Hugo laughs at something Anna says and then she laughs at some quip of his. Emil watches her body language. My god, he thinks, she's flirting with him! There's no doubt about it!

He turns and walks away from the cafe rapidly.

He walks for hours, head down, smoking one cigarette after another. His path takes him along the Donaukanal, crossing one bridge in one direction and then another back, heading up for a while, then crossing again and coming down the other side, all the while barely glancing at the busy waterway. It's only on the bridges that he pauses, and then it's to consider whether to throw himself into the river. What future does he have?

Passing through the Wettsteinpark, Emil is forced to take a detour because of a *Heimwehr* brigade marching toward him. Their green loden hats with those ridiculous grouse tail feathers once made him laugh, but those days are long gone. The power of the Pan-German and National Socialist paramilitary organizations is growing daily. Anti-semitism is more acceptable than ever. On the next bridge, the Friedensbrücke, he adds that to his list of reasons not to live.

He stands on the bridge feeling empty, painfully empty. The strong wind makes it hard for him to light his cigarette, the second to last in his pack. Emil shelters against one of the heavy steel struts and tries again, his hair blowing into his eyes, but his lighter is no match for the wind. He curses softly. It makes no difference. The flame will not catch.

Then, "*Scheisse!*" he cries loudly as a gust of wind snatches his cigarette. He grabs after it helplessly as it blows it over the railing of the bridge. "*Scheisse! Scheisse! Scheisse!*" he shouts, pounding the railing, watching the cigarette spin and toss in the breeze and finally land in the water. He stamps his foot. "*Scheisse!*"

"What are you so angry about?" Gisi, walking home from *Gymnasium*, comes up behind him. "Oh," she says, seeing the lighter in his hand, and following his eyes to see the cigarette floating down the canal. "Is that so bad? Was it your last one? But you can buy more right over there." She points to the newsstand at the foot of the bridge.

Emil turns and looks at her in surprise. His flash of anger is gone like the cigarette down in the canal. Instead he feels embarrassed—in fact, deeply ashamed—to have been seen so completely out of control.

"No, no," he says, attempting to pull himself together without much success, "It's more than the cigarette. So much more." He wants to talk then, to tell her everything that went through his mind as he walked along the canal, as he stood on the bridge ready to jump. "Do you have some time? Maybe we could have a coffee and I could tell you."

Gisi looks at Emil. He looks terrible. He's shaking. She'd never seen him in such a state. She'd never imagined he could be in such a state.

She says, "Yes, alright. It isn't so late, is it? I don't have a watch."

Emil looks at his. "It's 5:30."

"Sure, let's go."

Gisi has no idea what to expect when she and Emil sit down in the cafe. They walked for three blocks without saying a word. Several times she tried to open a conversation, but before she could formulate the sentence she knew it was wrong. Finally their coffee comes, and one word is enough.

"So?" she asks, and a tumble of words come from Emil: the bank crash, his father's involvement in it, the loss of his mother's inheritance, and finally Anna's betrayal.

When he pauses at last, she says, "Oh, Emil. I'm so sorry." Her heart goes out to him. "I knew about the bank. We talked about it at breakfast at home today—but it didn't occur to me that someone I know would be so affected." He shrugs helplessly. She continues, feeling angry now, "And Anna! How could she?"

He puts his head in his hands.

"My father could go to prison," he says without looking up.

"Why?" she asked.

Almost inaudibly, he replies, "If it comes out that they knew the extent of the debt years ago and didn't tell their shareholders, it's fraud."

"Oh god. Who knows that?"

"I have no idea. In the best case, only the partners, the men who were there the day I overheard the conversation. And me, of course. And now you. Or maybe most of the financial world."

"How distressing! I can only imagine how frightening that must be for you."

"And for my mother."

"Yes, your poor mother. Maybe you should go back to her now. She needs you, you know."

❧❦❧

Anna and Hugo leave the cafe together and walk over to Austerlitz-Hof, where Hugo and two of his older sisters have shared an apartment since their mother passed away two years earlier. Their father died long ago, in 1916, in the war. As Anna and Hugo walk under the great arches and through the complex, they pass several busy shops, the kindergarten, and the library. Across a pleasant courtyard is the building that houses the community art studios, where they are going, and the Austerlitz Cinema.

"Look!" Anna says, pointing at the marquee. "They're playing the new comedy, *Sturm im Wasserglas* (Storm in a Water Glass). I've been dying to see that."

Hugo looks at her curiously. "We could go together, of course, but wouldn't Emil be upset? I was already thinking that he wouldn't be happy that I'm taking you here to show you my handmade books."

"Yes, it's true. He probably won't like it, but as I told you in the cafe, we haven't been getting along very well lately. I doubt that he'll ever overcome his bourgeois upbringing. Sometimes I wonder what I ever saw in him in the first place."

Hugo's relationship with Gert isn't going so well either. In fact, they've barely seen each other in the last month. He'd been thinking maybe the attraction had been all on his side all along and had been hoping a time would arise when he could confront her with that idea.

"Well, if that's the case," he said to Anna, "then why not come back tomorrow evening and we'll see the movie? It's playing every night this week at 8."

Hugo's handmade books are stunning. They are small, not much bigger than Anna's hand, and each is unique, containing a single poem, hand-lettered in clear, upright calligraphy, one or two lines per page. Hugo makes the paper himself and binds his books in leather he dyes deep red with beets or dark yellow with onions. There are poems by Goethe, by Rilke, and of course by Josef Luitpold. Anna is enchanted.

"When do you find the time to create these wonderful pieces of art, Hugo? I thought you had a full-time job working for an optician now."

"Ah, I do, and that's a very fine thing. There aren't many jobs to be had," Hugo answers. "But when you're passionate about something, time changes its nature. It adapts and stretches to fit the creative process." He grins and raises his eyebrows. "You know how that is?"

She does. Suddenly it seems like she has all the time in the world.

CHAPTER 20

THREE VIGNETTES

September 1931
Vienna

Gisi drops her book bag and sits down at the kitchen table in her family's apartment in Alsergrund. Her mother smiles at her from behind the ironing board where she's pinning a paper pattern to a large piece of muslin. Her grandfather, sitting in his chair reading, looks up briefly.

"*Grüss Gott*," he says, and goes back to his book.

His words make Gisi's hackles rise. Over the past months, she'd come to associate the colloquial greeting with the conservative politics of rural Austria and southern Germany. But then, as always, she forgives her grandfather. He's old-fashioned, that's all. She kisses them both lightly and focuses her irritation on one of her professors instead. In general, she's loving her classes in the medical school at University of Vienna, but she always comes home from one of her lectures feeling almost angry.

"I'm so disappointed!" she says. "At such a prestigious university, Dr. Reiss is teaching us the most backward theories of race. Today he spent the entire session discussing the tension between the Hierarchical Model and Innate Superiority. He didn't even mention Human Equality."

"Why should he?" her grandfather asks. "It's unproven—

it isn't science. At least Innate Superiority is based on real science like head measurement. Human Equality is liberal fluff."

"But Opa, I always thought you were proud of being liberal in your thinking!"

"I am," the old man says, "but science is science. The white race has been proven to be innately superior again and again using a variety of measures. As a liberal thinker, I believe that with that superiority comes the responsibility to care for our inferiors."

"That's okay for now," she answers, not wanting to argue. "But Human Equality will be proven once the next generation is educated properly. Socialism, given twenty more years to reshape society, will disprove the current studies. I'm one hundred percent certain of it."

"Hmph. You won't change Africa," he says and returns to his book.

She has no answer. "I'm going out to meet friends. I'll see you at seven for supper."

Her grandfather doesn't look up. "Not Max, I hope."

"Papa!" says Helene sharply. "Gisi is old enough to choose her own friends."

later the same day
Brigittenau

Several people are already at the *stammtisch* at Cafe Rüdigerhof when Gisi arrives. Gert follows her through the door.

"You won't believe what I heard," she says as she slips off her jacket and slides into a seat. "Edith went back to England and got engaged!"

"Oh my god! To whom?" cries Toni.

"To that English doctor that she always talks about,

I think. His name is Julian, if I remember right. Or is it Alexander?" Gert can hardly stay seated. "She met him when she was studying Montessori there." Since rejecting Hugo's courtship, Gert has been seeing a fellow called Dieter, and is hoping for a marriage proposal herself.

"Are they getting married here or in England? Where are they planning to live?" Toni is very excited.

"I don't know," Gert says. "I don't know any of the details. I heard the news from somebody who heard it from somebody else at Edith's family's bookstore. Maybe Wolf will join us this afternoon and we'll hear some more."

"I think her photography business is doing so well here that she won't want to leave. And I understand her mother isn't well. I bet they'll come here to live," Gisi says.

"They won't if he's Jewish," puts in Leo. "Things are a lot better for Jews in England."

Gert says, "But Edith doesn't consider herself Jewish. Her father is a well-known atheist."

"That's true. But lots of people don't consider themselves Jewish, especially if their family has been secular for generations. All the same, if you have a Jewish name it can still be a problem," Leo says.

"I'm dying to hear more about Edith!" says Toni to Gisi and Gert. "I hope they have big wedding here in Vienna and we all get invited."

⊶⊱⋇⊰⊷

September 1931
Leopoldstadt

The Bloch house sells quickly. After all, the price Emil's parents were asking was well below market value, and

Leopoldstadt is a beautiful neighborhood. Fortunately, there was no mortgage—Ottilie's family had owned the house for many generations. With the proceeds, the family is able to buy a two-bedroom apartment in the same neighborhood, but Emil decides that the time has come for him to move into a place of his own.

After some looking, he decides on a room in a boarding house not far from the university. In the evening, all of the tenants, most of whom are students like him, gather around a long table in the dining room for a meal cooked by their landlady, the widow of a dentist.

It's a big change for him, and at first Emil feels unsure of himself in his new setting. His fellow tenants are a mixed bunch. Most of them are from the countryside or small villages in lower Austria and have plenty to talk about among themselves, but there are also a couple of rather rough Bulgarian boys who work as laborers in construction, a silly blond girl from Brno, Czechoslovakia, and a Russian girl who is so shy Emil isn't sure if she knows any German at all. The only one of his fellow boarders he thinks he might have something in common with is a tall, thin chemistry student from Salzburg. At least he's from a reasonably large city and is studying something serious. Emil thinks he'll ask the young man, whose name is Rolf, to join him when he goes out for a beer with Johannes and Walter the next time. In the meantime, he settles into his room, works harder than usual on his studies, and tries not to imagine what could happen if the truth about the Creditanstalt failure comes out.

Since the initial crash, several other Austrian banks also failed, and the collapse even spread to one of the larger banks in Germany. Emil's father sits at home reading the newspapers every day, too depressed to go out to look for work. His mother busies herself with selling the furniture and art that doesn't fit into their new apartment, which is much too crowded anyway. She cries as piece after piece is carried away. Emil has to force himself to visit them on Sunday afternoons.

He hasn't seen Anna since they had one last fight at the cafe, or Gisi, or for that matter, any of the Brigittenau group in weeks. He can't throw off his feeling of depression.

CHAPTER 21

RAIN

February, 1932
Brigittenau

It's raining in February.

"Bizarre!" says Anna, shaking off her umbrella as she enters Max's shop. "The bulbs are already starting to come through the snow."

"Hey, stranger!" he calls from the workshop in the back. "Don't get the seats of those chairs wet!"

"What does it matter if you never sell them?"

"Which I never will if they have water spots on them. Come in the back. I'm working on something new."

Anna moved out of their family home when a room in a shared apartment in Austerlitz-Hof became available, and she hasn't seen her brother in a couple weeks. She edges through the cluttered showroom, picking her way carefully between the many chairs and tables made of scraps of steel and iron left over from their family's metalworks. Though there are some matching sets of chairs placed around tables, as Max uses up the supply of scraps, more and more of his pieces are necessarily unique.

"Who would want this in their house?" Anna points at a heavy-looking chair made of scraps of iron welded into something that looks like the frame of a throne.

"That's one that took on a life of its own. Sometimes they do. You start putting a couple of pieces together and then the pieces themselves tell you what to do next. What, you don't like it?"

"This is how you use your time and our father's materials," she sighs. "What's that you're working on now?"

"A lamp. I'm interspersing these pieces of wood Leo found with these steel cylinders. Take a look at the drawing." He holds it up. "It's Hugo's design."

"This one I like! I think it's a beautiful lamp! Hugo is very good, isn't he?"

"Brilliant. Are you still seeing him?"

"Off and on. He's more interested in his art than women, I think. I figured my moving into the same complex as him would make a difference, but he's still busy all the time."

"Huh. Maybe I'm seeing him more than you then. Did you know he got me a sale?"

"I didn't! How did he do that? He's a terrible salesman. He can't sell his own books."

"You do know he's sitting on the governing council for Austerlitz-Hof now?"

"I suppose I did know that. It's one of the reasons we never see each other."

"It's a very good thing! He convinced the acquisitions committee to buy two of my tables with eight matching chairs to put in the game room in their newest building. It's my biggest sale ever."

"Do you have that many matching chairs?"

"I have six here. The last two I'll have to bring down from our apartment."

"You'll have to replace the leather seats on those," she says. "You wouldn't want spots on the seats."

"Yes, I should do that. The seats are a little stretched out on the ones we've been using, too. But the framework on both of them is like new."

"Well, that's some good news at least. There isn't much of that around."

Max looks up from his work. "Yes, there is. It's very good news that Papanek was elected to city council last month. And that Felix is now directing the full party choir instead of just the youth choir. And also that Franz got a job working for the city of Vienna, a real, paying job."

"Yes, you're right. I guess there's a little light in these dark times. How are you and Gisi doing?"

"It's something like you and Hugo, I think. She doesn't have much time for me. Her classes at the University take much more of her time than *Gymnasium* did, and I think she's made new friends there whom she sees after class."

"You don't think her grandfather is influencing her? You told me he was still angry with you over the clock."

"There's that, too. He claims it's not the clock he's mad about, but that I'm irresponsible in general. She says she doesn't take him seriously, but I don't know. Anyway, when I get paid for the tables and chairs going to Austerlitz-Hof, I should have enough money to either pay to have the damn clock repaired or—since the family insists they don't care if it's ever fixed—I'll buy Gisi a beautiful watch." He smiles, but it's obvious that the broken clock is still worrying him.

"But, Max, you can't do that!" cries Anna. "First you have to pay Papa's bill at the coffee house, which is so long overdue, and then whatever debts you've been accumulating for the materials here! Gisi's grandfather is right—you *are* irresponsible!"

"Anna! For heaven's sake! This is my money that I earned with my work! I'll pay back the cost of my materials, but I'll be damned if I'll pay for Papa to sit at the cafe getting drunk day after day. He isn't old. He could be here trying to sell his blasted security gates. He's the one who got us into debt in the first place. If I can get the business back on its feet by being creative, that's where my profits will go. Anything extra is mine to spend as I like."

"Suit yourself. I don't know why I care. It isn't as if he's done anything for me either, that father of ours." She turns to go. "The lamps will be beautiful. I'll come back to see them when they're done."

a couple weeks later
University of Vienna

Gisi runs to catch the tram. She had a question for the professor after class, and now she's six or seven minutes late. The steady rain is making the melting snow so slippery that she almost falls twice before realizing that it would be safer to slow down and miss her usual tram and take the next one. She changes her pace and catches her breath. Why on earth had she rejected the umbrella her mother offered as she left this morning? Now her shoes are soaked, her winter coat is soaked, and her hair is lying in dripping strings across her forehead. She dreads the thought of the state of the books and papers in her drenched book bag.

As she passes the Hall of Mathematics, she notices Emil coming down the steps, looking dapper regardless of the rain. He sees her at the same time and calls out,

"Hey! Gisi, wait! Look! I've got a big umbrella!" She doesn't want to do it, but she slows down again.

"Hello, Emil," she says miserably. He holds the umbrella out over her and says,

"Look at you! You must be freezing. Let's get you dried off! My place is just down the street. We can sit by the stove until you're decent to go."

A few minutes later Gisi's clothes are hanging on the line above the huge tiled stove that serves both as a heater and the cookstove in Emil's boarding house. Her wet papers are pinned up in a neat line next to her clothes, and her books are hanging open by their spines. Even her shoes are pinned to the line. The landlady lent her an enormous robe and she is sitting huddled against the side of the warm stove while Emil lounges on a kitchen chair, long legs propped up on the wooden bench that goes around three sides of the stove.

"Do you want to call your family to say you'll be late?" asks the landlady.

"I can't," Gisi answers. "We don't have a phone."

"Maybe you can call a neighbor?" Emil suggests. "It'll be a little while before your things are dry."

"We use the phone at the *Tabak*, but I wouldn't want to ask him to run all the way to my family's apartment in this weather," she answers.

"I'll call there anyway," says Emil. "Just in case there's someone going that way."

"No, no, please don't. My grandfather and my mother know that sometimes I can't be home on time. You've already done enough."

Emil looks at her seriously. "No, Gisi. I can never do enough to repay you."

She's surprised. "For what?"

"For saving my life that day on the Donaukanal. You know I would have thrown myself into the canal if you hadn't come by."

Chapter 22

Discord

April 26, 1932
University of Vienna

"What's new?" Emil says as he sits down with Johannes, Walter, and the newest member of their coffee group, Rolf. He shakes the hand of each of his friends.

"For me, the news is that I'm starting to look for a job seriously," says Walter. "I finish my studies in July. It's a tough market even with a good degree." He signals the server and indicates that it will be four coffees as usual. "Do you think we should go inside? It's cool out here."

"I don't know," says Emil, looking at the sky. "The clouds look a little threatening right now, but I'm sure they'll clear."

Johannes replies, "It's not too bad out here. I'm glad for the fresh air." He turns to Walter. "I agree that it's hard to find a job now. I'm in the same situation—I'll be done this summer too. I hear the best way to get a position now is to volunteer in the firm you hope will hire you for a period. But who can afford to do that?"

"Or to know someone in a high position," Walter says. "Or even better, to be related to someone." He pauses to light everyone's cigarette. "Unfortunately, I don't know anyone well enough in the chemical industry to ask for a favor."

Emil adds, "I have one more year to go, but I doubt things

will be any better next year. It's looking worse for industries of all kinds." He thinks of his father, rooted to the settee, and his mother, still in tears.

"What about going to someone in your party and asking for a favor?" asks Rolf. "I'll be going back to Salzburg when I finish my studies, and I'm almost certain my father will know someone through the party who can pull strings for me."

"I'd prefer to get a job based on my own merits than through a connection," Emil says.

Johannes adds, "I'm sure we all would. Why else would we be working so hard on our studies? Sadly, it's rarely the way things work anymore."

"Or ever did," Rolf says. "Sorry to be so cynical, but who you know has always mattered more than how hard you work."

Emil takes a drink of his coffee and from the corner of his eye notices Gert passing by. He hasn't seen her since he and Anna stopped seeing each other. She looks good, Gert, made up perfectly and beautifully dressed in a light blue two-piece outfit.

"Gert! Hi! Over here!" he calls out, and she turns and smiles in recognition.

"Emil! How nice to see you!"

"Come, sit down, meet my friends." High heels clacking on the tile, Gert makes her way to the table. She sits down gracefully in the chair Rolf pulled over from another table.

Emil introduces her. "Rolf, Walter, Johannes, this is Gert Wald, a friend I haven't seen in ages. Gert, tell us what you've been up to."

Gert describes her work as a seamstress for a well-known designer, and they all laugh when she talks about some the wealthy people whose houses she visits to take measurements. The men share some funny stories about the people they worked with, the next order is for beer instead of coffee, and the afternoon seems considerably warmer and sunnier than it had earlier. By the time she leaves, both Johannes and Rolf have written down the number where Gert can be reached.

"So which of you will ask her out first?" asks Walter as they watch Gert walk down the street.

"Me!" say Johannes and Rolf at once and everyone laughs again.

They're interrupted when the server brings another round of beers and puts a copy of the day's *Neue Freie Presse* on the table. "The election results, gentlemen."

Rolf picks up the newspaper. "Listen to this." He reads aloud. " 'Austrian Nazis make a strong showing in provincial elections capturing 16% of the vote in Vienna, 18% in Lower Austria and 22% in Salzburg.' How about that? Not bad at all!"

Emil is taken aback. He never considered what party these friends might be affiliated with. He'd never thought to ask. He waits to hear how the others will respond to Rolf's comment. No one says a word.

Rolf looks up. "What?" he says. "Am I sitting at the wrong table?" He looks at each of the others carefully, picks up his bag and walks out the cafe, leaving his beer untouched on the table.

CHAPTER 23

TABLES

May 7, 1932
Austerlitz-Hof

"Excuse us!" Max calls out as he and Hugo maneuver the bulky metal frame of one of Max's tables along Stromstrasse on their way to Austerlitz-Hof. "Coming through!" Fortunately, it's already the second of the two—it's a very long walk from Max's shop to the housing complex. Leo and Felix are a few blocks behind them bringing the heavy glass tabletop, wrapped carefully in a blanket and tied with rope. The eight chairs are still at the shop. Max hopes they'll be able to get them onto the tram, one by one, though it will take eight rides.

Anna, Toni, Gisi, and Gert are already admiring the first table, assembled and cleaned, as it stands near the window of the new game room.

"It's so elegant!" says Gert. "The glass top looks just beautiful with the sunlight on it!"

Anna, though proud of Max, is nevertheless skeptical. "It isn't very practical, though. People will get fingerprints all over the glass."

"I'll make tablecloths for the tables!" says Toni. "I can stitch together the small pieces of cloth left over at work. They're all just piled up under the looms."

"You'd better ask before you take them, Toni. Remember when I almost lost my job over off-cuts of the fabric we use to make dresses at my work? I've never dared to ask permission to take another piece, though I know girls take them without asking almost every day," say Gert.

"Girls who aren't Jewish," Anna says drily.

"And they probably make dresses at home and sell them," Toni adds. "I know. But I've never taken any offcuts so far, and I'll ask permission. I like my supervisor. She's my union leader. I think she'll be generous, especially when she hears where the scraps are going and what they'll be used for."

There's a commotion near the front of the building, and the women see Max and Hugo angling the second table frame through the doors. Ten minutes later Leo and Felix bring the glass, and once it's unwrapped, the table is set up near its twin. The men leave immediately to walk back to get the chairs.

"This is going to take a very long time!" Toni says. "Maybe we should think about a meal. Hey, I have an idea. Why don't we cook here and eat together at the new tables? Anna, do you have to sign up in advance to use one of the big kitchens here?"

"You do, and it's Saturday today, so it's pretty likely that they'll be taken, but I'll check."

Two hours later, the two tables are pushed together to create one large one, and the chairs are all in place. The curtains from Anna's apartment work well as tablecloths, and the friends are enjoying big bowls of soup while laughing about how hard it was to bring the tables and chairs from Max's shop.

"For the rest of my life, I'll remember standing at the back of the tram, my chair hanging over the railing, when that huge guy with the suitcase got on!" laughs Felix. "I practically had to hang off the back myself—while holding onto the chair!"

"You must have been worried about crushing your precious musician's fingers against the railing!" Leo comments. Felix is the only one in their large family who was given music lessons, though all the children are musical.

"Leo. Don't forget that I was never allowed to go ice skating with the rest of you because I might damage my hands!" Felix retorts.

Gisi is surprised. She's never seen the brothers squabble.

Anna looks at Leo so sharply he feels it.

Gert changes the subject. "It was kind of your friend to let us put our pot on the stove she'd reserved, Anna."

"But more than a little crowded with all of us peeling turnips at once in that tiny corner of the room!" laughs Gisi. "But it was fun! That guy you're dating sounds great, Gert. I can't wait to meet him."

"I hope we can find time for that soon. He's almost done with his studies at the University you know, and then he might have to go back to Salzburg for work—but with any luck, he'll find a job here in Vienna and be able to stay."

"Gert, you didn't tell us about your new romance!" Leo frowns.

"Men aren't interested in that sort of thing, why should I tell you?"

At that point the door opens and they turn to see an older man come into the room. He spots Hugo and comes over to speak to him.

"Oh!" Hugo says. He turns to the group and announces, "The government just resigned. Buresch couldn't build a parliamentary majority."

"Well, that's the end of any chance that the SDAP will ever be part of the ruling coalition again," says Max.

"There hasn't been a chance of that in years," Leo says.

Max adds, "But it's worse now. The right wing is gaining power so quickly, it's frightening,"

"It is frightening," Gisi answers. "But the SDAP still holds Vienna."

Leo says, "And we're setting a beautiful example for the whole world to see!"

"*Prost!*" calls out Hugo, holding up his glass. "To this elegant new table and chairs, to social housing, and to Vienna, our Utopia!"

"*Prost!*" comes the enthusiastic reply from everyone at the table.

Chapter 24

Paying Back What's Owed

May 21,1932
Brigittenau

Max divides the money he received for the sale of the tables and chairs into five piles: one to pay back the cost of the glass, leather, and other materials he'd bought on credit over the past months; one for expenses that would be incurred by the business in future months—electricity, water, welding supplies, hardware, and the like; one for the rent and household expenses—he and his father eat out more frequently now that Anna isn't there to cook, so he added extra to that pile; one for a little pocket money for himself, and the last one to save to hire someone to repair the clock.

Earlier, he'd considered finding out how much Seppe owed his cafe, but he decided against it. Now he's thinking maybe he should at least ask. On the other hand, the last two of his piles are already very small. It's so disappointing, those tiny piles of schillings. Finally, full of resentment, he locks up the money in the back of the shop, gets out his bicycle, and sets out for the Josef Weiss Cafe to ask what Seppe's bill comes to. Halfway there, he turns around, goes home, opens the shop up again, and gets the money he'd set aside to save. After all, he knows from experience that it's the family of the cafe owner who do the suffering when customers don't pay their bills.

As Max parks his bike, he sees that one of the lower panes of glass in the front window of the old cafe is broken. He looks over the piece of wood patching the hole to see his father and his cronies sitting around their *stammtisch*, mugs of beer in front of them, laughing. They make him sick. What gives them the right to sit there all day and laugh?

He doesn't even say hello to Seppe, whose back is turned to him anyway. Instead, he looks for the wife of the proprietor, whom he finds in the kitchen. Paying his father's bill takes nearly all the remaining schillings, but the look of relief on *Frau* Weiss's face when he counts out the money and hands it to her makes Max feel better.

Herr Weiss walks into the kitchen as he is leaving.

"Josef, look," *Frau* Weiss cries, holding out the handful of schillings toward him. "Max just paid Seppe's bill. It's almost enough to replace the glass in front!"

"I saw that," Max says. "How did it happen?"

"*Ach*, a gang of boys passed by last week chanting anti-Jewish slogans, and one of them kicked it in with his big boot. It happened in the middle of the day! Not even your father's fine security gate could stop it from happening."

That was it! Max suddenly realizes why Seppe seemed to have eternal credit at this coffee house. But that gate must have been paid for years ago!

"Here," Max says, handing them the last of his savings. "Take this, too. I'm sure we owe it to you. Will it be enough to replace the glass?"

"Oh, Max, this isn't necessary!" *Frau* Weiss says.

"But it will pay for the window," points out her husband. "Thank you, Max, you're good man. Sit down and I'll get a beer for you." Ignoring Max's objections, he pulls another chair over to Seppe's *stammtisch*. "Sit!" the cafe owner says.

Seppe stops in the middle of his joke and looks up. "What's this?" he asks. "My very serious son deigns to have a beer with us? A real beer?"

Max greets the men without smiling and sits down. Josef sets the beer in front of him.

"Did you see the paper?" Dolf asks the men at the table. "Dollfuss managed to form a coalition government of Christian Socialists, the Agrarians, and the political wing of the *Heimwehr*."

"So Englebert Dollfuss is our chancellor now? No one even knows who he is!" says Fredl.

"All I know about him is his height," adds Dolf. "He's about the size of my ten year-old son! How will he see over the podium?"

Seppe chortles. "I heard he once broke his leg climbing up a ladder to pick a dandelion!" The group roars with laughter.

"But to be more serious," says Jakob, catching his breath, "did you hear that a plot against Dollfuss has already been discovered?" His friends listen with great interest. "Yes, just this morning, someone left a mousetrap outside his door!"

Even Max laughs this time.

CHAPTER 25

MOVING ON

June 20, 1932
Emil's boarding house

" And what about you, Emil? What do you think this jolly peasant chancellor of yours, Dollfuss? Does he have a chance of bringing together the warring factions in your country?" one of the Bulgarians at dinner at the boarding house asks.

"I'm sure I couldn't say," Emil answers, spooning some soup into his mouth cautiously. "Politics has never interested me." Since learning of Rolf's political leanings, he's more careful than ever of what he says at the table. His curly red hair and aquiline features don't look Jewish, and so far no one has brought up the subject, but he feels uncomfortable around Rolf. In fact, immediately after the incident in the cafe following the election, Emil started to look for a new place to live.

"Dollfuss is very clever," says a student from a remote village in the Alps. "He makes me laugh."

"I like him, too," says someone else. "He's a man who gets things done!" The discussion is generally positive, but Emil makes his excuses early and heads back up to his room to study.

The quiet Russian girl, Zlotka, follows him up the stairs.

"I think maybe you and I have little to say downstairs for similar reasons," she says as they reach the landing.

He turns and smiles at her. "Perhaps," he says. She's very pretty, petite and blonde. Though they've lived in the same boarding house for months, this is the first time she's spoken to him directly. He takes a chance. "But I'm afraid this isn't the place to discuss it. Shall we meet somewhere after classes tomorrow to talk?" Her eyes glisten.

At four in the afternoon the next day, Emil and Zlotka are sitting side by side on a bench under a chestnut tree in the university botanical garden.

"So what's your theory, Zlotka? What's the secret we share that makes us so silent at the dinner table?"

She laughs. What a delightful laugh she has, he thinks. Then she purses her lips and says, "You are a communist, of course, like me!"

Emil scratches his head as if thinking. "No, I'm not a communist," he answers. "I was being perfectly honest when I said I wasn't interested in politics. If there is a secret that we have in common, it must be something else."

Zlotka is clearly disappointed. Frowning, she brushes a wave of her thick blond hair out of her face.

"You're not even a Social Democrat?"

"Well," he answers. "I do lean that way. And I've actually been to quite a few SAJ and SDAP meetings. I even attended the Youth Internationale a few years ago."

"But you're not completely convinced?"

"I try to keep an open mind. I like to ask questions. The question always matters more than the answer to me. I don't know if I'll ever be a true believer in anything."

"Very interesting." She looks at him intently. "Ah, then, if asking questions is so central for you, I have another idea of what we might have in common."

"Yes?"

"I think we're both Jewish!"

He laughs, "That's right! And who would know by looking at either of us!"

The following month Emil finds a room in another boarding house, not quite as nice as his current one and a good deal further from the university, but also a little less expensive. The landlady, *Frau* Rosenthal, is the widow of a tailor and is Jewish. Because the school year is ending, she has two rooms available, so Zlotka is able to rent the second one. Emil tells Johannes, Walter, and the tenants at his old place that he's moving because his new room is so much more economical. Walter smiles conspiratorially at Zlotka but Emil doesn't notice.

As Emil is carrying his and Zlotka's things out of the house on a Saturday afternoon, Rolf comes home to the boarding house. He doesn't offer to help. Instead he snorts derisively at Emil and sneers,

"Cheap Jew. I always knew you were one of them. Good riddance, vermin!" and he slams his door.

Chapter 26

The Ants

October 5, 1932
Austerlitz-Hof

Anna wakes up early. It's just about a month since she began working as an assistant teacher in the kindergarten at Austerlitz-Hof. That day, substitutes were replacing all the new teachers so they could tour other schools.

With Papanek in his new position at the Ministry of Education adding his perspective to Otto Glöckel's brilliant progressive ideas, education in Vienna has never been as exciting. The world watches as the city school system is transformed from one intended to preserve the class system into one set up to break it down.

The new teachers, all recent graduates of the university or of training programs like the one Anna had attended, gather in the community meeting room of the school in her complex before setting out on the day-long tour. Anna is chatting with a friend when she sees Papanek arrive. She breaks off her conversation and makes her way over to greet her former youth leader. He's as glad to see her as she is to see him.

"Anna! It's so good to see you here! How are you? And how is Max? The group is still meeting regularly?"

"Most of us are, yes," she answers, and she updates him on the doings of the members of the Brigittenau group. "We formed strong bonds under your guidance, and I think we've all done well."

"I'm glad to hear of your continuing commitment to Social Democratic values, and I'm very happy to see so many strong, intelligent women like you taking up the task of working with the next generation. You know how strongly I believe that it's here in the schools that the real transformation of society will take place."

"And I agree with you," Anna says. "It's a privilege to be doing such important work."

The tour breaks into smaller groups to go to see model classrooms in several different schools. Anna's group, led by Papanek, walks a few blocks to one of the new *Einheitsschules,* co-educational schools for all social classes with a common curriculum for children all the way up to the age of fifteen. Traditional schools divide the students into tracks with different curriculums that groom them to fit into a hierarchical society.

"The point is to abolish educational privilege based on class, to encourage the full development of intelligence and talent wherever it might be found, and to eliminate the personal, social, and economic costs of premature selecting out at age ten, as it's done under the old system," explains Papanek. "This school in particular demonstrates both the structural and internal reforms necessary to complete the change. We'll be visiting a class of eleven and twelve-year olds, just the age at which the old system divides the population into rigid tracks."

Although Anna went to primary school and *Gymnasium* in Vienna under Social Democratic governance, as well as completing a degree in education, she's surprised at the way the experimental classroom is organized. She and the other new teachers are encouraged to circulate in the room, and to sit down at the low round tables where students are working in groups with the head teacher or one of several assistant teachers sitting among them. There isn't even a podium for the head teacher in the room!

The entire approach to education is different. Instead of trying to make every child fit into a uniform curriculum, instruction is based on the child's immediate environment and prior experience. The classroom is full of movement and noise, since the pupils are expected to be active rather than passive participants in the process.

Most startling of all to Anna is the lack of strict division between subjects and hours. All subjects from language and mathematics to art and music are taught through a logical series of what Papanek called "self-evidently relevant" central topics. The current topic in the classroom Anna is visiting is "Systems," which apparently includes the rain cycle, the human body, ancient numbers, the family, and city government.

Anna follows a small group going outdoors to observe an ant colony. The teacher tells the children to either sit quietly where they can see what the ants are doing near the anthill or to follow a single ant at work, and to record their observations by using drawings and diagrams as well as writing in their notebooks.

Forty minutes pass as the children observe and record what they see. Anna is amazed at the focus and the attention span of the children, especially some of the boys, whom she predicted would use the excuse of following an ant to escape from the group and have some fun. When the teacher calls the group back together at an outdoor table to share their observations, everyone comes immediately.

"So, what did you see?" the teacher asks.

"I noticed how beautifully regulated the colony is!" one boy calls out. "The ants march just like soldiers. I followed an ant to that tree," he pointed, "where he.."

"Or she!" says a little girl.

"Okay," says the boy. "Or she, found a dead bug. The ant picked a little part of it up and brought it back to the ant hill. After that, a whole line of ants followed him..."

"Or her!" cry all the girls in the group.

"Sheesh," says the boy, "or her, to the place where he—or she—found it, and then each of them carried a piece of it back to the colony."

A red-haired girl calls out, "Cooperation! That's one of the signs of a well-functioning society!"

"Yeah," says another of the boys. "I saw that happen too. They were all in a line, head to butt, carrying pieces of something back to the ant hill. And when I stepped on the line of ants, the ones behind my foot just went around their dead friends and kept bringing back the booty." He laughs derisively.

"Oh, Wilhelm! How could you do that!" a girl cries. "You are so mean!"

The teacher doesn't respond. Instead she asks what other observations the children have to share.

"I love the way they work together and help each other. Each one has its own role. They're a true community," says one boy.

Another one shares, "I think I saw them put up defenses to protect the colony when I got too near and my shadow went over it. A lot of them hurried back into the hill but some of them stayed outside acting like guards."

At the end, the teacher assigns the children to write a short essay about how the ant colony functions as a system for homework.

Red Vienna

As they walk back to the class, Wilhelm, the boy who stepped on the line of ants, hangs back.

Only Anna sees him go back to the ant hill and demolish it with his foot.

CHAPTER 27

GERT AND ROLF + WALTER'S JOB

October 11, 1933
Grinzing, outside Vienna

"Der Alter Bach-Hengl has always been my favorite *heuriger*," says Rolf as he and Gert step off the tram at the last stop in the center of Grinzing. It's an unusually warm fall day. They've seen each other a handful of times since they met the previous spring, but this is their first full day out together. "It's a very short walk. Is there another one that you would prefer? There are several not far from here. We could go a little farther if you'd like to stretch your legs a bit first."

Gert considers the height of her heels momentarily and answers, "No, your favorite is fine with me." The choice between high heels or comfortable shoes had caused her considerable anxiety that morning. "I like all the *heurigen*." She smiles. Gert always looked forward to the first fall wines and the convivial atmosphere of the traditional wine bars. And right then, she adores the way Rolf's straight blond hair is catching the low sun. "This is the perfect time to be here."

"For me, it's a little late in the year. I prefer the new wines earlier in the season. But we'll have plenty of choices now."

"The weather is perfect, anyway," says Gert. "The leaves just turning, the clear air."

"That's certainly true. I remember years when it was so cold at this time of year that you expected to see the snow at any moment."

Two minutes later they're passing through the big green gates into the vine-covered courtyard of the ancient restaurant. Several cozy-looking buildings with high pitched roofs surround an open space. On either side of Gert and Rolf, people of all ages, many in traditional *dirndls*, *lederhosen* and feathered hats, are clustered around long wooden tables. The atmosphere is lively and pleasant. To Gert's left, a group of people are gesturing with great animation, while on her right others are engaged in quiet conversation.

"It makes no difference who's in power," Gert hears one man saying as she passes. Another is quoting Rilke. A middle-aged couple looks deep into one another's eyes.

"What would you like?" asks Rolf as they sit down between a family and an elderly couple. "Naturally, I prefer their own wines but there's a broad selection available."

"I'll have whatever you're having," says Gert. She is suddenly feeling shy in front of Rolf, who seems so intelligent and sure of himself. What is it about this man that tempers her usual boldness?

A stout and pleasant waitress, her ample breasts showing above the low cut of her *dirndl*, comes up to them. "Ah, a pair of young lovers!" she smiles. "What would you like to start with? How about a liter-liter, one liter of the Gruner Vetliner, our white wine, and another of sparkling water?"

"Yes, that would be excellent, and a cold platter of meats and cheeses, please," says Rolf without consulting Gert. Surely that would have offended her if it had been Hugo who'd done it.

Minutes later, the wine and food arrive.

The sun warms her back as Gert leans forward on her elbows to listen to Rolf tell a story about his family bringing him and his sister to this *heuriger* when they were children and the family visited Vienna.

"We were allowed to run around a little bit as long as we didn't disturb the adults. I would hide there, behind that tree," he nods toward a tree in the corner of the courtyard, "and my sister would pretend not to be able to find me. She's two years older than I, you see, and wasn't always happy to play with her little brother. But here..."

Gert pulls herself upright. Her lightweight wool jacket feels warm. The jacket, with its cinched waist and shoulders higher and straighter than usual because they're padded, is part of the new suit she'd finished making so late the night before that she was worried she'd have circles around her eyes today. The chestnut brown wool she'd used came from the mill where Toni worked. Toni's discount price was even further reduced because the piece had a section where the weave was irregular, but of course that was no problem for Gert—she knew how to cut around it and to use the parts she couldn't cut off in places where no one would see. She pulls off her jacket languidly, sleeve by sleeve, to reveal her best white blouse and the pretty belt around her small waist.

An accordionist playing melodies that everyone knows ambles by.

"Mmm, this is so easy to drink," she says as she adds a little more wine to her glass. She already feels woozy, so she eats more of the cheese and bread. It's *Bergkäse,* her favorite, on a thick chunk of dark rye bread.

"Tell me about your childhood," Rolf suggests, and Gert does, and then Rolf shares more stories of his own. They switch to a slightly sweeter wine, and Gert finishes off the last of the salty, fatty sausage on the platter. The conversation meanders from their favorite songs and pieces of music to the cinema.

When that wine is gone, it's time to order dinner. Gert is

relieved when Rolf takes charge and asks for roasted pork with potatoes and sauerkraut for them both.

She would like to wash her hands and to use the toilet before the food comes, but she isn't at all sure she would be able to walk without swaying, so she decides to wait a bit and not to drink any more of wine.

"We'll have the Sturm now," Rolf calls the waitress back and tells her. Turning to Gert he says quietly, "The Sturm is freshly fermented, so it's a little less alcoholic. Don't mind the cloudy look—that's why it's called the storm."

"Thank goodness," Gert replies. "I'm not sure I could have managed another glass of ordinary wine." And thank goodness Rolf is so considerate, she thinks.

"Have I told you how the *heurigen* originated?" he asks, paying no attention to her last comment or to the fact that she is nodding yes to his question as she cuts into her meat. "The story begins with a declaration by Emperor Franz Josef II in 1788, allowing anyone to sell home-made beer or wine. No permit was required." Gert knows the story well but she doesn't feel like saying so. A hearty piece of roast pork is a rare thing for her and she is intent on enjoying it to the fullest. "It came about when several inn-keepers in a small town complained to the Emperor that their Lord was only allowing them to sell the wine he made." If Hugo had been telling the story, she would have pointed out that it was 1784, not 1788, and in Gorz that it happened, and that the Lord was Count Delmetri, but she lets Rolf go on. Her father told that story every single fall when he took the family to out to a *heuriger*, and she and her sisters used to make fun of him by imitating the way he told it.

The Sturm arrives at their table, the clouds swirling in Gert's glass as Rolf pours it. The light is low by then. Many hours have passed, she realizes, and she barely noticed. She admires Rolf's profile as he thanks the server. What a beautiful straight nose he has and such a strong jaw and chin. Gert's mother taught her the importance of a good chin. "A weak chin indicates a weak man," she says firmly and often. Well, Gert thinks, here is a strong man.

They share their upbringings, both in pious Catholic homes, both losing their faith as they grew up.

"My mother still goes to church four or five times a week, can you believe it?" he says.

"Mine never leaves her rosary behind. She keeps one hand in her pocket or purse, and I can see her lips moving subtly as she prays as she works or walks. It's such nonsense, isn't it?"

The light, sweet wine goes down easily, and Gert is leaning comfortably on the cushions propped against the wall behind her. She'll have to go to the toilet soon, she thinks, but not yet. By the time they finish their apple strudel, and the last of the Sturm, she isn't sure she can walk anywhere.

Rolf, ever the gentleman, takes her arm as they walk back out onto the street. Gert thinks she might vomit, but fortunately she's able to hold it back.

"I'm not sure we should attempt the tram ride home, my dear," Rolf is saying in the distance. "Shall we take a room in this inn?"

Gert must have said yes. The next morning she finds herself sharing a luxurious feather bed with a man she barely knows. But looking at his hair spread across the pillow and his beautiful nose, she knows one thing. This is the man she loves and will marry.

October 19, 1933
two days later
Emil's cafe

"So, did you hear that Walter got a job after all?" asks Johannes as he and Emil sit down at their table in the cafe. "A good one too!"

"No! He was so discouraged! He was certain his degree was a waste of time and effort! Where?"

"That's the key to it. It's not in Vienna. Not in Austria at all, in fact."

"Where, then?"

"In Switzerland. At Sandoz Laboratories in Basel, for a handsome salary, too. He's a fortunate man in that sense, our Walter."

"He is. I was in Zurich not long ago. It seems Switzerland is doing better economically than Austria right now," Emil comments. "I wouldn't object to going there myself."

"Not I!" Johannes says. "I wouldn't want to live among such self-satisfied, smug, and secretive people. The Swiss, hah!" He almost spits out the word. "They never let on where they stand, but they're always certain theirs is the best position."

Emil laughs. "What's more, their version of German is excruciatingly painful to listen to." He turns. "How about you, Johannes, have you found work?"

"Unfortunately, no, not yet. I'm assisting in one of my professor's classes at the university, but it barely pays for coffee. My parents are still paying my rent. It's embarrassing to be so poor."

Emil sighs. "Things are certainly not improving here in Austria. Did you see there was another bombing in Styria? The Austrian Nazis blew up a provincial government office with a homemade bomb. No one died, thank God, but there were some serious injuries."

Johannes shakes his head. "You know? The longer I'm in the position I'm in, still dependent on my parents after having graduated from University, the more I begin to understand their anger."

Chapter 28

Christmas

December 22, 1932
Alsergrund
7:30 in the evening

"Papa, do you have your bag? Gisi! Where are you?" Helene calls.

Gisi is still packing her textbooks into her book bag. She, her mother, and her grandfather are going to visit his sister and her husband in Tannheim, Tyrol, for Christmas, as they have almost every year since Gisi can remember. This time, though, she will have to study while she's there. Medical school is definitely harder than *Gymnasium*.

As always, they plan to take the night train to Innsbruck, arriving at six in the morning, and then the local train to the village. The ride will take over nine hours, so they plan to stay in Tannheim for nearly a week. Gisi has been looking forward to the visit for months. When she was a child, it was by far her favorite event of the year.

Great Aunt Greta and Uncle Clemens's daughter, Gisi's mother's cousin, Basia, and her husband, Hans, have two daughters of their own, Litzi and Theresa, both a little older than Gisi. The three girls spent many memorable holidays together cross-country skiing, playing in the snow, or sitting

153

by the fire sharing stories. Now that they're older, they're still close.

The family was last together in June for Litzi's wedding. Litzi was almost twenty-four when she married, late for such a beautiful girl. This year she would be joined at dinner on Christmas Eve by her new husband, Horst. Theresa, at twenty-one, has already been engaged for a year. Her wedding is planned for a year from March, when her fiancé will be done with his military service.

Although Gisi fully intends to study on their way to Tannheim, it is after nine o'clock in the evening when they leave the station in Vienna, and the soothing motion of the train soon puts her to sleep. She sleeps almost the whole night even though the third class seats are made of hard wooden slats with very little leg room between them, and of course they don't recline. When the train finally reaches Innsbruck at six in the morning, Gisi and her family have to wait an hour in the cold station for the local train to Tannheim to arrive.

The second train is much more comfortable because the seats are upholstered, but it's full of tobacco smoke, and three men in their coach are having an animated conversation even though it's barely seven in the morning. Studying is impossible.

One of the men, wearing a black cap pulled low over his eyes, says to the others, "Did you hear? We doubled our membership in the provinces this year!" He raises his arm in a Nazi salute. Gisi shivers and tries to ignore them.

The man opposite him answers, "Doesn't surprise me. In my village alone, almost all the men and more than half the women have joined our party. And it's no wonder, with the economic situation getting worse and worse."

"I shouldn't say anything, but my nephew was involved in the bombing of that bridge last month. My sister worries, of course, but I have say I'm damned proud of that boy," says the third.

"That's right, and so you should be. He's a brave boy. We need kids like him to cause as many disruptions in the system as possible."

"The other thing we need to do is to convince our leadership to join forces with the German Nazi Party," says the man in the cap. Both of the others object.

"Don't be a fool! Austria needs to remain independent!"

"Why give up our autonomy? With the way our party is growing here, we'll be able to take control of the Austrian government within a year of two. Then things will change for the better fast, you'll see!"

The fellow in the cap says, "But how do you think we'll be able to do that without money and arms from the Germans? We aren't rich, you know."

"Not yet. Now we're only a bunch of provincial folk— farmers, miners, workers—but many of the new members of the party are *burghers*. The middle and upper classes are beginning to hear us. After all, the Jews oppress them as much as they do us. It's just a matter of time."

"Opa? Mutti?" says Gisi quietly. "Maybe we can find seats in another car?"

"No, no," *Herr* Berger replies. "I want to listen. This is better than reading the newspaper."

⊕⊰3⊰⫶⊱⊱⊕

The day before Christmas Eve is a busy one. The kitchen is already crowded with Helene, Basia, and Greta all cooking and baking at once, so Gisi puts on her boots, her winter coat, scarf, hat, and mittens, and joins her great uncle and grandfather on a trek into the woods to find a Christmas tree. The two old men are still strong and hearty, but they find plenty to complain about.

"You see what a mess they made cleaning the forest floor here?" says Clemens.

His brother-in-law answers, "It looks okay to me."

"Well, it's not. You don't know what to look for. You see how they left all those small trees there?"

"I should think they'd make good replacements for the ones cut down over there."

"No, they're the wrong kind of tree. They're pines. They have soft wood, and the ones they cut down were hardwoods. Cleaning the forest isn't a job just anyone can do. You have to know how to do it."

"You know how to do it right? Do you actually do it?"

"I can't with this bad knee."

"*Ach*, I know all about that. I can barely make it up and down the stairs in our building."

Gisi lets them talk while she wanders a little farther into the woods. The snow makes a soft carpet on the forest floor, muffling the voices of the old men. The deeper into the woods she goes, the more entrancing the silence became.

A light snow is falling. All around her the leafless branches catch the snow, creating a breathtaking panorama of black and white with an occasional dash of green from a pine or spruce. She breathes it in, reflecting on how deeply she loves this place, and her beautiful country, Austria.

"Gisi!" Her grandfather's voice interrupts her reverie. "We found the tree!" She follows her snowy footsteps back to the clearing where Clemens has just cut off the top of a pretty evergreen.

"It's perfect!" she says, smiling, and the three turn back toward the village. With the tree over her great uncle's shoulder, they walk through the falling snow single file, all equally in awe of their surroundings.

When they came back to the family house, Basia and the

others have moved the furniture around so a small round table is now sitting by the front window. They set the little tree in a heavy pot filled with stones and water on the table, and the women decorate it with nuts, dried fruit, and the delicate glass ornaments her great aunt keeps in a box in the attic. Very carefully, they clip on the candle holders and insert the small white candles that would only be lit once, the following night, on Christmas Eve.

The next day there is more cooking and baking, and Litzi and Theresa arrive. The three young women sit together peeling vegetables.

"So, how is it to be married?" Gisi asks Litzi. "Is it as wonderful as we are supposed to believe?"

"Of course it is, even better, I bet," answers Theresa for her sister. "I can't wait for my own wedding day."

"Theresa is right. Being with Horst day and night," she giggles, "is almost as much fun as being with you two!" Then very softly, she says, "And I have some exciting news to share that I haven't told anyone yet."

"No! Already?" says Gisi. "So soon?"

"Oh, Litzi—just what I wanted to hear! Are you certain?" Theresa can hardly keep her voice down.

"Well, I'm three weeks late now, and I'm usually very regular, so..." Litzi whispers conspiratorially.

"Congratulations!" says Gisi. "I hope it goes well." She's thinking about a girl in her neighborhood who left school suddenly to get married and died giving birth prematurely a few months later. She was only seventeen. The rumor was that her husband beat her. But Litzi would never marry a man who treated her badly.

Horst arrives just as they are about to sit down to dinner. He spent the day with his own family in a neighboring village and had to wait for a cousin to drive him over to Litzi's family celebration. A big man with a shock of blond hair slicked back onto his head with grease, he has an infectious smile and sparkling blue eyes that make everyone like him right away. Though it is obvious he could hold the attention of the whole room easily, he is deferential to the older men, who were telling stories of their childhood in Tannheim when he arrived, and gracious to the ladies, pulling their chairs out one by one as they come into the crowded dining room.

As Horst pulls Gisi's chair out, she notices that he smells strongly of *gluhwein*, but why shouldn't he? He just came from celebrating Christmas with his family. Her family had enjoyed the warm sweet wine with Christmas cookies that afternoon, too. She was the only one who'd abstained.

Dinner is sumptuous. First, each person is given a bowl of rich goose broth with one *Speckknödl* at its center. The round boiled bread dumpling with bits of bacon in it is sprinkled with festive fresh parsley from the pot in Greta's kitchen window. Gisi likes *Speckknödl* so much she wishes she could have two, but the dumplings are almost big enough to fill the soup bowl, and she knows the huge meal is just beginning.

The fish course follows. A large carp, caught by Hans the day before and kept alive in the bathtub until the last minute, is served in *sulz*, a savory gelatin. It's the part of the meal Gisi likes the least, but she politely picks out the bones and does her best to smile as she eats the cold fish. She likes the *sulz* even less, but fortunately there are tasty boiled carrots in it, which she enjoys. Theresa doesn't like the carp dish either. The cousins make eyes at each other as they watch their relatives enthusiastically sop up the last of the *sulz* on their plates with pieces of the kaiser rolls Gisi's mother baked that morning.

Next comes the main course, a goose stuffed with chestnut filling, served with red cabbage. The family has the same argument about who gets which piece every year, the wings and legs being the prizes, but Gisi is happy with anything as long as she gets lots of the crispy, salty skin.

It's accompanied by Basia's speciality, *Schlutzkrapfen*, dough-and-egg crescents with hearty potato filling boiled in salt water and served with brown butter and parsley, and a medley of root vegetables: white beets, rutabaga, turnips, parsnips, and carrots.

After a short break during which the men smoke cigars while the women clear and reset the table, the *Zelten*, a special Tyrolean fruitcake, is served. Greta baked it early in the Advent season because the longer it's left to mature, the juicier it is. Made with dried figs, pine nuts, raisins, hazelnuts, walnuts, and almonds, and seasoned with aniseed and cumin in addition to the more conventional fruitcake spices, this year's *Zelten* is exceptional. The lightly sweetened whipped cream on the side of each plate and on top of the coffee adds the perfect touch.

After dinner the men settle down in the sitting room with glasses of schnapps and the women clean up. Throughout the meal the conversation was light and filled with laughter, but afterwards the men begin to talk politics.

Clemens, a strong believer in the wisdom of uniting all the German-speaking countries, is, naturally, a member of the local Pan-German party. He and Josef, Gisi's grandfather, who has been a Social Democrat for nearly 50 years, have been arguing politics for almost that long. Hans, Clemens' son-in-law, isn't very interested in politics but voted Christian Social in the last election. He usually doesn't say much during the older men's discussions. Horst, it turns out, sympathizes with the political wing of the *Heimwehr*.

"Ha!" cries Clemens when Horst reveals his inclination. "Now all we need is a Nazi and all of Austria will be represented right here in our family."

Josef says, laughing, "Luckily, we can all appreciate a good argument without anyone getting hurt."

"It's not an argument; it's a discussion," says Clemens, pouring everyone another drink.

"So, what do you think of Dollfuss?" he asks the others, and the voices begin to rise.

In the kitchen, the three young women are drying and putting away the good china.

"Horst is wonderful, Litzi," says her sister. "He's such a gentleman."

"And very kind," adds Gisi. "He asked my mother questions that made me feel like he really wanted to know her. I think she's falling in love with him, too."

"I do feel very lucky," answers Litzi.

"I think we're all very lucky," Theresa says as she hangs her damp towel on the railing mounted all around the tiled stove. "We have everything we need: family, friends, a snug house, good food, and a warm fire."

Gisi thinks back to the hungry faces of the children in Edith's photographs, and wishes that everybody could say that.

CHAPTER 29

GERT, TONI, AND GISI + AN OPPORTUNITY

December 31, 1932
3 pm
Gert and Toni's apartment

Gisi, Gert, and Toni are sitting huddled around the heavy iron radiator in Toni and Gert's apartment. Every so often it hisses but it barely warms up at all.

"This place is either much too hot or freezing cold," says Gert. "There's no middle ground. I'm sorry you came to visit on a day when it's so cold here, Gisi."

"Too cold is only marginally worse than too hot," Gisi answers.

Toni adds, "At least you can open the window a little when it's too hot."

"In any case, we have this deliciously hot chicory coffee," Gert says, handing around the steaming cups. "Happy New Year!"

"May 1933 be an improvement over 1932!" says Toni as they clink their cups.

"That won't be hard," Gisi says. "But it doesn't seem very likely either. In any case, *Gutes Neues Jahr!*"

"How was your holiday in Tyrol?" asks Toni.

Gisi tells her friends how it went. "It was wonderful, of course," she finishes, "but in some ways I felt uneasy there.

My family in Tannheim lives a very different life to ours here. Of course, their politics are different, more conservative, but I have a sense that our differences run even deeper. I can't really explain it. Sometimes I feel more at home with Max's family, even though they're so much less comfortable than my family in many ways."

"I definitely feel more comfortable in Leo's family than in my own," Toni says. "They're poorer than my family—and there are so many of them—but they're always laughing. And they sing and play music together! My own family never seems to have enough. My mother in particular wishes she'd been born into the bourgeoisie. She even has a special accent for talking to people she thinks are above her in status. I can't stand it."

"That's funny," Gisi responds. "I've never heard her do that."

"That's because your family is from the same class as ours."

Toni adds, "Leo's family speaks Yiddish when the grandparents are around. I can barely follow it. There are all kinds of expressions they use that even if I can figure out what the words mean, they make no sense to me."

"You're quiet, Gert. What's Rolf's family like?"

"I haven't met them yet because they live in Salzburg, but I think they're even more conservative than your family in Tyrol, Gisi. They're very religious, maybe even more than my mother, which is hard to imagine."

"Do you know which party they belong to?" asks Toni. "Or, for that matter, which party Rolf belongs to?"

"I've never asked. As to his parents, I assume it's one of the more conservative Pan-German parties, or maybe they're Christian Socials. Rolf rejects much of what they stand for, so I think he's probably more leftist than they are, but to be honest, it's never come up. Our relationship is more about having fun than serious issues. I find it refreshing. We never argue politics—we never even discuss current events."

"Huh," says Gisi. "I find that a little discomfiting. Politics are important. If you never even discuss what's happening in the world, you're part of the problem. It's our duty to take responsibility in improving everyone's quality of life."

"I'm not as sure about that as I once was. You know as well as I do that not all the people in the housing complexes are happy with the culture the party is trying to impose on them," Gert says. "Rolf told me a story about someone he knows who moved into Austerlitz-Hof who is going around convincing people there that you pay for all the services by toeing the party line. His friend says it's not worth it and is looking for a place in his old neighborhood."

"People like that aren't happy because it's too big a change for them. People don't like change, even if it's change for the better," points out Toni, standing to collect the cups. "Anyone want a little more? The pot isn't empty."

"I'll take some," says Gisi. "You should talk to Rolf, Gert. Soon. Especially if you're considering getting married."

"I don't know if I can. I love him."

Gisi looks at her sternly. "Do you want me to do it? I'm not afraid."

Gert sniffles. "No, I'll do it."

❧❦❧

January 12, 1933
Vienna
Emil's boarding house

"There's a letter for you," Emil's landlady calls from the kitchen as he comes through the door of the boarding house after the day's lectures.

"Thanks, *Frau* Rosenthal," Emil says, taking off his gloves. "*Ach*, it's bitter cold out there!" He picks up the letter from the table by the door and slits it open with his penknife.

"It's from my friend Walter in Switzerland," he tells *Frau* Rosenthal, who would surely want to know, and he climbs up the stairs to read it in his room.

Sitting on the bed, he slips the letter out of the envelope:

Basel, Switzerland
January 11, 1933

Lieber Emil,
I hope you are well and enjoying the beautiful winter in our lovely home city. I can imagine the snow on the rooftops and on the trees in the parks. I do miss Vienna, and especially our lively conversations and chess games at the coffee house.

Here in Basel we have just as much or perhaps even more snow than usually falls in Vienna, but it is not quite so cold. Yesterday, in fact, I saw the sun showing her face, which is somewhat rare here at this time of year, so I went out without my gloves. I thought perhaps the snow was beginning to melt. I was wrong, however, and my hands were terribly cold all day.

Basel is an ancient and beautiful city of about 100,000 people, so it is much smaller than Vienna and considerably less crowded. It sits on the Rhine River where Switzerland, Germany and France meet. As I recall, you have never had the opportunity to visit here. Isn't that so? Basel is a city of exceptional charm and culture, having the highest concentration of museums in the country. It also has a delightful old city center, some exciting modern architecture, and, of course, the Rhine.

My work with Sandoz Laboratories goes very well. The research is stimulating, my colleagues are a pleasure to work with, and the laboratories are modern and well-equipped. Indeed, it is an entirely world-class enterprise, and I feel most fortunate to have found a place here.

It is in regard to Sandoz that I write.

It has come to my attention that there is a position that will soon become available for which you might be particularly well-qualified, even if you haven't finished your degree yet. It requires just the combination of pure and applied mathematics and engineering that you have focused on for all the years we've known each other. A team at Sandoz is experimenting with designs with an extraordinarily fast calculating device, or "computer."

Perhaps you would like to visit me here and I could arrange an interview for you? Of course there are no guarantees, especially since you have one more year of study to complete as well as a thesis to write, but I suspect that you and my colleague, who is heading the new calculator project, will find you have much in common. I believe it is worth a trip to Basel to find out.

Please give my best regards to your parents and to our friend Johannes.

Freundliche Grüße,
Walter Schmidt

Emil rereads the letter several times. It's a most tempting offer! He writes back the same day, suggesting that he travel to Basel in two weeks' time when there is a short break in his classes.

Red Vienna

the same day
Gert and Toni's apartment

When Toni comes home from work, she finds Gert lying on her bed crying.

"What's the matter, Gert?" she asks. "Did something happen at work?"

"No," sobs Gert. "It was on my way home."

"What happened?"

"I ran into Emil."

"Emil! Anna's old flame? I haven't seen him in years, though I think Gisi is still friends with him."

"He was with Gisi. She's helping him with some kind of job application."

"What wrong with that?"

"Nothing's wrong with that. It's what they said to me!"

"Which was?" Toni hangs her jacket on the coat tree.

"Emil said that the reason he moved out of his old place last year—the place he shared with Rolf before Rolf got his own place, you know?—was that he found out Rolf is a Nazi."

"What? How can that be true? You've been going out with him for a whole year! Surely he would have told you— or it would have come out somehow."

Gert looks up at her friend. "We never talked about that sort of thing. He's always the perfect gentleman. I never asked."

"Maybe Emil is just paranoid. Some Jews are, you know, because there's so much persecution."

"Maybe. I hope that's true. I love Rolf. He's saving to buy me a ring so we can get engaged officially. He was going to take me to Salzburg to meet his family next month."

"Well, you'd better ask him straight out before you make a commitment to him."

Gert sobs. "I already did make a commitment. He asked

166

me to marry him and I said yes! I haven't told anyone because he asked me to wait until he could buy the ring."

"Oh, Gert, this is such a mess."

January 15, 1933
three days later
Toni and Gert's apartment

"So, did you ask him?" Toni asks Gert. They're sitting at the table on a Sunday afternoon peeling potatoes.

"No, I couldn't make myself. We went to see a funny film and I couldn't find an opening. Our relationship isn't like that—we don't ask each other serious questions."

"But you know what Emil said about him."

"I know. I feel so weak," Gert says miserably.

"Listen, Gert, Gisi and I have supported you so far. We haven't told a soul—but you really have to ask him. Or just break up with him."

"Of course you haven't told anyone. You're both going out with Jewish men! Who are you going to tell?"

"If you can't make yourself ask him or break up with him in person, how about if I help you write him a letter?"

"That's so cold! I love him, Toni. You don't get it!"

"I'm going to get out some paper right now. I'll start, you can add what you want and then copy it over in your own handwriting. If you can't do it, maybe I should find another place to live."

"Oh, Toni, don't do that. We've been best friends since school—I don't want to find someone else to share your place with."

"Then you don't have any choice." She gets up and washes her hands before pulling two sheets of stationery out of a drawer and sitting down at their little desk.

Dear Rolf, she begins. *I am so sorry to have to tell you that*

Red Vienna

I found out from friends that we have some irreconcilable differences....

Gert pushes aside the heap of potato peelings, puts her head on the dirty table, and heaves with sobs.

CHAPTER 30

FIGHTING DEMAGOGUERY

February 4, 1933
Cafe Rüdigerhof, Brigittenau

"Well, now Austria really has something to be proud of," says Hugo sarcastically. "Germany has made our native son, Adolf Hitler, in my opinion the most dangerous of all the Nazis, their Chancellor!"

Leo puts his coffee down on the table and lights a cigarette, adding, "I read in today's paper that in Hitler's first speech to the Reichstag, he promised that in four years the German farmer will be raised from his current state of destitution, and unemployment will be completely overcome. In four years—that's ridiculous! We've been in power here since 1918 working on exactly those issues and even with all our successes we can't claim that. And so many simple souls, especially those who are desperately poor now, believe he can actually do it."

"*Schrecklich!*" says Toni. Terrible. "Do the people who voted him in have any idea of what they have done? To give a man like that so much power?"

"Of course not. Most of them feel they're still suffering because of the Versailles Treaty, and to a certain degree they are. Germany did get the short end of the stick there. The people who support Hitler think he can change that somehow," Max says, a wry look on his face.

Toni takes umbrage. "Austria suffered even more at the end of the Great War. After having such a massive empire we're a tiny land-locked state now. One big city and a lot of mountains. But Austria hasn't fallen for a demagogue," she points out.

"I don't think the German people have any idea of the danger. They believe the propaganda. They're unhappy and they think Hitler will solve their problems by ridding the country of what they see as the cause," Hugo says.

"What's that? The Treaty of Versailles?" asks Gert.

"Don't be a fool, Gert," says Anna, who just arrived. "It's very simple. The Jews are the problem. It's the Jews that need to be gotten rid of. Everyone knows that."

"You're right, of course, Anna. What I'm worried about is how he will go about doing it," Gisi adds. "It could get much worse than it already is."

"I don't want to even try to imagine that," Toni says.

They're sitting at their *Stammtisch* waiting for Edith to drop off some flyers Hugo designed for the SDAP candidates in the upcoming municipal elections. Leo printed them at work the last several years, but recently the owner of the small press he works for switched parties and he rescinded his permission for Leo to use the press on weekends for SDAP and SAJ publications. Because his boss supports the Christian Socials, he'd allowed another of his employees to print Christian Social flyers instead. Leo has been looking for work with a more sympathetic printer, but while he's looking a new position, Edith volunteered to get the flyers printed at a place she knows.

Max continues the discussion. "I hear that some of the Jews are beginning to leave Germany voluntarily. Quite a few are going to Palestine."

"Good idea, even though Palestine sounds like a god-awful place." Leo says. "It's not so easy to pack up your life and leave a place you've lived in your whole life. Even if you're young. I certainly wouldn't want to leave my friends and family and emigrate to another country."

"And who would want to live in the desert in north Africa anyway?" agrees Max.

"Did you read in the paper that Hindenburg limited freedom of the press in Germany? From now on, we'll be hearing less and less about what's really going on over the border," adds Hugo.

A biting wind blows into the cafe as Edith enters, the stack of flyers in her hand.

"Here they are! A few more than you asked me to do. They look good, don't you think?" She holds one up. They do look good, as good as the ones Leo printed.

"Thank you, Edith," Hugo says. "I'm pleased. Sit down. Have a coffee with us."

Edith looks at her watch. "Sure, I have a little time." She tucks her camera bag under a chair and makes herself comfortable. "So what's new? What are your plans for the next months?" A lively conversation follows. Edith explains to the group that she has a new job with the party leadership, rotating between between neighborhood groups to cross-fertilize ideas.

"Great idea," Hugo is impressed. "With us, you're in the perfect position to do that since you're getting our flyers printed for us."

"Can you tell us what some of the other district level groups are doing?" asks Gisi.

"Well, the group based at Julius-Ofner-Hof is planning an information campaign to warn people of the danger of falling for demagogues like Hitler. I offered to get their flyers printed, too, but they have a press right there," she tells them. "But their point is a good one. People are frighteningly susceptible to demagogues. Any political leader who seeks support by appealing to the prejudices, fears, and hatred of ordinary people rather than by using rational argument is dangerous. It tears apart of the fabric of society. Hitler is the perfect example. It could just as easily happen here, of course—a populist leader could rise up and take power."

"Educating people about demagogues is a good idea. We should do something like that here," suggests Gisi.

"More flyers, more posters!" says Hugo. "I'm in!" He pulls out a sketchbook and starts to draw. "I'll start to work on a cartoon."

"I think printing more flyers will be too expensive. Do we really know if anyone is paying attention to the ones we're putting out now?" Max asks.

Leo chuckles. "Could be they're wrapping their garbage in our beautiful flyers. Do a good cartoon, though, Hugo, and maybe we can get it in the *Arbeiter Zeitung*."

"That would be preaching to the choir. Everyone who reads the *Arbeiter Zeitung* already agrees with us on issues like this," comments Hugo.

Toni has an idea. "How about doing a series of talks in each of the local housing complexes?"

"What about doing them in the beer halls and coffee houses? That's how Hitler spreads his ideas," Gisi suggests.

"Great idea," says Edith. "You should do it. I'll pass your ideas along to the other groups. Keep me posted." She picks up her camera bag, says good-bye to them all, and is gone.

"So, none of us asked about her engagement," Toni says. "What's going on with that?"

"We should have asked her. I haven't heard a word about it from anyone else," Gisi answers. "Maybe it wasn't true."

"What I heard was that the man she was so-called 'engaged' to is married with two children," says Toni.

"That'll complicate matters," laughs Leo.

Max asks, "Have any of you seen her brother Wolf lately?"

"I think he's off studying film at the Bauhaus in Germany," Hugo says. "I should be so lucky."

"Well, next time any of you see either of them, ask," Gisi answers. "I'm dying to know more."

CHAPTER 31

MEETINGS OVER COFFEE

March 7, 1933
Cafe Rüdigerhof, Brigittenau

M ax closes the shop early to meet with the others at the coffee house. The news that Chancellor Dollfuss had eliminated the parliament hit the press earlier that week, and that on the same day, it had been announced that the Wartime Economy Authority Law, an emergency law passed in 1917, would be used as a basis to rule. It gave Dollfuss significantly broader powers than he had under the parliamentary system.

In fact, every day that week brought what seemed like earth-shattering news. Wednesday, the National Council couldn't agree on how to settle the railway workers' strike. When an agreement was finally reached, irregularities were found in the vote, and Karl Renner, leader of the SDAP, resigned as Chairman of the Council.

"You've all heard how it came about? It was apparently one of our people. He passed his voting card on to be handed in by someone else while he went to the lavatory," Hugo says. "And they called that a voting irregularity."

"Renner shouldn't have resigned. He should have fought it," says Leo.

Hugo shakes his head. "He took the high road, though, and he's out now."

"If it wasn't true, it would be unbelievable," says Max. "That one man responding to the call of nature could cause the cascade of events that led to the downfall of democracy in Austria."

After Renner's resignation, Rudolf Ramek, a Christian Social, had been named Chairman. He declared the previous vote invalid and called for a new vote. Another uproar followed. Ramek then resigned, and Sepp Straffner, leader of the Pan-Germans, became Chairman, but he also stepped down immediately. The resignations of Renner, Ramek, and Straffner left the house without a speaker, so the session couldn't be closed and the National Council was incapable of acting. Not knowing what to do next, the members of the Parliament left the chamber.

In response, Chancellor Dollfuss had declared a constitutional crisis. The parliament had "eliminated itself," a crisis not provided for in the constitution. Dollfuss then set up an authoritarian government without a parliament. The establishment of wartime rule gave him complete authority.

"It's what he always wanted! He wanted to be head of a fascist state from the beginning!" Gert is saying as Gisi joins them.

"That's not true. Don't you remember that he wanted to make peace between the parties at first?" Toni answers.

"What does it matter now what his intentions were then?" asks Leo, looking grim. "We have a completely authoritarian government now. Democracy in Austria is dead."

"It's as bad as Italy," says Hugo. "Dollfuss always did admire Mussolini."

"That's why I said he always wanted to be a dictator," Gert points out.

Max adds, "It's a coup d'état, really. Renner, Ramek, and Straffner fell right into Dollfuss's hands."

"At least Dollfuss isn't likely to let Austria merge with Germany," says Felix.

"Small comfort when one man now controls the power over all economic activities and over war and peace indefinitely," Max points out.

Toni wonders, "Should we continue our new education program? Having Dollfuss as dictator doesn't diminish the rising power of the Nazis and the dangers of demagoguery, but I think it's risky to continue."

"Dollfuss isn't a Nazi. Or a demagogue. It's possible the rule of a strong hand will calm things down a little," Felix says.

"One can hope," says Gisi, "but I think the Nazis are far too pleased with how fast their ideas are spreading to stop now."

"I think they'll be more dangerous than ever. And we all know that Dollfuss's party, the Christian Socials, are barely less anti-Jewish than the Nazis anyway," Leo says.

Felix adds, "I wonder how soon it'll be before it's too dangerous for us to even hold meetings or give talks."

"Especially in the beer halls. I already find them frightening. I don't think we can ever convince the kind of people who go there of anything. I vote to stop taking our education programs to the beer halls," Toni says.

"But we shouldn't be driven by fear of what might be," Max answers. "I say we go ahead with the talks as scheduled. I think it would be a big mistake to let ourselves be intimidated at this point."

"I agree."

"Yes."

"You're right," come several responses.

Toni looks down into her coffee. "I think we're making

a mistake. You think you can change the minds of men who don't care about the same things you care about. I don't think it's safe anymore."

"Okay, you made your point, Toni. We'll go ahead, but I think we all need to keep our eyes and ears open to gauge the response of the groups we address," says Hugo.

"It's the energy of the mob that I'm afraid of," Toni continues. "Hitler tries to whip that energy up."

"And he succeeds," says Gisi.

Toni isn't done. "I don't want any of us to be in the position of having that mob energy turned against us. If one of us says the wrong thing…"

"Or one of them thinks he heard the wrong thing, even if we didn't say it," Gisi is as worried as Toni.

"And there's another thing to be careful about. Dictators use spies to keep the peace. We should be very careful before trusting newcomers into our movement now," adds Hugo. "It's more important than ever that we aren't portrayed as rabble-rousers."

Max stands up. "All the same, I'm not ready to give up. Let's meet on Tuesday, and listen to Leo practice his speech for the beer hall."

⊷┅ӠᚼӃᚼƐᚼ⊷

March 12, 1933
University of Vienna

Gisi smiles when she spots Emil at the bottom of the stairs when she comes out of the lecture hall.

"Hallo!" she calls, "are you waiting for me?"

"I am. Do you have some time? Can I take you out for *Jause*?" He turns to walk toward Cafe Landtmann and she runs down the stairs to catch up. "I have a dilemma I'd like to hear your thoughts on." They hadn't seen each other since he returned from his visit to Basel two weeks ago and she'd been wondering how it went.

"Sure," she says, "but my group is expecting me at the coffee house, so not for too long."

Cafe Landtmann is a step up from their usual coffee house, but it's closer to the tram stop, so it seems like a good choice. Emil, though he can rarely afford it, still enjoys a little luxury whenever he can manage it.

"I'll have a *Melange*, and a *Schillerlocken*," Gisi tells the waitress in the frilly black and white apron. She had noticed the extravagant pastry in the case as they walked in.

"For me, a *Buchteln* and a *Verlängerter*," Emil says.

As Emil shares the story of his visit to Walter in Basel and the interview at Sandoz, he watches Gisi eat the pastry slowly, with delicate and precise movements, even though he knows what a rare treat it must be for her.

"This is wonderful, Emil. Thank you so much for the delicious pastry," she tells him. "But what's your dilemma? Have they offered you the position?"

"Not yet," he answers. "But I can apply. The application process is a competition. A very interesting problem has been laid out, and the successful candidate will be the one who offers the best solution."

"That sounds like just the sort of challenge you enjoy"

"It is indeed. The issue is how much of my time it would take. My days and nights are already full with my studies. But if I wait until I've completed my master's degree, the position will surely be gone."

"The company doesn't mind if you haven't completed your degree?"

"Not if I solve the problem elegantly enough."

"Ah, I see," says Gisi. "It's a risk. I suppose it's possible that you could fail your last exams because you put so much time and effort into solving the problem, and also fail to get the position at Sandoz."

"Exactly." He stirs a second lump of sugar into his coffee.

She thinks for a few moments, taking another bite of her pastry, "Can you imagine a better position you might find here in Vienna after you graduate?"

Emil considers the idea as he savors the *Powidl* in his pastry. "No, not really. No one I know of here is even dreaming about the kind of device Sandoz hopes to produce."

"Then you should at the very least think seriously about applying."

"That much I've already decided to do. It's too good an opportunity to throw away without serious consideration. What I have to decide now is whether to commit to the time it will take or not."

"Do you know," says Gisi, pushing the last crumbs of the pastry into a neat pile at the center of her plate, "in my psychology class, we've been talking about how the creative process works, about how we come up with new ideas or solve intractable problems."

"Yes? Have they figured out how it works?"

"Well, there's been quite a lot of observation done, and a series of steps in the creative process has been suggested."

"What are they?"

"First, preparation. The problem must be carefully defined, its elements identified, older solutions studied, and any necessary research done."

"Naturally."

"Then, surprisingly, the problem must be left alone, like bread left to rise, or a baby to gestate."

"Well, that part wouldn't be so hard to do with all the work I have for my classes now."

"The gestation period lasts until the solution arises on

its own, via inspiration. It seems that truly new solutions to problems aren't found—they find you."

"Ha! Brilliant," Emil smiles broadly. "I can think of many times the best solution to a problem came to me after a good night's sleep or a hike in the mountains."

"Or even a walk in the woods. Genius strikes; we don't create it, or make it, or do it. It comes. But there is still one last step: verification. An inspired solution doesn't always work in the real world. It has to be tested."

"Impressive," says Emil. "I think I'll give it a try. I'll find the time to do the preparation and then see how things go. Thank you. That's a good solution to my dilemma."

She licks the very last of the whipped cream off her fork.

"I'm glad I could help," she says, getting up to go, "but now my friends are waiting and I have to run."

"Of course," Emil replies, helping her put on her coat.

How I wish this young woman were free, he thinks as he watches Gisi hurry down the street. I would ask her to marry me tomorrow.

Chapter 32

Radios and an Arrest

May 13, 1933
Brigittenau
Max's shop

Max lifts the radio out of the excelsior in the box, brushing off the last of the dusty wood packing material as he sets it on his workbench and plugs it in. Slowly and carefully, he turns the dial until the crackling sound disappears and a voice comes through the cloth-covered speaker. It's the news.

"Bavarian Justice Minister Doctor Frank and an entourage of German officials arrived this morning in Vienna," the announcer is saying. "But instead of the usual fanfare they expected, the Viennese officials meeting them immediately informed the Germans that their presence was not particularly desired by the government here."

Max smiles, but he doesn't want to hear the news now. Instead he turns the dial until he finds a Mozart piano concerto. Much better. He's pleased with his recent purchases, three Minerva radios in modern wooden cases which he plans to sell in the shop. He leaves the music on as he clears a table in front of the small front window, unpacks the second radio, and sets it up so people walking by on the street can see it. Then he puts a carefully lettered sign in the window announcing that he is now selling radios as well as furniture.

He stands outside the store looking at the window. The sign is too big—you can't see the radio. There are too many words and the writing is too small—it's almost impossible to read. Going back into the store, he pulls the sign out of the window and goes to his workshop in the back. He turns the piece of cardboard over and writes in much bigger capital letters BUY RADIOS HERE. But when he tries it out, the sign still takes up too much of the little window. There's nothing to do but take the sign out again. This time he carefully cuts it down so it only says RADIOS. Finally he's satisfied with the window, so he heads to the workshop to unpack the third of his new purchases.

Max's lamps have been selling surprisingly well, and he'd bought the radios with the profits. Now that the three of them are all unpacked and one is displayed in the window, he begins to work on assembling another lamp. With the money he'll earn from selling the radios and lamps he should be able to have *Herr* Berger's clock repaired. He knows the old man wants the clock fixed even though he insists that he doesn't. That's why he's so grumpy around Max. Max hasn't given up on the possibility either but this is the first time in a very long time that he feels optimistic. Once the old clock is repaired, he plans to ask Gisi to marry him. After all, he's twenty-two now and owns a thriving business. Well, a small but thriving business. A business with great promise, in any case.

At that happy moment, the bell in the front of the business interrupts his thoughts and someone walks in through the front door.

"Hallo?" Max calls out.

"Hallo," comes the reply. It's Hugo, looking discouraged.

"What's the point of trying to sell radios now?" he asks Max after a demonstration of the marvelous new devices.

"With Dollfuss shutting down more and more of the sources of news, everything we hear is censored."

"You can enjoy the music."

"The hand-picked music."

"Oh, come on, Hugo! It's not as bad as that."

"It is, Max, it is. Every day it's worse. We're moving into a era when less and less truth is being told in the public arena. And you'll see, it'll only get worse. There's already more propaganda than truth available."

Max doesn't want to hear it. He's excited about his radios. "That's so, I'm sure. But come over here." Hugo moves closer to the big wooden case holding the radio. Max is leaning over it. "Listen." He's turning one of the dials very slowly. The radio emits a crackling sound with occasional whistles. Then a voice breaks through calling out a series of numbers. "There it is!" cries Max. "With a little knowledge and care, you can tune into shortwave transmissions and foreign broadcasts on these Minervas. The more of them I sell, the more we can work around the restrictions."

"Hm," says Hugo, lifting his eyes a little. "That's encouraging, at least. You'll have to show me how to do it. With the new ban on public demonstrations and strikes, people will know even less about what's going on. I think your radios could help—and that does give me a little hope. But I came here to tell you something else." He sits down in one of Max's many chairs. "I don't know if you've been aware of it, but since the May Day demonstrations two weeks ago, the police have been all over Vienna arresting Communists. I heard that almost five hundred have been picked up. Dollfuss is apparently very concerned about Soviet interference here."

"And he's leaving the Nazis alone? I think they're the more dangerous of the two groups by a long shot, don't you?"

"Personally, I agree with you. But the Communists are supported by Russia, and for the time being at least, the Nazis here are resisting becoming a wing of the German Nazi Party. That's possibly why Dollfuss is leaving the Nazis alone, I don't know. The Nazis were outlawed at the same time as the Communists, of course, but the news is that Dollfuss's Fascist government is currently only routing out Communists—but everywhere, all over the country."

"Huh. Our paramilitary wing, the *Schutzbund*, was outlawed too."

"But so far they haven't been rounded up either. Fortunately. I don't know why—I just hope we won't be next. Now that I think of it, it occurs to me you're taking a chance, selling theses radios here."

"As far as Dollfuss and his people know, these are ordinary radios, only capable of spreading their propaganda and playing music. Hardly anyone knows what shortwave radio is. I think I'm safe."

"For now," says Hugo. "Are you coming to the cafe later?"

"Naturally. What else would I do when I close this afternoon?"

<hr>

later in the day
Cafe Rüdigerhof

"You won't believe what I heard at work," says Gert. "You really won't!" Her eyes twinkle with pleasure at the juiciness of the story she's about to share.

"What is it?" asks Leo, looking bored. He puts down his newspaper. "Someone we know is getting married?"

"No, not this time," answers Gert. "Do you think that's all

we women think about? This is a lot more important than something like that."

"Is it good or bad?" Gisi wants to know that first.

Gert thinks for a moment, pursing her very red lips. "Bad, I would say."

Anna stares. Where did Gert get that lipstick? It is lipstick, Anna is sure.

"But you're not quite sure? If it's good or bad, I mean?" asks Max as he hangs his sweater on the back of the outdoor chair in front of the cafe.

"Come on, tell us!" says Toni.

"All right. This is it. You know how Hugo told us the government has been rounding up all the Communists?" Gert looks all around the circle of friends.

"Am I missing something?" Gisi says. "I didn't know that was happening."

"It's been going on ever since May Day," Hugo tells her. "All over the city and the countryside, too. But just the Communists, not the Nazis or the *Schutzbund*, even though they've all been banned."

Gisi makes a long face. "Why am I always the last to know?"

Gert says, "Because your nose is always in a book! Now listen. Last week, just outside the Goethe bookstore, the police stopped and arrested another Communist." She pauses for effect. "Who do you think it was?"

Toni wrinkles her brow, and pushes a black curl behind her ear. "Who do we know who's a Communist? Their party leadership, of course..."

"Who said we know this person?" asks Max.

"Why else would she be telling us this story like she is? Of course, we know the person who was arrested," says Gisi.

"There are the people who write letters to the newspaper defending the Communists..." suggests Leo.

"No, this is someone who was arrested for *spying*," Gert says. "Not someone whose sympathy for the Communists everybody already knows about."

"A relative of someone's? A brother or sister? A cousin?" asks Max.

Felix asks, "Or is it someone who's well-known? A public figure?"

"No, no." Gert answers quickly but then stops. "Well, yes, you could say a public figure. In certain circles, anyway."

"All right, Gert, tell us," says Hugo, "Enough of this game."

"Okay," says Gert, fluttering her eyelashes a little and pausing for effect. "It's Edith!"

"Edith!" The group all talks at once.

"No!"

"Our Edith?"

"How could it be Edith?"

"What would Edith see in the Communists?"

"She's in jail?"

"But her father owns Goethe, the Social Democratic bookstore."

"Who was she spying on?"

"Oh my god," Gisi cries. "She must have been spying on us!"

❧❦❧

May 14, 1933
the next day
Max's shop

In the back of his shop, Max is listening to the news on the radio as he screws a bulb into one of the new lamps.

The announcer is reading the news. "The German Reich

has responded to the Viennese officials telling the German minister Doctor Frank that he is not welcome in Vienna by imposing an exorbitant visa fee for all Austrians entering Germany."

"Well," Max tells the radio, "I, for one, had no desire to go to Germany even before exorbitant visa fees were applied." He looks around. The shop looks cheerful with all six of the lamps on, but it's too expensive to leave them on, so one by one, he switches them off.

As he returns to his work area, the bell sounds and Anna comes in.

"So, did you hear the news about your friend Edith?" she asks, easing her way through the crowded display room.

"She isn't particularly my friend. Is she yours?"

"I guess not! So much for the queen of blending social justice with publicity."

"It's a shame," Max says. "She did a lot to change the perception of who the poor are, but I suppose she thinks the Soviets are doing a better job alleviating poverty than we are. I wonder how long she'll be in jail."

"She's out already."

"Is that true? They let her go home until the trial?"

"They did, and she took full advantage of it."

"What do you mean?"

"She's already in England. You know that doctor she was having an affair with? Well, yesterday he arrived in Vienna to rescue her. They flew to London last night. And I hear they got married this morning!"

CHAPTER 33

THE PATTERN

May 21, 1933
a cafe near Emil's boarding house

"Personally, I think it's a very good thing that we only have one party now. Dollfuss was brilliant to merge the Christian Socials and the Pan-Germans into the Fatherland Front, with the *Heimwehr* as their paramilitary," Johannes says. "The last thing we need now is infighting." He puts out his cigarette and takes a sip of his coffee.

"That's alright with me, but what I wonder is, what are the banned parties doing? They won't actually give up their beliefs, will they? Wouldn't they all just go underground?" asks Zlotka, lighting a new cigarette and offering Emil and Johannes a light. The three of them are sitting in the sun outside their regular coffee house.

A gentle spring wind carries the fragrance of the blooming trees past their table. It's the first time in weeks that Emil has come out from under his work to join his friends. That day, he finally gave in to the call of the breeze at his window. For several weeks he had tried Gisi's suggestion of doing the preparation for his application to Sandoz, and then leaving it alone to focus on his classes, but so far the inspiration he was waiting for hadn't struck.

"Let them all crawl back into their holes, " says Johannes.

"I'm sure the Communists already have, the ones who escaped the raids. And I suspect the SDAP's paramilitary, the *Schutzbund*, has, too. The Nazis? For the time being also. But take my word, the Nazis won't stay hidden for long. They'll be back in force, and it's my bet that it won't take more than a few days."

Emil sighs. "You're probably right. Dollfuss can try to keep the peace by decree, but I'm not sure it will work in the long run."

"I believe he's making a deal with Mussolini for Austria to serve as a buffer between Italy and the German Reich, and on paper this time," Johannes says.

"*Ach*, it gives me a headache to think about it," says Zlotka, putting a hand to her head. "How fortunate for me that I'm just a student here and not a member of the Austrian Communist party!" She smiles. "Emil, tell me, have you sent in your application to Sandoz?"

"I haven't, and I suspect it may be too late now. I have no idea who else is submitting a solution to the problem or how long they'll wait for the perfect candidate."

"But you haven't heard from Walter that somebody else has been hired for the position?"

"No, but the committee could well be deciding between applicants. I haven't even come up with a solution yet, much less written it up. I'm beginning to think the push-on-through method of problem-solving might be more effective than the incubation method that Gisi recommended."

"At least you've been able to keep up with your classwork."

"That's true, but in addition to solving the Sandoz problem and keeping up with my classes, I have my thesis to complete before my degree is finished. It's rather overwhelming at the moment. In fact, I shouldn't be here at all now." He looks at his watch, drinks the last of his coffee, and stands up. "It was a pleasure to spend time with you both, however brief." Tipping his hat and bowing to each of his friends, he turns and walks away.

"I worry about him," says Zlotka.

Emil doesn't go home to study or work on the problem for Sandoz. Instead, he walks back toward the University. It's four in the afternoon, he thinks, just in time to catch Gisi as she finishes her classes.

As he walks, he reconsiders the Sandoz position. It does seem like a dream come true. Basel suits him, the job suits him, and Switzerland's policy of remaining neutral suits him. It would be good to get away from all the tension in Vienna, especially among the members of the Social Democratic group. They're much more worried about the political situation than most of the people he knows. In fact, it drives him a little nuts how worried they are. He has a hard time taking seriously the dark perspective on life they, even Gisi, seem to have adopted in the last couple of years.

He's ready to put some distance between his parents and himself, too. It isn't that he doesn't love them; it's just hard to watch them encouraging each other in decline instead of supporting each other in recovery. His father could look for work. For that matter, his mother could do the same. But instead, they stay at home, often not even dressing, his mother complaining constantly about what they lost, his father complaining constantly about his mother. If he got the position at Sandoz, he could send them some money every month, which would probably alleviate his mother's anxiety considerably and hence his father's too.

He pulls his light sweater on more tightly. The weather is changing, blue skies clouding over, and the pleasant breeze is turning cold.

The problem Sandoz gave him to solve shouldn't be impenetrable, he thinks. He has the background in math and in engineering to solve it. The thing that's stopping him from moving forward with it is that it's so much more complex than anything he'd ever tackled before, and so far, he hasn't even been able to discern a pattern in it. If Gisi's creative problem-solving method had yielded some kind of pattern, and then he could have gone ahead and solved it. He drops his finished cigarette into the gutter and figures he'll have another look at the problem when he gets home.

A few big drops of rain fall, and suddenly it's pouring. Emil pulls his sweater over his head and walks faster. He doesn't have an umbrella with him. The wind is growing stronger, driving the rain hard into his face, blowing him backwards, soaking through his clothes. Another couple blocks to go. Should he stop somewhere? No, he'd miss Gisi. He runs.

Two minutes later he's nearly at the Landtmann Cafe, only a block from Gisi's tram stop. The wind and rain are too much. He needs to stop for a moment and dry off a little. He slows, wipes the water out of his eyes, and pushes open the heavy glass door to the cafe.

"Emil!" calls a voice. He looks up, and there is Gisi, sitting at a table with her friend Elsa.

"Look at you!" she cries. "You're as wet as I was when you took me to your boarding house last winter."

"I am," he laughs, looking at his drenched clothes dripping onto the tiled floor. "It's exactly like that time you ended up at my place with your clothes soaking wet. Are you going to make me undress so you can dry my clothes?"

Elsa laughs too and asks Gisi, "Did he really make you undress?"

"He did," she answers. "Well, it was actually his landlady who insisted that I take off my wet clothes, and she gave me an enormous robe to wear while she hung them by the stove to dry."

"I probably shouldn't undress here." He looks around the elegant cafe. "What do you think?" Emil cocks his head slightly, raises one eyebrow, and looks at each of the young women. "Do you think anyone will appear with a big soft robe for me to wear if I take my clothes off here?"

Gisi smiles. "I think you should go into the restroom and see if you can squeeze some of the water out of your clothes and dry off the best you can, and then come and sit down with us. We're celebrating the results of Elsa's nursing exams."

A few minutes later they are having rich coffee drinks topped with sweet whipped cream and Emil is trying to explain the Sandoz problem to them.

"That many calculations would have to be solved simultaneously?" asks Elsa. "I can't imagine how it could be possible!"

"When you describe it, the image of Toni's loom comes to mind," says Gisi. "So many threads being worked simultaneously."

Emil stares at her. "That's it!" he cries out. "That's the pattern I've been looking for! I think I can solve the problem!"

Chapter 34

Peter

June 20, 1933
Cafe Rüdigerhof, Brigittenau

Hugo joins the group late that afternoon. When he finally arrives, he's holding the hand of a little boy, about five years old, with frizzy red hair and glasses almost exactly like his.

"Well, I did it," says Hugo, sitting down. "I went to Berlin—I paid that exorbitant visa fee, but it was worth every penny—because look who came home with me." The boy looks out from behind the big man shyly. "This is my nephew, Peter." He pulls Peter forward gently and then turns and addresses the waiter, "A chair for Peter, please. And some hot chocolate if you have it."

A chair is procured from the next table and Peter climbs up and sits down. He leans toward his uncle, tiny in the big chair, and Hugo puts his hand over the boy's. Everyone greets Peter warmly, but the little boy barely responds.

"Let me tell you some of what is happening in Germany. Peter is here for a good reason, and his parents will be coming as soon as they can sell their apartment.

"As you know, we hardly hear the news from Germany, and what we do hear can't be trusted. I have to tell you, though, having just been there, that the news isn't good at all." Hugo looks at Peter, who seems smaller than ever sitting in that adult-sized chair, picks him up, and settles the boy on his lap. Then he continues, "Since April 1, all Jewish-owned shops and businesses in Germany are being boycotted."

"Oh, no," says Gisi.

Hugo goes on, "Peter's father, who's a gentlemen's tailor, only gets by because so many of his customers are Jewish. The great majority of his non-Jewish clients are honoring the boycott."

The waiter brings a coffee for Hugo and some hot chocolate for the boy. Holding the big cup with both hands, Peter tastes his drink tentatively and then drinks it all down in big gulps.

"There's more bad news. As most of you know, my eldest sister Hilda, Peter's mother, has been teaching Austrian Literature at the University there for several years. She already had one strike against her because she's Austrian, no matter that she is married to a German, but on April 7, a new law was passed barring Jews from holding any civil service, state, or university positions. Hilda had to clean out her office and leave the same day."

"*Schrecklich,*" say Gisi. Awful.

"It could happen here any time, believe me," Leo says. "They already bombed the shop of that Jewish jeweler and killed him, right here in Vienna."

Anna reaches over and wipes some of the chocolate off Peter's face with her handkerchief.

"It could indeed. Even so, I wouldn't have gone to Berlin to get Peter if there hadn't been another factor. Peter, who as you can see is small for his age, has been bullied at school. Last week, a few days before I went to Berlin, my sister called to tell me a gang of bigger boys had followed Peter home, throwing stones at him. Isn't that so, Peter?"

The little boy nods his head sadly. "They broke our front

window with a great big rock," he says, barely looking up. "And the next morning, when I woke up and came downstairs, it was all dark in our apartment because Vati had boarded up the window." He sniffs and looks into his empty cup. "And then, when Mutti took me to school, those big boys were waiting for me in the school yard. So Mutti took me home again and I didn't go to school after that." He wipes out the inside of his cup with his finger and sucks on it.

Hugo continues. "I went to get Peter as soon as I could, and now he can stay with me, and join Anna's kindergarten class at Austerlitz-Hof."

"Welcome, Peter!" comes from around the table as coffee cups are held up in a toast to the little boy.

"But my cup is empty," Peter protests.

"Well then, we'll have to get you some more hot chocolate," says Toni, standing up to go to find the waiter. One cup of hot chocolate is already an extravagant treat, but this is an occasion that merits two. Gisi stands up too and follows her friend.

Once they were out of range of Peter's hearing, Gisi says to Toni, "I certainly hope Peter's parents can get out soon—it will be very expensive."

Toni shakes her head. "I know. I don't want to hear what it already cost Hugo to get Peter out."

"Did you know that Germany is requiring citizens intending to travel to Austria to pay a thousand mark exit fee? I wonder if they had to pay that for Peter."

"Probably."

"Then his parents will have to pay it twice more, in addition to the cost of replacing the window, and of moving their things here. I hope they can sell their their apartment for enough to pay for it all."

"It certainly won't be easy," Toni says, scanning the cafe for the waiter.

When Gisi and Toni return to the table, Hugo is saying, "And there's even more bad news from Germany. Last month, there were dozens of public book burnings."

"No!" says Toni as she sits down.

Felix says, "How awful!"

"Whose books were burned?" asks Max.

"All the books by Jews, by political dissidents, and by a long list of others not approved of by the Reich," Hugo answers. "The frightening thing is that it happened all over the country, in small villages as well as in the big cities."

"Very disturbing," says Leo. "It shows you how deep and wide-spread the anti-Jewish sentiment is."

"It's probably just as wide-spread here," says Felix.

"At least Dollfuss is working hard to keep a lid on it," adds Toni.

"For the time being," Max says.

"Well, the Nazis seem to have stopped planting bombs in places frequented by tourists since Dollfuss took full control," continues Felix.

"It's no wonder he decided to put his foot down after that terrible street fight in Innsbruck between the *Heimwehr* and those Nazi students! That was really awful," Toni says. "So many injured and four killed."

Leo says, "I'm embarrassed to admit it made me smile when Dollfuss responded to that by prohibiting the Nazis from wearing their brown shirts in public—and then the Nazis countered by parading through the city shirtless but in silk top hats. Did any of you see the pictures of them?"

"I saw them in one of the papers. It was pretty funny," agrees Max with a chuckle.

"I didn't find it funny at all!" cries Gisi. "I'm so relieved that the Austrian Nazi Party is completely banned now."

Toni agrees. "I don't think anything about the Nazis is funny. But I do think Dollfuss is serious about keeping them down for good this time. He even expelled Theo Habicht, the Austrian Nazi leader who was Hitler's man here."

"That's right, and when he outlawed the party, Dollfuss appointed Commissioners of Public Safety to carry out his decrees in each of the states. It's in the provincial areas that the people are the most vulnerable to Nazi propaganda. I'm feeling hopeful about Dollfuss's recent moves, too. I think there is good reason to believe we're still safe here in Austria," says Hugo.

"And Peter is safe here too," says Anna, putting her hand on Peter's little knee.

Peter smiles up at her just a little.

CHAPTER 35

THREE STORIES

July 5 1933
Emil's boarding house

Emil returns from the post office to find Zlotka is waiting for him in front of their boarding house.

"Congratulations!" she cries, running up the street to greet him. "*Frau* Rosenthal told me you were going to mail your application to Sandoz this morning."

"I just came back from the post office," Emil smiles. "What a relief! Now all I have to do is to complete my thesis and hand that in. Then my fate is up to the gods."

"I think you should take a short break before you try to finish your thesis. It isn't healthy to work all the time."

"Of course it isn't, but I still don't know who else has submitted applications for the position at Sandoz, and I don't know when they will decide whom to hire. I'm sure all of the other candidates will already have completed their degrees. I'd be a fool not to finish my thesis and defend it as quickly as I can."

"But you have the rest of the summer to do it. No one will be at the university to receive it for several weeks— they're all on summer break. I've been thinking. Why don't we go on a short vacation together?" Zlotka's eyes shine up at him.

"A vacation? What's that?" asks Emil, raising that eyebrow.

She laughs. "Let's just go somewhere for a few days. Then you can get back to work. We could take the train into the mountains and go hiking." She shakes her head just a little and her blond waves bounce. She's a pretty girl, Emil thinks. Funny, I hadn't noticed that before.

"Maybe it's not a bad idea, to take a short vacation."

"We could stay overnight in one of the huts in the mountains. It would be fun."

"We'd go for two days?"

"Three!"

"Okay, three. Have you already got it all planned? I wouldn't be a bit surprised," he teases.

"Actually, I have. I was thinking we could go hiking on the Rax. It's not too far. We can take the new cable car up."

❦

July 5, 1933
Alsergrund

Gisi still has lunch at home with her mother and grandfather whenever she can manage it, but it doesn't happen as frequently as she would like. Her medical course is so demanding that, as often as not, she doesn't have time for a mid-day meal. She spends the lunch hours in the library studying. Anyway, food is more scarce than ever, and even with her grandfather's pension and her mother's meager earnings, there is rarely enough for three. At breakfast she eats as much bread as she can, drinks a glass of milk, and sometimes has a little cheese if she thinks her family can spare it. She buys an apple on her way to university and eats it surreptitiously in the library where food isn't allowed. When she comes home in the evening, there's always her mother's soup for supper. It's fortunate that the term will be over soon because Gisi has so little energy it's getting hard to keep up with the work. She's very, very thin.

On Wednesdays there are no classes in the afternoon, so she's usually able to come home in time for the noon meal. That July day her mother made her favorite, *Schinkenfleckerl*. Though there is almost no pork in it, just a few crumbles of bacon and the heel of the small piece of ham they had on Sunday chopped finely, there are plenty of long savory egg noodles. Gisi eats her pile of noodles happily and scrapes a little of what is stuck to the bottom of the pan onto her mother's and grandfather's plates before finishing the crunchy browned scrapings herself.

"My favorite part of my favorite meal," she says, licking the last of the salty taste off her lips.

"You won't be able to have *Schinkenfleckerl* if you marry Max, you know," says her grandfather, looking at her sideways as he pushes the last of the scrapings onto his fork.

Gisi is surprised. "What do you mean?"

"Jews don't eat pork," he says, folding his napkin and slipping it back into the silver napkin ring with his initials engraved on it.

"Don't be silly, Opa. Max's family doesn't follow old-fashioned customs like that. Only the Orthodox Jews do. His family is secular." She gets up to clear the plates.

"Old customs like that are hard to let go of. I'll bet he tells you he doesn't eat pork because he doesn't like it."

Gisi is offended. "He wouldn't do that! He doesn't lie. Anyway, I've seen him eating sausage lots of times, and that's made of pork." She doesn't mention that Max claims to be allergic to shellfish. He probably really is, she thinks.

"Religious ideas about things like what to eat and not to eat are dying out everywhere."

"I wouldn't be so sure," says her grandfather. "I heard on the radio that Dollfuss just reached a concordat with the Vatican giving the Roman Catholic Church much greater influence over Austrian schools."

"Austria has always been a Catholic country," says Helene. "We all had catechism in school. It didn't make good Catholics of us."

"This is different. He's trying to create a Catholic bulwark to hold back the Germans and the Soviets. He's in league with Mussolini. He's going to ramp it up. You'll see. Soon we'll all be required to go to mass and to eat fish on Friday."

"And how would that stop the Germans from taking over if they decided to? Or the Soviets?" asks Gisi.

Herr Berger wipes his mustache with his napkin. "I don't think fish on Friday by itself will do anything, to be honest, but a strong alliance with the Vatican could be very useful. The Church hasn't completely lost its power. You wait and see."

July 5, 1933
Brigittenau
Max's shop

Anna brings Max a fresh kaiser roll with butter and some little pieces of boiled beef on it for lunch.

"Mmm," he says, sitting down at his work table and taking a big bite. "What a nice treat."

"I left a little more of the beef in a pot of soup upstairs, too," Anna tells him. "This morning I bought a bone with enough meat left on it for the soup and a few sandwiches. I took some over to Hugo and Peter's place, too."

"How's he doing, our little Peter? Any sign of the parents coming?"

"He's lonely, I think. I'm sure it's very hard to be away from your family at that age. I think he's particularly close to his mother, too. He asks me to help him write letters to her every time I see him."

"But they aren't saying when they'll be here yet?"

"No, I don't think they know. It's ridiculously expensive. Hugo says they're probably going to try to sell all their furniture and carpets rather than paying what Germany is now asking for the privilege of taking their things out of the country. It's such a shame. He says it's her husband's family's furniture and includes some very good pieces. It seems like it'll still be a good long time before they can manage to come."

"How's Hugo doing? He hasn't had a child to care for before, and he's alone there now that both his sisters are married."

"Well, caring for Peter isn't entirely up to him. I stop in whenever I can to help, and so does Gert. It's lucky he lives in Austerlitz-Hof, too. There's excellent free childcare for the times when he's at work and Peter isn't at school, there's that wonderful playground, of course, and communal meals are available whenever Hugo remembers to sign up for them. Peter is still very shy, but he's starting to make a few friends, and it's obvious he loves Hugo very much."

"They look alike, those two. Have you noticed?"

Anna laughs. "Yes! I think they make a very delightful pair."

"Do you still like Hugo? Romantically, I mean?"

Anna thinks for a moment. "You know? I do. More than before even, now that he has Peter. I think he's wonderful with the boy. But it's more and more obvious to me that he prefers Gert to me, even though they fight a lot of the time when they're together—at least it seems like that to me. She's hard on him, I think." She sighs deeply. "Fortunately for me, it's a new world. Single women aren't looked down on the way they have been in the past. To tell you the truth, I'm seriously considering the option of being an outstanding example of a single woman for the rest of my life!"

CHAPTER 36

A SHORT VACATION

August 1 - 5, 1933
The Rax

Zlotka and Emil sit on slatted wooden benches looking out the big windows of the cable car as it moves slowly up the mountain. Once in a while another car moving at exactly the same speed as theirs passes by on its way down. The view grows more spectacular by the second.

"Oh!" cries Zlotka, taking her eyes off the scenery and looking fearfully at the other passengers "What's happening?" The cable car comes to a gradual stop and sways back and forth gently.

"People are getting on or off at the top and bottom of the mountain. It's nothing to be afraid of," Emil says. "If you look down at the station, you can probably see them."

Zlotka leans over so she can see where Emil is pointing. So do several of the other passengers. The cable tips as they all lean in the same direction. "Oh no," she cries, sitting straight again. "I'm making us tip over!"

"No, you aren't, silly," says Emil. "These cars are perfectly safe." There's a vulnerability about Zlotka that he finds appealing at times.

She looks relieved as the cables pull them upwards again. "I'm glad it wasn't broken. The scenery is incredible, but

I wouldn't want to spend hours so high above the ground swinging in a cable car."

The car continues its slow ascent.

Midway up, another car coming down and Emil and Zlotka's car stop at the same time. They hang side-by-side above the deep mountain valley. The passengers in the two cars smile and wave at each other before going back to appreciating the extraordinary scenery on their own sides.

"Look at that," Zlotka says, pointing at a new vista coming into view as they're pulled up the mountain again. In the distance they can see a picturesque Alpine village tucked into a green valley, and beyond it, snow-capped mountain beyond mountain as far as the eye can see. "It's so beautiful, it makes me cry." She dabs her eyes with the sleeve of her jacket.

When they look down, the station where they boarded looks like a toy.

Too soon they reach the top, and it's their car causing all the others to stop. Along with the other occupants of their car, Zlotka and Emil slip on their backpacks and step out onto the snowy mountain top. They're almost 1600 metres above sea level. Spontaneously they both draw a long breath. Then another. And another. Neither says a word. Neither can speak. They are flooded with awe.

At last, uncharacteristically tentative, Emil says, "You know what?"

Zlotka turns and looks up at him, smiling, her blue eyes glistening. "What?" she says softly, not wanting to break the spell.

"I know what's missing in Vienna, for all its charms."

"And what is that?" Zlotka asks. What a beautiful profile he has, she thinks. And those curls.

"It's the freshness of the mountain air. Vienna is sadly lacking in fresh air." He pauses to take another long deep breath. "But it's more than that, isn't it? There's some special quality in the air here."

"It's crisp and clean when you breathe it in, and crystal clear," she says. "I love it so much I can't breathe in enough." She takes another long, slow, deep breath.

Emil almost slips into a reverie. "Don't let anybody know you heard me say this," he finally says slowly, "but the air up here seems to imbue everything with a sort of magic." His eyebrow only rises the tiniest bit.

"Doesn't it! Every branch, every tree, every snowflake. Everything seems enchanted up here!"

They sit down on a wooden bench and pull their hiking shoes out of their backpacks.

"I love my hiking boots," says Zlotka, happily. "They're like old friends."

"I feel the same way," Emil answers, holding up one of his. "These boots have been with me during many of the best times of my life." He smiles at her. "Thanks for thinking of taking this vacation, Zlotka. I didn't realize how much I needed it."

For their first hike they choose the easiest option, a path that takes them up a gentle rise. They walk for nearly an hour barely speaking, through forests of firs and mountain pines, and alpine meadows filled with tiny wildflowers.

Finally they see a rustic mountain hut ahead.

"Do you know the story of these huts?" Emil asks. "One of the Social Democratic Clubs, the *Naturfreunde,* built them about ten or fifteen years ago. They still maintain them. It's such a good idea."

"It is. Now people can hike for days without worrying about where to eat and sleep."

"You know, I considered joining the *Naturfreunde* once. It seems like such a long time ago. Being here now and seeing how it is to come upon one of the huts after such a wonderful hike, I rather regret that I didn't join. But I'm glad those who did join are still at work here."

As they come closer, they can hear music. Six or seven people are leaning on the front of the cabin taking in the sun and singing. A man is playing the guitar.

Minutes later, Emil and Zlotka are welcomed into the hut by two enthusiastic young hikers.

The interior of the sturdy building is entirely made of wood with the exception of the big green enamel stove in the corner. The hut is as warm as the greetings the rest of the hikers give them as they arrive. Soon Emil and Zlotka are sitting at the long table having lunch, telling stories, laughing, and singing.

Their next hike, even more beautiful than the last, crosses above sheer cliffs and rushing streams as it takes them to the next hut, where they'll spend the night. After sharing big wooden bowls of hot soup made on the same stove that heats the cozy hut, they sleep in the crowded dormitory, huddled tightly against one another, bundled in their warmest clothes.

By the time the three days pass, Emil and Zlotka have shared the stories of their lives in detail, discovered their common love of wordplay, recited their favorite poems to each other, laughed until they cried, sang many songs, weighed the merits of socialism versus communism several times over—Zlotka almost convinced Emil of the superiority of communism—and have fallen thoroughly in love.

When they return to *Frau* Rosenthal's house, Zlotka bursts in and calls out to anyone who happens to be home,

Red Vienna

"Hallo, we're back! And we have some wonderful news—Emil and I are getting married!"

CHAPTER 37

A CATHOLIC CORPORATIST STATE

September 12, 1933
Cafe Rüdigerhof, Brigittenau

"So now Austria is officially a 'Catholic, ethnically German, Corporatist state,'" Leo says, reading Chancellor Dollfuss's words aloud from the newspaper. "Listen here. He says the new republic is, I quote, 'based on new principles and ideals which in reality are very old ones for a Christian and German people.' Well, that should appeal to a good cross-section of the people—even the Nazis if he's lucky."

"I'm sure that's the intention," says Max dryly. "Jews aren't included, you notice."

"And the only party that's legal in Austria now is the Fatherland Front, with Prince von Stahremberg, that old Nazi, running it," says Hugo. "We've got ourselves a true dictatorship now."

"Oh, come on, Stahremberg renounced Nazism years ago," Max points out, "Though he's a Mussolini fascist of the worst kind."

Leo adds, "And as Vice Chancellor and head of the Fatherland Front, he's clearly the second most powerful man in the country. Back to the monarchy, eh?"

"Did you read where Dollfuss says we should return to

the medieval guild system? He's basing the whole thing on some idea of Mussolini's," Max continues.

"That's right. Italian corporations are supposedly modeled on guilds," Hugo says.

"So we're going back to the Dark Ages. How depressing is that," says Toni, frowning.

Gisi looks at the others. She has never seen the whole group looking so dejected.

"All our hard work, all of Otto Bauer's visionary thinking, all these years of building a social democratic future, all down the drain," Leo remarks.

"That doesn't have to be true. I bet the other banned parties are sitting around their *Stammtisches* planning coups," says Felix.

"And, regardless of all that banning, we still hold Vienna," adds Gisi. "And we're strong—our union leaders have agreed to a General Strike if the Fascists occupy either Vienna's *Rathaus*, the union offices, or the Austrian Social Executive's office. The power of a General Strike shouldn't be underestimated." No one looks encouraged.

Max clatters up on his old bike and parks it.

"The BBC was certainly interesting today," he says, sitting down with the others.

"Oh, you heard Dollfuss's speech at the stadium? In front of 60,000 people here in Vienna and the whole world on the radio?" asks Leo.

"Yes, that, and more. Listen to this. According to the BBC, a truce between Dollfuss and the Austrian Nazis exiled in Germany is a real possibility now."

"A truce? I thought Austria banned the Nazis forever!" cries Gert.

"The foreign press is saying that the new fascist government might permit the inclusion of Austrian Nazi representatives," Max continues. "It seems that recent pronouncements by Dollfuss, and by Theo Habicht, the Austrian Nazi leader in exile in Germany, and by certain German Nazi leaders, are being seen as providing an opening for negotiations to end the standoff between Dollfuss and the Austrian Nazis."

"What! Damn that Dollfuss! That two-faced rat!" Hugo exclaims, hitting the table with his fist.

Gisi shakes her head. "Oh no."

"I always said that would happen," says Leo.

"Wait, it gets worse. The BBC also announced that Dollfuss had already outlined the terms for a compromise with the Nazis *some time ago* in an interview he did with a French newspaper!"

"Well, it's no secret that the news is censored here. Thank god you've got that radio," says Leo.

Max continues, "It seems that Habicht has defined the terms under which Nazis would consent to work with Dollfuss. He announced it in a Nazi broadcast from Munich on Sunday night. But the story is even more complicated than that. The day after Habicht's announcement was broadcast, Rudolf Hess, the German Nazi party leader, decreed that all outside fascist organizations—which would of course include Habicht's Austrian Nazis—were no longer entitled to claim affiliation with German Nazis. The decree even said that all the Nazi party branches were forbidden to deal with any such organizations. Every detail was taken care of."

"Oh, so the Reich doesn't want us after all? What a shame," says Hugo.

"Wait, I don't understand. Habicht and Hess contradicted each other?" asks Gert.

"It seems like they did, but the BBC analyst I listened to believes that what the Hess decree means that German Nazis are temporarily severing relations with their Austrian counterparts for a specific reason. The advantage of separating the organizations would be that the Reich could work directly with Dollfuss. You see? They're cutting Habicht out of the deal."

"Yes, but that's just speculation. The Dollfuss government is still setting up concentration camps to put the Nazis into. And they've just reintroduced the death penalty," Gisi points out.

"They're saying those measures are meant to contain Nazism, but that could change very easily. The concentration camps and death penalty could just as well be used for us, or for the Jews, at any time," says Leo.

"It's not good in any way you look at it. I'm beginning to think it's time to get in touch with the *Schutzbund* and talk about fighting back," says Felix.

"Fighting? Are you kidding? You want to start another war? Are you crazy?" his brother replies. "You're becoming blood-thirsty now?"

"No, not really," says Felix miserably. "I just want to hear some good news for a change."

Chapter 38

The Pawn Shop

September 20, 1933
Vienna
Max's workshop

Max empties his jar of coins onto the workbench and counts them out. Nowhere near enough to have the clock repaired. In any case, he'd pretty much given up on that again. But maybe, just maybe, he can buy Gisi a watch, not an expensive one, but one that would serve its purpose. He counts the coins again, slides them into his coin purse, and slips it into his pocket.

After carefully writing BACK IN 30 MINUTES on a piece of cardboard and hanging it on the door of the shop, he locks the door and sets out on foot. Maybe the watchmaker in his neighborhood will have something used and refurbished that he can afford.

The bell on the door of the watchmaker's shop rings as Max walks in, and *Herr* Fischer emerges from behind his desk, smiling.

"Have you had any luck learning to repair old clocks?" he asks, remembering Max from his last visit.

"Unfortunately, no. I only learned how hard it is." Max relates the story of his visit the clock museum and the difficulty of saving any money at all. "But finally, since I began selling lamps and then radios, I've managed to save a little." He empties his money in his coin purse onto the watchmaker's table.

Herr Fischer looks at the small pile of coins and shakes his head.

"I'm sorry," he says. "I don't have anything at all that you could afford. I wish I could help you, but unfortunately I can't. Why not try the pawn shop?"

Max shudders. He's familiar with the pawn shop. For several years he'd been going to some length to avoid walking on the block that the pawn shop is on because he didn't want to remember all the things that he took there in the first years after his mother died, when his father barely came home and he was too young to run the shop.

"So, you're selling radios now," the watchmaker says as Max is turning to leave. "Good ones?"

"Of course they're good ones. They're made by a company called Minerva right here in Vienna."

"They get good reception?"

"Very good. I carry three different models. Minerva makes twenty-seven different models, can you imagine? But I chose the ones with the cases that look best with my furniture."

"Do you have any that receive, what is it called, the special station my son uses to communicate with his friends?"

"Oh, you mean shortwave? In fact, two of the three models I carry do receive shortwave transmissions."

"Very useful. Very useful, indeed," says the older man. "Perhaps I'll visit your store and try out those radios. Maybe there's some kind of exchange we can work out. You get a watch, I get a radio. Let me think about it."

"That sounds like a very good idea," says Max. They shake hands cordially and Max leaves, walking in the direction of the pawnshop.

As he walks, he thinks, Fischer, is that a Jewish name? It sounds like it. But it could be a German name, too. Some names are both German and Jewish, and some are just German or just Jewish. What if this man discovers that almost all the radios Max sold are used to listen to foreign broadcasts and private shortwave messages, and he isn't on the right side? Suddenly selling radios seems risky. Max hopes the old man will forget to come to look at his radios. He'll look elsewhere if he ever has enough money to buy Gisi a new watch.

❧❦⊱3⊰❦❧

The pawn shop has one small window in which a jumble of dusty items are displayed, some jewelry, a camera, perfume bottles and atomizers, a few books, a record album, and two watches. The window is so crowded with things for sale and the glass is so dirty that Max can't see the watches very well, but it's obvious to him that both of them are men's watches. He sighs and pushes the door open.

Inside, the shop is packed tightly. Max can hardly make his way through all the items piled high on all sides to get through to the glass case at the back that serves as a counter. The pawn broker is standing behind the case talking to two men in long, old-fashioned coats and black hats. Orthodox Jews, Max realizes. He waits his turn and takes a look around the crowded shop. Unfortunately, he can't see into the glass case because of the two other customers, but he thinks it's very likely that that's the place where the rest of the watches are kept. The small window to the outside of the shop closed off with a piece of wood and locked from the inside of the store, so he can't see those watches either.

215

The three men at the back of the shop are deeply engaged in conversation, so Max picks up a book, leans against a pile of boxes, and begins to read. The book is one he's familiar with but has not read, Hugo Bettauer's *Die Stadt ohne Juden (A City without Jews.)* The dust jacket describes it as the Viennese author's best novel, a satirical response to the growing anti-Semitism in Austria. It's set in Vienna in the 20's, when the country had recently been humbled by defeat in the war and the collapse of the Habsburg Empire. In the book, unemployment and inflation are soaring and the politicians are on the lookout for scapegoats. The chancellor of Austria decides that the solution to the city's problems is to expel the Jews, so Vienna's hundreds of thousands of Jews are forced to emigrate. When conditions worsen without them, the Jews are invited back. The scathing satire caused a great controversy when it came out in 1924.

Recalling that its author had been assassinated because of the book and that the book itself was banned, Max is surprised that there's a copy in the pawn shop. He looks for a price on it—not that he can afford to buy the book or any book—but he can't find one anywhere on the little volume. Pushing some of the boxes he'd been leaning against to the side, he sits down on the one at the bottom of the stack and continues to read while the argument between the pawnbroker and the Orthodox Jews grows louder.

Finally the two customers shout something that sounds rude and, continuing to bicker among themselves, they stomp out of the shop, their long black coats brushing against Max's knees. Finally he's able go over to the glass case to ask the shopkeeper about watches.

"I feel for those guys," says the pawnbroker, looking after the two men. "In fact, I feel for all my customers. Well, almost all my customers. But how can I afford to return their items without full payment? They don't understand how many people are bringing me their things now. And no one is buying anything. Look at this place—you can't walk in here." He waves his arms at all the goods surrounding them. Finally he turns back to Max. "So, young man, what can I do for you? What is that you've brought to me this fine afternoon?"

"Nothing, actually. I've come hoping to buy something," Max begins.

"Is it that book?" the pawnbroker points at *A City without Jews*. "It isn't for sale. It's a banned book, you know. I leave it there so people like you will pick it up and read some of it. And be forewarned! I tell you, Bettauer was right. We Jews will soon be boarding the outward-bound trains." He looks at Max grimly. "But what is it you were looking for?"

There are boxes of watches, dozens and dozens of them: gold watches, silver watches, pocket watches, jeweled watches, ancient watches, watches on necklaces, watches on pins, chic modern watches, well-worn watches, never-worn watches.

Max doesn't return to his shop in half an hour as he intended that afternoon. He looks at watches for the rest of the day, sorting them into the boxes the pawnbroker gives him by type after he's looked at them. In the ladies' gold watch box, there are perhaps thirty watches. Max lays them all out side by side. Then he sees it: a watch with a simple face set in a round-cornered square with two tiny roses attaching it to a delicate gold band. It's perfect. He can imagine it on Gisi's little wrist perfectly.

Eagerly, he brings the watch to the counter, certain that, small and delicate as it is, he will have enough money to buy it. He empties out all of his coins next to the watch.

"How much is it?" he asks. "It's exactly what I was looking for. It couldn't be more perfect."

"I'm sorry," replies the pawnbroker sadly. "It's gold. It's worth ten times what you've got there."

"Oh," says Max.

"But I'm happy to set it aside for you. Maybe in a few months or a year, you'll be able to afford it."

"Maybe," says Max, pushing his coins back into his purse. "But it doesn't seem very likely."

"You never know," the pawnbroker says.

Max puts on his jacket and his cap. "Thanks anyway."

As he walks out of the shop, he hears the pawnbroker calling after to him. "Young man—don't give up hope!"

CHAPTER 39

ZLOTKA

September 20, 1933
Emil's boarding house

Though more than a month has passed since Emil and Zlotka announced their engagement at the boarding house, Emil still hasn't shared the news with anyone other than their fellow boarders and two of Zlotka's friends.

"Let's wait until we have a date," he says one day, and "After I defend my thesis," on another, and "Let's wait until I hear from Sandoz," the next. He hasn't mentioned his engagement to his parents or to Johannes.

As he walks to the university library where he plans to put the finishing touches on his thesis before handing it in, he thinks about his dilemma, as he does most days. It would have been much quicker to take the tram to the University, but he likes using the long walk to think things through.

The truth is that he regrets his impulsive proposal and doesn't know how to undo it. He knew it was a mistake the day after he and Zlotka returned from the Rax, but he hadn't had the heart to tell her. No, he tells himself sternly, it isn't the heart I'm lacking—it's the courage. He feels ashamed. But surely Zlotka has some idea of his mixed feelings. A whole month has passed and he hasn't agreed to a single one of her ideas about when and how to follow through on their promise. She must know, or at least suspect. On the other hand, he reminds himself, they share a bed every night. Oh god, what if she gets pregnant? They take precautions, of course, but there's no guarantee. This can't go on. He has to break it off. That day. That very day. And how many times have I said that, he asks himself.

As he looks through his work at the library, Emil realizes that there are no more changes to make, and that, to be honest, most of those he'd made over the last few weeks have been excuses for not handing the work in. He signs the last page with his name and the date. Carefully, he puts the papers back in order, slides the thesis into an envelope, walks over to his tutor's office, and leaves it on the receptionist's desk. What's done is done. His defense will be scheduled in about a week.

With a new sense of determination and a lighter step, he takes the tram home.

There are two letters on the hall table when he arrives, one for him, and one for Zlotka. Hers looks official, but he doesn't want to pry, so he doesn't look at it carefully before he takes his own upstairs to his room to open and read it.

His letter is from Sandoz and it's good news. The committee liked his solution and wants him to come back to Basel for another interview. He has to call the secretary of the department to make an appointment for next week or the week after. Hallelujah! Two hurdles passed in one day! He raises both his arms in a gesture of victory.

Then he sits down on his bed and lets all the tension of the past year fall from his body. He reads the letter over and over. He reads it aloud to the mirror. In an imagined scenario, he tells his father how well the second interview went and that Sandoz just offered him a position with a salary comparable to Walter's. It could happen—it really could. What a remarkable thing. In any case, his thesis is turned in and Sandoz has invited him back. A celebration is in order!

He takes the steps down two at a time to see who else is home. "*Frau* Rosenthal?" he calls, "Jacob? Anyone else home?" Zlotka would be still be at university, of course, but he is eager to share his news with anybody and everybody.

"Yes?" calls *Frau* Rosenthal from the kitchen. "What is it?"

"Sandoz wants me back for another interview," he calls back. "And I handed in my thesis today."

"How wonderful!" she says, coming out to give him a hug. "That's very good news indeed."

"It is. I have to make an appointment to go back for a second interview at Sandoz, but that's easy, because my thesis is done too. I'll try to make the appointment for immediately after my defense late next week."

"I'm so happy for you, Emil," says Mrs. Rosenthal, smiling. "But, tell me, what do you think could be the matter with Zlotka? She came in five minutes ago and went straight to her room without even saying hello to me."

"Zlotka? But she has a lecture this afternoon. Why would she come home at this time of day?"

Zlotka is lying on her bed crying. She holds the official-looking letter out to Emil.

Austria is deporting her. She has three days to make arrangements to return to Russia.

CHAPTER 40

SAYING GOOD-BYE

October 3, 1933
Westbahnhof station, Vienna

Gisi and Emil get off the tram at the Westbahnhof. He carries both his suitcases across the plaza to the station while she walks by his side objecting,

"But I agreed to come along to help you, and now you aren't letting me,"

"You're helping me by keeping me company," he tells her. "And by being the last friend I see before my new life begins."

As they reach the big glass doors, Gisi runs ahead a few steps and opens one of them wide for Emil. "It's the least I can do," she says laughing as he walked through with his baggage.

After Emil buys his one-way ticket to Basel, they sit down on a bench together to wait until his train is announced.

"So how are you feeling about Zlotka now?" she asks. "It's been a few weeks."

"I suppose I'm still feeling more relieved than anything else," he answers thoughtfully. "At first I was shocked of course. But I was never really influenced by her arguments for communism. In fact, I didn't take them seriously enough to even consider that she was trying to recruit me, or that she might be working for the Soviets."

"I'm sure it wasn't her politics that convinced you to propose to her," she says, smiling slyly.

He laughs. "No, it certainly wasn't that."

"Oh my goodness, what if she hadn't been sent back to Russia and you had actually married her?"

"Then I would be taking her to Basel with me now, I guess."

"Or going to Russia with her!"

"My God, what a disaster that would have been. It was actually pretty fortunate that it turned out the way it did. I knew she wasn't the woman for me weeks before she was forced to go back, but I'm embarrassed to tell you that I hadn't been able to figure out how to tell her."

Gisi thinks for a moment. "We were all terribly naive not to suspect her. I guess I was still reeling from finding out that Edith was working for the Soviets. Zlotka was so much more obvious—we knew she was a Communist, for heaven's sake—and not one of us saw it."

"To be fair, she probably wasn't spying on you or your family or friends. You barely knew her. I think she was just a good Soviet trying to add to the ranks of her party."

"So you don't know for certain what what she was up to? With Edith, the press made clear that she was spying on the SDAP, sharing our strategies and plans with the Soviets."

"No, I tried to find out, but no one would tell me anything except that it had nothing to do with me. I had to have that cleared up officially before I could accept the job in Basel. It was a close call."

"Oh, I hadn't thought of that. Could your association with her have stopped you from getting the job?"

"It certainly could have. Especially if our relationship had been longer or if I'd been even a little responsive when she'd tried to recruit me. She could easily have passed on my name to someone."

"I still can't believe you never suspected her."

"I think I thought of her as a non-practicing Communist, like so many of our friends are non-practicing Jews. Even when we were discussing Communism at the Rax, I thought it was just an exercise in argument for her, the way arguing against it was an exercise for me." He breathes out. "Well, what's over is over, and I'm ready to begin a new chapter of my life in Switzerland."

They stand and begin to walk toward the platform where his train is waiting.

"I'll miss you, Emil. I'm sorry you're leaving Vienna. But what an amazing opportunity you're being offered," Gisi says.

"It is, isn't it? I'm still having a hard time believing I got the job. They asked some very tough questions at the second interview. When I came home, I fully expected to hear that they'd given the job to one of the other candidates."

"But obviously you're the right man for it. Are you sad to leave?"

"I'm sad to leave some things, and especially some people," he says, looking at her for a long time, "but I think Basel will suit me."

It's you I'll miss the most, he thinks, but he doesn't say it.

Two minutes later he boards the train.

CHAPTER 41

ASSASSINATION

October 5, 1933
The Parliament Building, Vienna

Hugo cuts through the Parliament Building on his way to the Federal Housing Department offices as usual. It seems that more paperwork is required to run the Municipal Housing Program every month. He's already late for his next meeting when he turns a corner to find the corridor completely blocked with people. Ah, they're all petitioners, he realizes when he sees that each of the people in the hallway is carrying a sheaf of papers filled with signatures.

"I don't have a petition," he tells the others as he tries to work his way through the waiting crowd to get out the other side. It would have been better to walk all the way around the building, he realizes, but it's too late now. "Excuse me, I'm just trying to get down the hall," he tells a large man waving a handful of papers in the air. "Pardon me, I'm not trying to see whoever the official is that you're waiting for. I just want to get through this crowd," he says to another petitioner.

"The 'official' we're trying to see is Chancellor Dollfuss himself!" the man replies. "Be my guest, go on through if you don't have business with him." He steps aside.

"Dollfuss himself! Is that who you're all waiting for?" Hugo is surprised.

"Yes, the little bastard should be coming out of that door any minute," says another of the people in the crowd, pointing at one of the ornate doors.

If I wasn't already late I wouldn't mind seeing him in person, Hugo thinks as he slips between a couple of men in shabby clothes.

Just then, a small door to his right opens up and the diminutive Chancellor comes out, accompanied by *Herr* Friedrich Stockinger, the Minister of Commerce, and surrounded by a contingent of uniformed guards.

"He's over here!" the man next to Hugo calls out. The whole group turns in their direction. Dozens of petitions are thrust toward Chancellor Dollfuss, who stops and begins to take them one by one, responding politely to each his constituents.

"Sir, this is so important," says a young man with military bearing who had pushed his way to the front of the group. Chancellor Dollfuss takes the sheaf of papers from the man, glances at the top page, and starts to say something.

Before his words are out, the petitioner pulls a revolver from his jacket and fires two shots at the chancellor. Startled by the noise of a gun so close by, Hugo watches as one bullet hits Dollfuss's arm and the other just misses his chest. The shocked crowd pushes back as the Commerce Minister hurls himself at the shooter and knocks him to the ground where the guards are able to disarm him.

Chancellor Dollfuss stands very still, holding his injured arm.

"Don't let there be any fuss. No need to call an ambulance," Hugo hears him saying calmly to the guards. "Let me walk to the car. I'm fine."

As the Chancellor leaves with his entourage, some

members of the waiting crowd rush toward the assassin, now pinned to the ground by guards, and attack him with their walking sticks, umbrellas, and flying fists. As Hugo stands plastered against the wall watching, a considerable struggle ensues, but in time, the guards manage to hold back the attackers, get the shooter handcuffed, and walk him out of the building between them.

Hugo and the rest of the people who'd seen the attempted assassination are lined up and ushered out by more guards. As they pass a desk set up near the doors, each of the witnesses is asked to show his or her identification papers so their names and addresses can be recorded, and to describe exactly what they saw. It takes a long time. When Hugo's turn comes, and he explains how close he was when the shooting happened, he is taken into a side room where a secretary takes notes as he shares the details of his experience again.

Finally, much shaken, he stands outside the Parliament Building in the noisy group of expelled petitioners and others who'd heard the startling news. The meeting he'd been on his way to was over hours ago. He looks down at the housing papers he is still carrying and almost drops them into a nearby trash can.

They seem so insignificant, almost unbearably absurd.

❦

The next day
Brigittenau

Max, Leo, and Hugo huddle around the radio in Max's workshop while a cold autumn rain drenches the city outside.

"In response to the failed assassination of Chancellor Dollfuss, Prince Von Stahremberg, Vice Chancellor of Austria, immediately called upon all members of the *Heimwehr* to take up arms and report to the Ringstrasse," says the newscaster. "As I speak, tens of thousands of the paramilitary are gathering for a demonstration in front of the Chancellory to show support for Dr. Dollfuss, who is at home recovering from the bullet wound on his arm. According to a reliable source, Dr. Dollfuss told his inner circle that he only escaped death by a miracle. The people of Austria are deeply grateful."

"Not all the people," comments Max.

Hugo says, "He's better than a Nazi."

"So far," Leo says. "But I'm still convinced he's in secret collusion with them."

The announcer continues. "The would-be assassin has been identified as one Rudolf Dertl, a former member of the Christian Socialist paramilitary, who had been dismissed from the Austrian Army for political activities as well as reported cruelty to horses."

"He's a Nazi, that Dertl," says Leo. "I'd swear to it."

"Yes, he claims to be a Christian Social, but anyone can claim anything, no? Have they found his membership card?" Hugo asks.

"Why would a Christian Social try to assassinate a member of his own party?" Max adds.

Hugo responds, "It's a little too unlikely, in my opinion. What I worry about is that we'll get a response like we had in '27 when the Palace of Justice was burned. No matter who did it, our party will get the blame."

"Why would that happen?" asks Max.

"Because Dertl will implicate us," Hugo says.

"Huh. That could well happen," says Max, "We should prepare ourselves. Let's bring up the possibility at the party meeting tonight."

8 pm, the same day
Karl-Marx-Hof

They arrive discretely in groups of no more than three over a two hour period, yet it seems that everyone in Vienna still committed to the SDAP is gathered in Karl-Marx-Hof that evening—in direct defiance of the ban on large group meetings. Otto Bauer presides over the meeting, and as usual pushes for a non-violent response to the attempted assassination.

"I can't believe that, after all this time, with so much violence all around us, he's still holding on to his purist ideas of pacifism," the man sitting next to Felix comments.

"I agree with you," says another man. "Bauer may have been the great visionary of our movement at one point, but from the late '20's on, he's failed to appreciate the very real dangers of fascism and Nazism."

"We should have fought back when Dollfuss took over. That was our biggest mistake," says Felix's neighbor. "The SDAP members in the provinces were much braver than we Viennese were."

"That's right," a man in the row behind them says. "We're virtually at war now. It's time to leave idealistic dreams of pacifism behind and fight for our lives."

"You'll see, tomorrow or the next day, we'll hear that the SDAP was behind Dertl's attempt," someone says. "And it will be Dollfuss's people who are saying it."

"I say the only way to counteract that is to beat them to it, and get it out that Dertl's a Nazi before they call him a Social Democrat," says the first man.

"He *is* a Nazi. His whole family are Nazis. Fanatical Nazis. My sister works with his cousin," says a woman sitting behind them.

Max turns around to join the conversation. "You're

certain?" he asks. The woman is. She's even willing to introduce Max to her cousin.

"Great!" says Max "I think I know someone who could get that out on the radio all over Austria."

Their conversation ends when the meeting is interrupted by shouting.

"WE'RE DONE WITH THIS SO-CALLED PEACE!" calls a voice from the back of the room.

Someone else yells, "MOBILIZE THE SCHUTZBUND NOW!"

Then voices come from all over.

"OVERTHROW DOLLFUSS!"

"RESTORE DEMOCRACY TO AUSTRIA!"

Bauer's voice comes through the microphone above the din. "Let's not throw ourselves into a bloody civil war!" he cries. "There are better ways to deal with this issue!"

"I'll check with my contacts," Max tells the small group around him when the crowd quiets a little. "With any luck, we can get the news that Dertl is a Nazi out tomorrow morning."

He picks up his bag and leaves for home to see who he can reach on the shortwave radio.

❦❈❦

October 8, 1933
two days later
Max's workshop

"Ha! There it is!" says Max to Leo. "I just heard on the radio that they found Dertl's documents! He *is* a Nazi! They found his membership card and it's from the Nazi party, not the Christian Social Party. We were right!"

"That's certainly a relief, but I'm not sure we can overcome the bad publicity Dollfuss and his minions spread about us in the interim."

"But we scooped them. Our news went out first, and we were right!"

"I know, but people believe what they want to believe. Our press doesn't have the clout it used to. Too many of the people who've been voting for the SDAP for many years are disillusioned now, and they're easily sucked in by the lies and propaganda the Fatherland Front is putting out. And they're reading the *Fatherland Front* newspaper instead of the *Arbeiter Zeitung.*"

This time it's Max who is shaking his head. "It's true. I'm afraid we may be starting to lose our base. The workers are listening to the Right."

CHAPTER 42

THE FATHERLAND FRONT

October 29, 1933
along the Donaukanal

That fall, Gisi begins taking Sunday afternoon walks with Max instead of with her family. The break came a few weeks earlier when *Herr* Berger mentioned the broken clock once too often.

"That's it!" Gisi cried out in frustration. "Don't expect me to come along on Sunday when you go to the park! I'm finished." And she stomped down the stairs, making enough noise for the neighbors to look out their doors after her.

The sky is overcast that late fall Sunday, and the water in the Donaukanal and the buildings alongside it are as gray as the clouds. Max and Gisi amble slowly down the path, hand in hand.

They speak idly of the week that passed since they last saw each other. Max sold a lamp and two more radios. He plans to order four from Minerva this time, instead of only three. Gisi passed her anatomy examination with an almost perfect score. There'd been much to memorize! She received a letter from Emil saying how much he was enjoying his new job. They wonder how Peter is doing at Hugo's place and in school at Austerlitz-Hof. Max promises to ask Anna before their walk the following Sunday.

While Gisi watches a barge pass by slowly, Max pauses to read one of the newspapers posted on the wall next to the canal.

"Look at this!" he says, "The Fatherland Front seems to be changing its tune."

"Oh, I see what you mean," says Gisi, moving in closer to read the article he was pointing to. She tries not to wear her glasses in front of Max. "That's definitely the most anti-Jewish statement I've ever heard from them," They stand together, reading more of the articles on the front page of the daily paper.

"My god, look at this one!" cries Gisi, pointing to another article. "It says here that Austria is likely to be 'coordinated' with Germany in three to six months, and surely no later than August! What on earth does that mean? 'Coordinated'? Coordinated in what way? Are they planning a merger with Germany after all? It sounds like it to me."

Max looks worried. "'Coordinated with', huh. I have no idea what it means, but it's very disturbing."

"I know. It doesn't look like our Austro-fascist government is going to keep its promise to champion the church and leave the Jews alone after all."

"Or its promise to remain a separate country from Germany. It's very ominous. In my opinion, this article reads exactly like Nazi propaganda. But look at the banner! It's definitely the banner of the Fatherland Front, the official newspaper of the state."

"Oh my god," Gisi says, her heart aching. "What will you do if Austria merges with Germany and starts to treat the Jews the way they're being treated there? It does sound like that's what this article is implying. Surely you've thought about it?"

"Frankly, I have no idea of what I'll do if they actually merge, or even if Austria just takes on the same stand toward

Jews as Germany. I don't have the money to move to Paris or America. What's more, I have my father to think about, and Anna. And the business. And you! It isn't so easy."

"No, it certainly isn't. Look how long it's taking Peter's parents to come here, and how much it's going to cost them. You would need to go much farther away."

Max considers. "Maybe it isn't such a good idea for Hilda and her husband to come here now. This newspaper is really frightening. You know, I think we should show it to Hugo right away so he can warn Peter's parents." They turn and walk briskly in the direction of Austerlitz-Hof.

For a few minutes, neither of them speaks. The news is overwhelming.

Forty minutes later, Hugo and Leo, whom Max and Gisi found playing chess in one of the courtyards at Austerlitz-Hof, hurry back to the wall along the canal where the newspaper is posted. They want to see the article for themselves.

Gisi and Max stand back while the other two read.

"Oh no," Hugo says. "You're right. It's much worse than I knew. Worse than I imagined. It's obvious that some Nazi is influencing Dollfuss and his people. Maybe there's an infiltrator in his cabinet."

"Or it could be that this has been Dollfuss's plan all along," says Leo.

"You're right that my sister and her husband shouldn't follow Peter here now. It doesn't seem like it will make any difference anymore. Maybe I should try to figure out a way to get all three of them to Paris instead."

Sighing, Max says, "It sounds like we might all have to figure out a way to get out sooner or later."

"Wait a minute! I just thought of something! Don't move!" says Leo suddenly, and he runs toward the newsstand at the next corner. A couple minutes later he returns with another copy of the Fatherland Front paper in his hand.

"The paper on the wall is a forgery!" he says. "Look! Here's today's real paper. The headline story is about the arrest of another Nazi, some old Austrian aristocrat from Linz who was driving around with a swastika flag on his car."

"Aha!" says Hugo, grabbing the paper from Leo's hand. "Look closely! Compare the banners! If you look here you can see that the one on the wall is a copy, a very good copy, I have to say, but nevertheless a copy. You see where the A is narrower here? And the date is pushed to the left? It's subtle, but now that I see them both side by side there's no doubt in my mind that the paper on the wall is a fake."

"Oh my god, I am so relieved! I don't know why I don't suspect it myself," Gisi says. "It's obviously part of the national campaign the Nazis are conducting. My grandfather heard from his sister that they've been more active in Tyrol, too. They're hanging their flags in inaccessible places in the mountains that can be seen from far way, and they paint swastikas on cliffs where it's almost impossible to remove them."

"That's right," agrees Hugo. "They're doing things like that right here in Vienna. Did you know about the huge swastika banner they hung from the tower of the *Rathaus* last week?"

"No, right on City Hall? That was brazen. I wonder how they got in," comments Leo.

Hugo goes on, "They climbed up the outside of the tower, I heard. Of course their banner was removed immediately, even before pictures were taken by the press, but still. Right in the middle of Vienna!"

"And now this false newspaper," Leo says. "I wonder how many more copies there are of it? Why don't we spend a few hours looking for the forged copies posted on the walls and tear them down?"

"Let's do that," Max agrees. "I am unbelievably relieved that it's just a forgery. I swear I was ready to pack my suitcase and take the next train to Paris!"

CHAPTER 43

HORSEY RIDE

November 3, 1933
Austerlitz-Hof

Peter holds Anna's hand as they walk across through the streets of Austerlitz-hof on their way home from school. His parents still haven't come from Berlin. Peter looks anxiously for letters every day and on most days he receives one. Though the letters always cheer the little boy up, not much has changed for his parents. They promise to be with him as soon as they can, they say, but these things take time.

"But *Tante* Anna, when Mutti and Vati come, will they bring my bed? *Onkel* Hugo's settee is very hard, did you know that? I drew a picture of the settee for Mutti and wrote the word HARD next to it and I sent it to her. And will they bring Otto, my cat?" He asks about the cat every day, and Anna gives the same answer.

"I'm sure they will bring everything they can, Peter. I wish I could tell you more." She is a great believer on being honest with children. No use in making promises that aren't likely to be kept.

"Can we stop at the playground today, *Tante* Anna?"

She looks at her watch. "Okay. We have a little bit of time for that."

"Hurray!" he cries, running off to greet some of the other

Austerlitz-Hof children. He's already forgotten, thinks Anna. How I wish I could. She is having a harder and harder time shaking off the tension of the times. Violence is always just under the surface. It seems like it breaks out somewhere new daily. The ban on the Nazi party hasn't stopped all the bombings, especially in the smaller cities of Austria, or the graffiti, or the breaking of windows of Jewish businesses. She sits down on a bench with some other people to watch the children play.

"My husband has gone to Linz for training again," one of the other women says to another. "I can't imagine they would send for him if the *Schutzbund* wasn't getting ready to fight."

"At last! I have to say I'm glad to hear it," the other woman replies. "If I were a man, I would volunteer to fight myself. As much as I appreciate what the SDAP has done here in Vienna for people like us—after all, our old flat had no water or even heat in the winter—imagine how cold we were—I have to say I have a hard time understanding why the SDAP in Vienna just accepted it when the government disarmed the party."

"Well, I can tell you for certain that quite a few members of the party think the way you do, and there are more and more of us every day. My husband says the *Schutzbund* is rearming all over the country."

"Good! That's great news! If the party hates the Fascists so much, let the *Schutzbund* come and fight them here in the city. I'm sick and tired of being preached to by elitist SDAP members who think they can change human nature by talking," the second woman replies.

"Right. Telling us what kind of music to listen to and what kind of films to go to. Really, who do they think they are?"

"To be honest with you, my husband and I never go to

the hoity-toity cultural events they have here in Austerlitz-hof. When we have a little extra money, we go to the same *gasthaus* we always went to in our old neighborhood."

The first woman laughs. "Us too. And we never went to a single lecture after the first one put us both to sleep."

"When your husband comes home, we should go to the *gasthaus* together."

"Let's do that!" They both laugh.

As Anna walks Peter home, she thinks, so much for changing people by changing the culture, and she sighs.

Hugo is home when Anna and Peter arrive.

"*Onkel* Hugo, *Onkel* Hugo—you're already home! Give me a horsey ride!"

"Okay, my little one," says Hugo, grinning. He gets down on his hands and knees, Peter climbs onto his back, and they romp around the room.

"Giddy-up!" Peter calls out. "Faster, faster!" Hugo crawls faster and Peter squeals with delight. "*Tante* Anna, look at me! Look at me! Uncle Hugo is a horsey!"

"Oh, Hugo! And Peter! You two are so cute. I wish I had a camera."

"Mine is right there on the table," Hugo answers, panting. "Do you know how to use it?"

"No, how would I know that?" says Anna, laughing. "It's much too complicated. Stop, and I'll be the horsey. You can get up and take the picture."

"What, you're going to be a horsey in that dress?" Hugo asks. "Wait, I can lend you some trousers. They're on the hook on the back of the bedroom door."

"Okay, I'll do it," says Anna, heading into the bedroom. A couple minutes later she emerges in Hugo's pajamas.

Hugo and Peter both roar with laughter when they see her. "You look so funny, *Tante* Anna!" cries Peter.

Hugo says, "Okay, Peter, you get off, and your *Tante* Anna will be the horsey."

Anna gets down onto her hands and knees and Peter climbs on. "Giddy-up!" he yells as Hugo sets the camera up. "You're too slow, *Tante* Anna!" Anna does her best to crawl faster.

"Hold on," she says. "The horsey needs a break—the drawstring on the trousers has come untied. Let me fix it."

There's a knock on the door.

"Just a minute! Hold still you two," called Hugo as he takes another picture. "Who is it?"

"It's me," comes the answer as the door opens. It's Gert. She stares at Anna tying the drawstring on Hugo's pajama pants. "What on earth is going on?" "I'm having horsey rides!" cries Peter. "You get down too, and I'll ride on your back!"

Gert looks disdainful. "I don't think so," she says. "Hugo, I brought you some news."

"Oh," says Hugo. "What is it?"

Gert glances at Anna and Peter and says to Hugo, "Come into the hall and I can tell you."

"One moment, Anna, Peter," he says, and he follows Gert out the door.

"Hugo, listen" says Gert, once they are in the hall. "You need to be very careful now. I just heard from someone at my work that the Dollfuss regime is going to go after the SDAP leadership next. They've heard that the *Schutzbund* is rearming and they believe there's a coup being planned. Your name was mentioned as one of the co-conspirators."

"My name was mentioned? But no such thing is happening. I have nothing at all to do with the paramilitary wing of the party. I never have had—everyone knows I'm a dyed-in-the wool-pacifist. Why would they have my name?"

"I don't know, but I heard that you were believed to be part of the planning group."

"It isn't true."

"Still, you should be extra careful what you say and who you meet with," she says. "Now go back to your silly games. I've warned you." She turns and walks down the hall, her high heels clacking on the tile.

Hugo scratches his head and goes back into his apartment, deflated.

Chapter 44

Horst and Litzi

November 15, 1933
Alsergrund

It's Wednesday afternoon so, as usual, Gisi goes home for the mid-day meal. She hasn't even had time to take off her coat when her mother hands her a letter. It's one Helene had received from her cousin Basia in Tyrol that morning.

"I don't think we'll go to Tannheim for Christmas this year," Helene says. "Look what Basia writes about her new son-in-law, Horst."

Gisi takes the letter and unfolds it. She'd been concerned about her cousin Litzi lately because since her baby boy was born in September, Litzi has only written to her once. Usually they exchange letters every week or two. Of course Theresa writes to her regularly and everything seems fine, and Basia and Helene write to each other every week—Gisi had even seen the photo the baby Basia sent—but there hadn't been a word from Litzi. Was she angry with her? Theresa laughed that off when Gisi asked. Of course not, she'd written, Litzi is just busy with the baby.

Perhaps Litzi isn't well. Basia and Theresa had both mentioned that she had recovered from the birth quickly, but Gisi knew from her studies that new mothers sometimes suffer from melancholia for months after a birth. So, when she hadn't heard from her older cousin for more than two months, she'd written to Theresa to ask if her sister was depressed but unwilling to admit it. Not at all, Theresa had said, why do you ask? And then she'd continued at great length with the plans for her own wedding in March.

Gisi sits down at the table to read Basia's letter.

Liebe Helene,

It is very difficult for me to write this, so I will say it right away: it would be better if you and your family, or at least Gisi, do not join our family for the Christmas holidays this year.

As you know, Tyrol has been the target of many bombings and other acts of violence by the Nazi party these last months. Over the past weeks, it has become much worse. One no longer feels safe in the streets.

But the violence in general is not the reason I think you will probably prefer to stay in Vienna this year. After all, there is violence in Vienna too. Although the train could be a target, it's not that likely, and we would of course be safe in our own house here in Tannheim. The problem is rather that Litzi's husband Horst has revealed that he is, and has been for several years, an active member of the Nazi party, and a proud one too.

Unfortunately, Litzi loves him so much that he has been able to convince her to believe in the values of that terrible party, as well. She, in turn, is working on convincing her younger sister, although Theresa still argues with her. Theresa's arguments are becoming weaker and weaker, however, and I am starting to think that she argues only for the benefit of her father and me and her grandparents at this point.

Horst claims that he supports the Nazis for economic reasons. You know his family owns a hotel in the mountains. He says that since the border between Austria and Germany has been closed and the 1000 mark visa fee imposed, the tourist business here in Tyrol has dropped by more than 60%. That may well be true. It seems that Horst's family and other hoteliers have banded together to demand that the borders be re-opened. The group doesn't admit that they are almost all Nazis, but everyone knows it's true. It's certainly true that tourism would benefit from the borders being reopened, but so would the ranks of their party, which Horst tells us now fully supports merging with the German Nazi party.

I think what the young people find appealing about the Nazis and their various campaigns in our area is that they shake things up to show their power. The Nazis promise that once they are in control, they will make big changes and return Austria to what it was before the Great War, when it was a mighty empire. Horst is a hero to Litzi, going out at night and creating havoc, like a bandit in the movies. Sadly, Litzi has also fallen into the trap of pointing the finger at the Jews as the cause of whatever Horst and she see as their problems, both petty and great.

Here in the countryside, in the small village where they grew up, my girls hardly ever met a Jew. Your Gisi's Max is the only Jew they know much of anything about, and they have never even met him in person, but I am sorry to tell you that his name is mentioned over and over as the instigator of some plot to hold Gisi back, or as a conspirator in a plan to deprive us all of something necessary. It is hard for me to believe.

Of course, you are all most welcome to join us at Christmas this year, as always. Or, perhaps you and Onkel Josef would like to come on your own, and Gisi could spend the days with friends in the city? I think Gisi would be terribly unhappy to spend her time here listening to her cousins try to convince her that Max is a member of a despicable race, as I heard Litzi call the Jews the other day.

I am distressed and embarrassed to have to tell you all

of this. I wish I had more power over my children, but if you could hear the conversations—I can't really even call them conversations—the rants, that I have to listen to at the dining room table every Sunday, you would understand.

Ganz liebe Grüße an Onkel Josef und Gisi,
Basia

Gisi reads the letter twice. She can't believe what she's reading. How could Litzi, and probably Theresa too, fall for such nonsense. After all they'd shared and all the fun they'd had together through all those years, how could they believe such things about the Jews? She folds up the letter, hands it back to her mother, and goes to the bedroom without saying anything.

Closing the door to the little room, she picks up her pillow and throws it at the bed as hard as she can. How could they, she thinks. How dare they! Litzi, whom she wanted to grow up to be like for so many years! She throws the pillow hard onto the bed over and over. Theresa, her closest confidante for so many years—how could she? She slams the pillow onto the bed again.

Then she lies face down on it and sobs.

Chapter 45

The SDAP's Response

December 7, 1933
Karl-Marx-Hof

"It is resolved then. We unanimously agree that a strong response to Stahremberg's declaration is necessary. The time for a decisive action has come." Otto Bauer stands in front of the SDAP leadership council. The group is joined by British, French, and Belgian delegates. Once again, they're disobeying the ban on large meetings, but events demand it. Reporters from most of the Austrian newspapers are present too, as well as foreign correspondents representing several countries.

Two days earlier, Prince Von Stahremberg, leader of the *Heimwehr*, declared openly and publicly that the *Heimwehr* desired an entirely Fascist State. The city of Vienna was the last holdout, with its Social Democratic mayor and city council.

"It is better to copy a good thing than to make a new experiment of dubious value," Stahremberg had said. "The *Heimwehr* does not wish to subject to terror or persecution those who in the past have belonged to another party, but if necessary, *we are willing to use brutal methods to attain our end*. It is unbearable for Austria, and especially for the population of Vienna, that the Marxists are still in the

Rathaus. The real birth of the new Austria will be when a Federal Commissar enters Vienna's *Rathaus*!"

The government of Austria had effectively declared war on the city of Vienna.

The speeches given by the council members and their international supporters in response to the declaration are passionate and articulate. One after another, the leaders of the movement stand before the group and remind the members of their strength. Social Democracy as manifest in Vienna is Socialism's greatest accomplishment, its pinnacle, its acme! The municipal housing system is the greatest example of integrated urban living ever created! Never in the history of mankind has such a large-scale implementation of high-minded ideals occurred! Especially in these hard times, the experiment must be allowed to continue—the world is watching! Reporters write furiously and the keys on stenography machines clack loudly.

"These talks are remarkable, as inspiring as the ones at the Second Internationale," Hugo comments to Max, smiling. They're sitting together at the meeting representing the Brigittenau group.

"They are, aren't they? It warms my heart to hear such eloquence," Max says. "I'm very much looking forward to sharing the texts of the speeches with the rest of the group when they're published in the paper tomorrow. They'll give everyone some hope, and god knows, we need it."

In the end of the meeting, it's agreed that the official response of the SDAP is to be a reaffirmation that a General Strike will be called if the *Rathaus*, Union offices, or the Office of the Austrian Social Executive are taken over by the Fascists. Several factions of the party, some of them quite angry, argue for a promise to call up the *Schutzbund*, but they're outnumbered. Bauer appoints a committee to draft the formal response to be delivered to Stahremberg's office as soon as possible, and the meeting breaks into sub-groups.

Max and Hugo go down the hall to meet with the other district level leaders. Unexpectedly, Otto Bauer and Julius Deutsch join them. The two men both look considerably more worried than they did while speaking to the larger group.

Bauer speaks first. "Regardless of the support of the socialists from other countries and the enthusiastic speeches we just heard, we have to face the very real fact that Dollfuss and Stahremberg's threats are real and more dangerous than ever." He pauses and wipes his brow. "It's come to this: we have to adjust our levels of organization and make plans to keep the party functioning even if Julius and I and the other upper level party leaders are arrested— or worse."

Max shudders.

Deutsch continues. "Each of you will have to be ready to take on the responsibilities of the people above you in the hierarchy, and the people below you will need to be prepared to take on the work you do."

"Starting tomorrow, you'll work closely with us and the level of leadership above you so that you're familiar with what we're responsible for and you'll be able to continue the work if the party is forced underground. We need a strict contingency plan in place which allows for the possibility of continuing arrests, after Julius and I are gone, after Papanek and Luitpold are gone, after any or all leadership is gone, and also after you are gone," says Bauer. "You'll have to coordinate with the people above you to learn their responsibilities, systems, and contacts. The best way is to shadow them, to be with them when they perform whatever it is they do to make the party function. It will take some time, and it must be started immediately. In turn, you will have to work out ways to train those below you in the hierarchy to take over if need be."

"We hope never to use the plan, of course, but we would be fools not to prepare for the worst. Let's start to work out the details now."

December 8, 1933
Cafe Rüdigerhof, Brigittenau

The next morning, Hugo arrives at the cafe early. After hanging up his hat and coat, he goes over to the newspaper rack where the day's papers hang neatly on their wooden rods. He pulls out the *Arbeiter Zeitung* first and lays it out on a table. Oddly, the article about yesterday's meeting isn't on the front page. It isn't on the second or third page either. In fact, it isn't in the paper at all. Hugo checks the date. Yes, it's today's paper. Something must have happened, he thinks, and the deadline was missed. He breathes deeply. Unlikely, but not impossible.

After sliding the *Arbeiter Zeitung* back into the rack, he takes the *Neue Freie Presse* out and lays it on the table. The evening's meeting isn't mentioned there either. Nor is it in any of the other papers.

He sits down, stunned, and orders a coffee. Could it really be that the Fascists had managed to censor the entire event? That the SDAP isn't even being given a chance to respond publicly to the threat against them?

As the others arrive, he tells them what happened.

"Then it's worse even than we thought," says Leo. "We aren't banned yet, but we've lost our voice."

Max adds, "I didn't hear anything on the radio either. I thought I had just missed it."

"Let me run over to the *Tabak* and see how the foreign papers covered it," offers Gert, heading out the door. "You said all those journalists were there last night! I'll bring copies of the papers back so we can see their coverage."

"And I was so worried that we were disobeying the ban on large meetings," Max continues. "I expected them to raid us any moment through the whole event. But they decided to turn the tables and ignore us."

"It's so disappointing," says Gisi. "It makes me feel powerless. Their tactics are effective at wearing us down."

"It's true," Toni says. "Some of the most ardent Social Democrats at my work have nothing to say now when the followers of Dollfuss begin to crow."

Anna adds, "The same workers who supported us all these years—and who are still benefitting from our programs—are turning against us. I hear it in the laundry at Austerlitz-Hof, in the playground, everywhere."

"What I don't understand about Dollfuss is why he opposes us at all. It would have been so much better for him if he had allied with the SDAP from the start. He would have all the workers behind him now, instead of only the most dissatisfied ones," Gisi points out.

"It's true. If he'd accepted Bauer's offers of help and they'd worked together, the Nazis wouldn't be gaining so many followers now," adds Max.

"That was certainly a big mistake on Dollfuss's part," agrees Leo. "Instead, he made the choice to woo the rural peasantry and the aristocracy. Why would two disparate groups like that think that they have any goals in common?"

Hugo says, "Actually, historically speaking, it isn't such an uncommon coalition. It's often the way that demagogues maintain their position. When a demagogue is in charge, the intelligentsia is powerless or holds only symbolic power. In Poland, for example..."

Anna glares at him and interrupts in mid-sentence. "Don't lecture us, Hugo. Let's focus on the here and now." Hugo looks hurt.

Leo glances at his friend sympathetically and picks up the conversation. "Well, I've never trusted Dollfuss's anti-Nazi rhetoric. He's just waiting for the right moment to drop the pretense."

"Any day now," says Max. "Any day."

The door opens and Gert returns from the newsstand empty-handed. There is nothing about the meeting in the foreign papers either.

"Maybe the groups arguing to recall the *Schutzbund* are right," Leo says. "Maybe a civil war is inevitable and we aren't facing the facts."

⊷⊶⊱⊰⊷⊶

Max walks Gisi home, bundled in their warmest coats, hats, and scarves against the chill December wind. Everyone agrees that it's unusually cold that year.

"Where do you think it will go? Will the Fascists move forward and try to take Vienna, or do you think it's just an empty threat?" Gisi asks.

"Well, even if it wasn't in the papers, they must know there'll be a General Strike if they do. The great majority of the workers are still with us, and a General Strike would be disastrous for the economy. I don't think they can afford that much disruption. I think it's just a threat; they'll hold back, at least for now."

"But what if they do take over, and we strike but the strike fails, and it turns out that Leo's right and they've been negotiating with the Nazis all along? What if they make a deal with Germany for an *Anschluss*, a merger, and we become part of the Third Reich? Or even if Austria manages

251

to remain independent but it becomes just as dangerous to be here as it is in Germany, especially for Jews?"

Max doesn't answer right away. Then he says, "Beyond going underground here in Vienna? Because that's what I promised the party I would do—just yesterday at the leadership meeting. There's an elaborate plan in place so that we can continue operating from underground if they start to arrest us."

"If even that becomes impossible."

"In that case of course I'd be forced to figure out some way to leave the country. I've already thought about it, actually. If it comes to it, I'd like to go to Paris."

"Paris! That would be my first choice, too. The French are the most open to foreigners, especially in Paris. It's so international there. Jews will be surely safe."

He smiles at her. "Shall we go together, then? We could get married!"

Gisi looks up at Max. "Did you just ask me to marry you? That would make me very happy!" she says. "It's a wonderful plan."

"Now we just have to figure out how to make it possible," Max answers, and they kiss for a long time.

CHAPTER 46

TO PEACE

January 10, 1934
Max's workshop

"Hallo? Are you back there?" Gisi calls as she comes into Max's shop. "It's cold in here!"

"Come to the back," he answers, opening the door that divides his workshop from the display room. "I've got the coal stove going back here, but it doesn't heat the whole shop."

Gisi closes the door behind her, pulls off her gloves and warms her hands over the little stove. She isn't ready to take off her coat yet. "It's bitter cold outside," she says. "I haven't been able to get warm all day."

"Me, neither," Max answers. "I've been working right beside the stove and I'm still cold. Let me heat some water up and we'll have some of this." He holds up a bag of chicory coffee. "I refuse to call it coffee, but it does make you a little warmer."

"That would be good." Gisi sits down, unbuttons her coat and takes off her boots. Leaning back, she puts her feet up on the box of coal next the stove. "It's the political situation as much as the weather, you know? The violence everywhere is chilling."

"I don't know about that," he replies, a bit of a twinkle in

253

his eye. "I'd say things are heating up." She laughs in spite of herself. Max always can make her laugh.

"You're right. Things are heating up. Did you see there were over a dozen bombings in Vienna just in the last couple days? Right after the government starts making use of the concentration camps and its promises of the death penalty against the Nazis, they increase the number of their attacks. It's brazen—it's as if they're daring Dollfuss and the *Heimwehr* to make them into martyrs."

"Any one of those bombings should merit a death sentence under the current law. Ten of them were in Jewish neighborhoods, too, did you notice that? I almost feel offended that they missed Brigittenau."

"Yes, but it's probably just a matter of time. I know they say they're relatively harmless bombs, but several went off in Leopoldstadt. One was only a block from Gert's parents' place. Thank god, no one was injured, but they blew up every one of the telephone boxes."

"I heard that a Nazi demonstrator was killed in the riots in the provinces, in Klagenfurt, I think. It was a fellow who'd just been released from one of the camps where he'd been sent for doing something else violent, I don't know what, " Max says. "But he was part of a group who were demonstrating outside the Fatherland Front newspaper office there yelling '*Heil Hitler.*' It was too much, too blatant, so the *Heimwehr* attacked them. A few people were injured and the one guy died. And that wasn't the only violent Nazi protest. They were held all over the provinces. Luckily no one else died."

"I know. My cousins in Tyrol probably took part." She sighs. "I still find it hard to believe that they both got sucked in by the propaganda."

Max pours some of the steaming chicory coffee into their cups. "It's a rural/urban conflict, you know, like so many others throughout history. You're a city girl and they're country girls, even though you're cousins." He takes a drink of his coffee, makes a face, and adds a little more beet sugar. "I've been thinking about it lately. The country folk in their traditional clothing and their traditional values are siding with the pious Catholics and the aristocracy because they all favor a strict hierarchical society with authoritarian leadership. On the other side are the workers in their caps and coveralls," he points to his own, "who live in the urban industrial centers, where we've been well-served by the unions. We tend to side with the free-thinkers and intellectuals who believe in democracy and social justice: the intelligentsia that Hugo wanted to talk about the other day when Anna interrupted him." They both think back to that moment in the cafe. "Anna was so rude, wasn't she? Sometimes I could hit her," he says.

Gisi takes a long drink. She doesn't feel like talking about Anna, even though she shares Max's sentiment. She looks into her cup. "I think this is good, even if it isn't coffee. It's hot and it's sweet and that's good enough for me." Taking another sip, she says, "Yes, the rural/urban split plays a big part in the polarization of Austria right now. And there's also the nationalist/internationalist divide, which fits right in with country versus city split. People who grow up in a small rural place, and have little or no contact with people who are different than they are, become the nationalists. They want to protect their world as they know it. People who grow up in large cities where they have to learn how to get along with people from different backgrounds sooner or later realize the value of learning from and working with people from other cultures. We become the internationalists."

"*Ach*," Max replies. "It's easy to analyze and philosophize, not so easy to make changes for the better."

"Especially when everybody involved has a different idea of what 'better' means!"

"But we aren't helping ourselves very much. Even the SDAP is divided into factions who are always fighting each other," he goes on. "Our wing is pleading with Dollfuss to let us join him to create a united front against the Nazis, while the *Schutzbund* is stockpiling weapons to fight him."

"The *Heimwehr* is divided too. One wing follows Dollfuss blindly, another faction follows Stahremberg in demanding pure Fascism based on Mussolini's system, and the third wants us to merge with Germany."

"It's true. We humans don't seem to know how to live in peace. Even those of us who proclaim it as our highest value." He refills their cups, stirring a little of the beet sugar into each one. Raising his cup, he says, "To Peace!"

"To Peace!" she responds smiling a little and clicking her cup against his. They take sips of the sweet ersatz coffee.

Gisi's smile doesn't last long. "Did you see that graph in the paper that showed how many more Austrians favor an Anschluss, a merger with Germany, now? It's over two thirds again. For a long time a lot of the Nazis were opposing it, but now they're all in favor."

"But wasn't it over 80% already a few years ago, when the SDAP was still supporting a merger? During the Weimar Republic period in Germany? Before Hitler came into power?"

"You mean when supporting an Anschluss was about economic health and collaboration on social goals? When it was about redressing the wrongs in the Versailles Treaty? When it was about peace?" She smiles wryly. "The numbers who supported it were higher then, yes, but what's so popular now would be a merger with a very different Germany. And unfortunately, an Anschluss has many more supporters now that it's about promoting nationalism and anti-Semitism."

She puts down her cup. "Support peaked at 80% just before the Nazis started setting off so many bombs all over Austria. I think that was a big mistake on their part. If they'd pushed for a referendum instead of turning up the violence, we'd probably already be part of greater Germany."

"How do you know all that? You forgot to resign from the People's League when Hitler became Chancellor of Germany?"

"No," she laughs. "I just follow it in the paper. It seems important to me."

CHAPTER 47

A LITTLE HOPE

January 13, 1934
Cafe Rüdigerhof, Brigittenau

"**W**hoo hoo!" Leo cries gleefully, reading the morning paper as he and Toni have coffee together at his place. "Some good news! Listen to this! It's all out in the open now. Yesterday the police raided our local Nazi leader Alfred Frauenfeld's apartment and, what do you think? They found him in his living room, deep in conversation not only with two other prominent Nazis, Senator Schattenfroh and *Herr* Suchanwith, but also with—listen to this—Count Johann Alberti, the commander of the Lower Austrian *Heimwehr*! The guy who's supposed to be Stahremberg's top commander in the fight *against* the Nazis. The tide is turning at last—they caught them red-handed!"

"Well, it's about time these things came out. I've always agreed with you that that kind of collaboration has been happening all along," says Toni. "So, what happened? What did the police do?"

"They arrested them all. Oh, but wait a minute, I'm still reading the article... oh, I see this actually happened the day before yesterday, but they blocked the press from reporting it right away, even the foreign press, until an official *Heimwehr* communique was released." He sighs, and he reads aloud:

"'The communique briefly recounted the incident and said that Alberti had been relieved of his duties and arrested.' That's not so bad, I guess. Even if they took an extra day to let us know."

"It's as it should be. They should arrest him and try him and all the rest of the collaborators. I hope they all get what they deserve." Toni takes a bite of the *Punschkrapfen* she'd brought them from the bakery downstairs.

But Leo isn't finished reading yet. "Ah, ah, ah. There's more. In a later dispatch, it says they've already released Alberti! And why did they release him so soon? Without paying bond or having even a preliminary hearing? It was so he wouldn't have to miss the *Heimwehr* leaders' conference yesterday."

Toni grimaces. "For god's sake. I'm sure a good portion of the *Heimwehr* leadership shook his hand and commended him on his excellent contacts. They probably felt sorry that he had to be arrested for a few hours. Poor Count Alberti in that cold jail cell without even a glass of good schnapps to warm him."

"I'll bet Alberti is their regular liaison with the Nazis, and has been for a long time," Leo continues. "The *Heimwehr* knows that there's more than a good chance they'll be working with the Nazis sooner or later. They have so much in common after all. They're all Fascists and they're all anti-Semitic, though in different degrees. What more do they need in common? Why not plan ahead?"

"But why let that incident go public at all? Do you think it was a mistake to let it get into the paper?"

Leo thinks for a moment. "No, it was probably their own factionalism biting back at them. Vice Chancellor Fey is supposed to be rabidly anti-Nazi, so he might have set the police on them. The paper also says that the two Nazis, who really are their top people, were sent off to a concentration camp. They didn't get released so fast. Well, at least there's that. Maybe they were willing to throw Alberti under the bus, albeit very temporarily, to catch those two Nazis."

"That would be good, I suppose. Sort of. At least they got the Nazis."

"Or there might be a feud going on between Alberti and Fey. There are plenty of ways it could have happened and then come out."

Toni is still looking through the paper. "Oh, you could be right. Look here. They've made Fey Commissioner of the Police now. There's a statement by him down here." She points. "Strong words! He's says he's going to cleanse the public services of all concealed Nazi influence and stamp out Nazi terrorism once and for all."

"One can hope, I suppose," Leo said, putting the last piece of the pastry in his mouth. "but it all sounds like more propaganda to me."

❧⚕❦⚕❧

January 13, 1934
Peter's school at Austerlitz-Hof

Anna puts on her boots and buttons her coat, pulls on her hat, tucks in her scarf and slips on her gloves. She picks up her bag, heavy with students' notebooks that she would add comments to tonight, and makes her way through the crowds of children leaving the building at the end of the school day.

The cold air buffets her as she stands at the top of the steps scanning the playground for Peter, whom she walks over to Hugo's place every afternoon. There he is, wild mop of frizzy red hair popping out at the center of a circle of children.

Oh no, she thinks, looking at the group more carefully. Not again.

From her position at the top of the stairs, Anna can see Peter well. He's very red in the face, his fists are clenched tightly to his sides, and he's standing still as a statue. A group of bigger boys surrounds him, gesturing and calling out.

Before Anna can run over to intervene, Peter explodes like a little bomb, arms flailing, hitting the boys closest to him as hard as he can. The others don't hesitate to join in the fracas. They knock Peter to the ground quickly and pile on top of him. Anna drops her bag and rushes into the group, pushing the growing crowd of children aside. One by one she pulls the boys off Peter: one, two, three, four of them. More adults push their way in to help and the offenders are taken off to the headmistress's office.

After dusting Peter off and giving him a big hug, Anna walks the little boy, wallowing in tears, over to the nurse's office. He's bruised, full of cuts and scratches, and very dirty. His shirt and trousers are torn. His rucksack is gone.

"How did it happen?" she asks, brushing him off again.

"They were calling me Carrot Top and Four Eyes," Peter said, wiping his nose on his sleeve. "They always do it."

"But we've discussed that so many times. We just talked about it yesterday. All children with red hair or glasses get called those names. Remember I told you that some of the children don't mean it in a nasty way? That they just don't know any other way to say hello to you?"

"I know all of that, but this wasn't like that. Those boys were saying it to be mean to me."

Poor little Peter, Anna thought, you get called both names and then you give the nasty kids exactly the response they're looking for: tears. "You're right. They probably were being mean. And when they see that calling you names bothers you, they do it more."

Peter sobs loudly. "That's exactly what happened. They were doing it more and more, until I just couldn't stand it." He looks up at her through his big glasses, which Anna now sees had a long crack across one lens. "Will I get in trouble?"

Anna looks at the little boy sadly. "We'll see. You probably will. I'm pretty sure that I saw you hitting them first, didn't I?"

"But they taunted me! And that wasn't the first time at all. I think hitting them back was the right thing to do!"

"I guess you'll know that when you see if they keep on teasing you, or if they stop." To fight or not to fight, the eternal debate, thinks Anna. She remembers the last SDAP meeting.

Peter's teacher is already waiting at the nurse's office. "We'll clean him up, find some other clothes for him, and then we'll talk a bit. You go and see if you can find Hugo, Anna." The teacher and the nurse are undressing Peter carefully, tending to his cuts and bruises as they go. "I tried the telephone, but I didn't get an answer. He could still be at work, or at the coffee house, or maybe he's in the communal workshop he uses for his art projects?"

Anna gives Peter another hug and hurries off, but Hugo is neither at home nor at the workshop. He's probably still at work, she thinks, looking at the time. It isn't uncommon for him to be at work after the shop closes. The optician is happy to let him make his own hours, so long as the orders are filled on time and the lenses are well-crafted. Good jobs like that are hard to find.

She checks her purse. Not enough change to get to there by tram. She'll have to walk.

Halfway to the optical shop where Hugo works, she passes Cafe Rüdigerhof. Realizing there's a good chance Hugo is there, she pushes open the door and steps into the old cafe. Across the room, she spots Leo and Toni at their regular table, but Hugo doesn't seem to be there. She looks at her watch again. He should be done with work about now, even if he did work late, and he stops here on his way home most days. She'll ask the others if it's likely he'd be there soon.

"Have any of you seen Hugo? I thought he might be here at this time of day," she says, joining the group.

"He should be here any minute," answers Toni. "Why don't you sit down and wait?"

As she hangs her coat on the coat tree and pulls up a chair, Anna joins the conversation. "What sounds like more propaganda?" She feels uncomfortable under Gert's suspicious glare.

"Oh, it's just Fey making more meaningless threats," says Leo, smiling. "Hello, Anna! What brings the strongest single woman in Vienna here to our humble cafe?" Anna has been sharing her new goal of being an exemplary single woman with everyone lately.

Toni stands and gives her a light hug and two quick kisses on the cheek. "It's good to see you. How have you been?"

Anna answers, "Not very well at all at the moment."

"Oh dear! Why not?"

"Peter was in a fight with some other children today."

Toni cries, "A fight! Oh no! How is he?"

"How on earth did that happen?" asks Leo. "Peter doesn't strike me as the fighting type."

Anna relates the story. "I'm not even sure the boys who were teasing him were Austerlitz-Hof children. They were probably neighborhood kids who come to the playground in the complex after school."

"There's no reason to make an assumption like that, Anna," says Leo. "Socialist children are still children." Anna wants to argue that the methods they're using in the schools substantially reduce violence and bullying, but she stops herself. She doesn't know which boys were there in that big crowd of kids, and, being honest with herself, she had recognized at least two of the boys she'd pulled off Peter. They were definitely Austerlitz-Hof children.

"Okay, you're right. Boys will be boys, I suppose. In any case, it doesn't help matters that Peter tends to overreact to what the other children consider jokes," she finishes.

"He's a very sensitive child—I see that as a good quality. We should all be more sensitive," says Toni.

"Poor little guy," says Leo. "Things are getting worse in Germany, too. I'm sure his parents must be having a very hard time now. Jews have effectively been banned from working, so nobody at all comes to Hugo's brother-in-law for tailored suits anymore, and nobody is interested in buying their household goods. There's no one to buy it—all their potential customers are selling their own furniture. I don't know how his parents will ever be able to pay the exit fees."

"So you've heard from them?"

"No, not me, not recently anyhow, but I did hear from my brother that all the Jewish and leftist musicians who can afford the fees are streaming into Vienna now. They're telling terrible stories."

The door opens again letting in a rush of cold air and this time, Hugo. A minute later, he and Anna set off for the school.

Chapter 48

The Account Books

February 7, 1934
Austerlitz-Hof

Hugo writes the figures carefully in the big account book that is spread out on the desk in front of him. Pulling out a piece of scrap paper, he copies the numbers one more time, and adds them up from the bottom of the column to the top and again from the top to the bottom. He does it another time by hand and once more on the mechanical adding machine. The numbers still don't add up. Without the support of the federal government, the finances of the municipal housing system are stretched to the limit. In fact, a fair bit beyond the limit, as he can see from his unsuccessful attempts at balancing the books. Austerlitz-Hof is no exception. Realizing there is nothing to be done about it at the moment, he closes the heavy book and hefts it back onto the shelf next to the others.

A loud rapping at the door surprises him. "Who's there?" he calls out, pushing his chair away from the table. It's early in the morning, early enough that most of the residents of the complex wouldn't even be up yet. Who could it be? Who knocked like that? Before he can cross the room, the door swings open and half a dozen armed and helmeted *Heimwehr* soldiers fill the small office.

Hugo backs up against the desk holding his hands up. "What's the matter?" he asks, trying to keep his voice clear and steady. "What have I done?" Gert's warning from a few weeks ago comes back to him. Is it true that they have his name on a list of conspirators?

Will they take him away now? It's so early. Will anyone be up and out yet to see it happen if they do arrest him and take him to jail? Or will he just disappear? Lately there are more and more stories about people who disappear.

To his immense relief, one of the officers answers gruffly "It's not you we want. We don't even know who you are. It's this office we want," he looks around the small room, "and those books." He points the tip of his bayonet toward the shelf of account books. "Take your things and get out of here."

Two of the soldiers are already pulling the huge books off the shelf, and two others have stationed themselves outside the door. The remaining soldiers keep their bayonets pointed directly at Hugo as he puts on his boots, coat, scarf, and gloves, and hurriedly leaves the office.

With barely a pause to tell the one man he passes on his way out of Austerlitz-hof what just happened, Hugo rushes to catch the tram to Karl-Marx-Hof where he hopes to find the members of the SDAP leadership. He needs to tell someone above him in the party hierarchy about what occurred. With any luck they'll know why it's happening and whether similar takeovers are going on elsewhere—and they'll already be planning some kind of a response.

As the tram pulls up to the massive new housing complex, Hugo sees *Heimwehr* guards standing at the main entrance there too. A fierce-looking soldier holds up his machine gun to bar Hugo from entering. The meeting halls are all occupied by the *Heimwehr*, the guard tells him. "And don't bother going over to the offices of the *Arbeiter Zeitung*," he snarls. "They're occupied too."

So that's it, then. The Fascists are taking Vienna, thinks Hugo, just as they've taken every provincial capital in Austria, one by one, since January 1930. But this time, they aren't taking it over through an election. This is a coup.

Obviously, the time for the General Strike has come.

Rather than going back home, he walks over to a nearby news kiosk and stands on the far side of it where the soldiers can't see him. He picks up and glances at a copy of the previous day's *Neue Freie Presse,* but he doesn't read it. Instead, he pretends to be looking at the paper until out of the corner of his eye, he sees two members of the SDAP's central committee coming out of another entrance to Karl-Marx-Hof, deep in conversation. Leaving the paper at the kiosk, he follows the two men at a distance for about a block, and when he's certain no one is watching, he catches up and discretely joins them.

The other SDAP members tell him that a General Strike has indeed been called, and word of it should be going out via the union leaders any moment, unless, of course, their offices have also been taken over, which would obviously make communication more difficult. The leadership council will be meeting at Otto Bauer's home in Leopoldstadt in the afternoon, but it's extremely important not to be seen going there.

The two of them, in fact, are fortunate the *Heimwehr* guards had believed their lies about who they were and had let them pass out of the complex. They'd told the guards that they'd been at Karl-Marx-Hof inspecting the security system for the federal government, they explain to Hugo, but before they could pull out their papers to prove it, the guards' attention had been drawn away by some commotion in the courtyard, commotion that happened to be instigated by some other SDAP members for that very purpose. The two of them plan to take trams going in opposite directions now, and later make their way to the council meeting in Leopoldstadt with great care.

Leaving the two "inspectors" at the tram stop, Hugo thinks for a few moments, and decides that he'll go to see Gert before trying to make his own way to Bauer's place later in the day. Who knows when they will see each other again?

In addition, Gert and Toni are both members of the textile workers union. They'll probably have heard what's going on. He takes the tram back to Brigittenau and walks the four blocks to the women's apartment house. When he knocks on the door of their place, though, neither of them is there. Disappointed, he takes another tram, and then walks several blocks to the dressmaker's shop where Gert works. It's closed.

Next he tries the woolen mill where Toni works as a weaver. There's no sign of a strike happening, but the workers aren't there either. He feels increasingly uneasy.

In addition, if he takes one more tram, he'll have no money left for trams for the entire week! He walks back to Austerlitz-Hof.

It's nearly three in the afternoon by the time he gets back. He can see from the tram stop that no *Heimwehr* guards are standing at the main entrance of the complex, and when he goes in, he's much relieved to find the housing office unlocked and unoccupied. The account books the soldiers had taken down are piled up in three untidy stacks on the table. Why would anyone want them anyway? It doesn't make any sense to him.

Outside, the courtyard is buzzing with conversation. It doesn't take Hugo long to find out that SDAP offices and meeting halls were occupied all over Vienna. At the *Arbeiter*

Zeitung, the offices were taken over, the presses stopped, and no morning edition of the paper had been printed. Then, at exactly 2:30, all over the city, the soldiers took note of the time and they walked out of the places they'd been occupying, all of them at once. No explanation was offered.

Had a General Strike ever been called? No one is certain. The factories let out for lunch as usual but as far as anyone knew, there was no definite word of any collective action in response to the brief occupation. All the same, hardly anyone had returned to work.

Hugo decides he'll put a few hours of work in that day, after all. The task of carefully grinding lenses will give him a chance to think things over. In addition, the owner of the optical firm he works for is a good member of the party and a generous man, and Hugo knows there's work that he should be doing. So, instead of crossing the city to join the leadership group at Otto Bauer's home, he heads to the optician's office. He'll find out who was at the meeting at Bauer's place, what was said, and what was decided later on.

The optician is glad to see him. "So, my friend, here you are at last! What's happening that has so many people looking worried?" Hugo takes off his winter coat, settles in at his workbench, and shares his experiences.

"In the end, I have to tell you, I'm not sure what really happened," he says. "It seems most likely that the *Heimwehr* were ordered to occupy as many of the smaller SDAP offices as possible, plus all of the meeting rooms we generally use, and the *Arbeiter Zeitung* offices and press, all for a certain amount of time, and then to leave. As far as I know, they didn't take over the *Rathaus,* or the union offices, or the office of the Austrian Social Executive, which meant we weren't under any obligation to make good on our threat of a General Strike." He shakes his head quizzically. "They certainly gave us a good scare, though. What strikes me in particular is how effectively they managed to stop us from communicating among ourselves."

"It was a show of strength then."

"Yes, that's what I think, too," Hugo says, placing a lens carefully into his machine. "And it worked—I felt completely powerless, rushing all over the city the whole day looking for answers and finding out so little."

"So it was a successful exercise on their part," says the older man.

Hugo dusts off the lens. "It was. It most certainly was."

CHAPTER 49

APOCALYPSE

February 12, 1934
Vienna, Austria

At 11:46 AM on a cold morning, the power goes out and the trams stop all over the city of Vienna.

Minutes later, Leo, hurrying to meet Toni for lunch, crosses the Ringstrasse near the University to see a long line of tram cars standing silently on the plaza. Surprised, he approaches some conductors and drivers who are standing in a group smoking and talking animatedly.

"What's going on, comrades?" he asks.

"We don't know," says one of the men. "There's no electricity."

Another of them offers, "We've heard that the Fascists are shooting workers in Linz and that a General Strike was called there. All we know for certain, though, is that the power has been cut at the central station so none of the trams can go anywhere."

"It could be an accident somewhere—that's happened before—or it could be sabotage—I wouldn't put it past the Nazis to shut the whole city down—or it could be the call for a General Strike," another adds, "and communication is so disrupted that we haven't heard the details yet."

"If they're using troops and heavy artillery on our

comrades in Linz, which is what I've heard, then there'll be definitely be a strike, and it'll most likely lead to a civil war," says a third.

As Leo starts to ask another question, a young man in a blue cap runs up to them. "I'm from the *Arbeiter Zeitung*," he says breathlessly. "The presses are shut down again. This morning the Government sent the police to raid the Workers' Club in Linz looking for a cache of weapons that they believed the *Schutzbund* was storing there. The *Schutzbund* leader gave his people the order to resist and they managed to lock the police in the cellar. But then police reinforcements arrived and began shooting at the building from the outside with machine-guns. Our people returned fire. It seems Dollfuss gave his men a free hand, so the full force of the artillery was turned on the workers. High-powered weaponry. It was war." He pauses for a moment.

"Oh my god, did people die?"asks one of the drivers.

"Many died," answers the boy. "Many. I don't know the number, and frankly, I don't want to think about it." He stands still then, wiping his brow, staring at the ground. At last he looks up and says, "I'm also supposed to tell you that a General Strike is beginning now, throughout Austria." He turns and hurries off toward a group of people in workers' clothing standing outside of a cafe to deliver his message to them.

"Under the circumstances, will the *Schutzbund* everywhere be ready to fight?" Leo asks the men in general.

"Of course," answers one of the drivers. "We all knew it would come to this eventually."

Another adds, "There's nothing left to do but to fight. Our backs are against the wall."

"The hell with pacifism!" a third says. "I always knew it was a mistake."

At about the same time, at the *Rathaus*, Hugo is leaving a particularly stressful housing meeting. When he walks out the door into the hallway, he finds himself surrounded by *Heimwehr* holding machine guns and rifles. He stops walking. This is it, he thinks, and he breathes out deliberately.

Trying to appear calm, he turns to the stiffly upright soldier closest to him. "What's going on?" Hugo hears himself asking.

"Mayor Seitz is being asked to step down. His office is just around the corner, there," the soldier points with a brief nod of the head. "Get out of the building as quickly as possible."

Karl Seitz has been mayor of Vienna since 1924, presiding throughout the height of the Social Democratic experiment. At 65, he is physically frail, but as spirited as ever.

"Out! Get out of my *Rathaus* immediately!" Hurrying down the hall, Hugo hears Seitz roaring from his office door. Despite the clamor all around by then, Seitz calls out, "I am still the legally elected *Burgermeister* of this city! I will not yield to threats! I yield only to force!"

Hugo stops, and turns back to see what's going on. Seitz's brave statements are in vain. Force is being duly applied by the soldiers. The elderly mayor, followed by all the councillors and officials he could gather, is being dragged away by the soldiers.

Hugo, stunned, still feeling as if he is outside of his body, makes his way out of the building and through the barbed wire barricades which are rapidly being hammered into place around it. The *Heimwehr* are everywhere, setting up gun-nests, bringing in tanks, pointing machine guns down the major roads in every direction. Mechanically, he

Red Vienna

walks over to the SDAP's party headquarters in the Rechte Wienzeile. The great gates are locked.

Overwhelmed, he walks back toward Austerlitz-Hof on eerily quiet backstreets.

⚙━✳━⚙

In a small apartment at Karl-Marx-Hof, Max is demonstrating how to use the radio that an elderly couple, Franz and Else Schiffer, bought from him earlier in the day. He'd packed the bulky radio up in its wooden crate and carried it over to the couple's place. *Herr* Schiffer cleared a space on the bookshelf, and Max set the radio on it and plugged it in. He's explaining how to use the shortwave band when there's a great commotion, like the sound of dozens of people running, in the hall outside the apartment.

"This way!" shouts someone. "I know where the cache is!" More speeding feet pass the door.

"Where are they? Where are the guns?" come other voices.

"Bricked up in the cellar, behind the storage area! Bring tools!" cries a third.

Max opens the door a little and calls out, "What's going on?"

Someone shouts back, "It's the *Heimwehr*! Karl-Marx-Hof is under attack!"

"We're getting the weapons!" says a man, pausing at the door for a moment. "Can you handle a gun?"

Max tells him, "No! Sorry," and he shuts the door firmly and locks it.

Inside the apartment, he leans against the wall, horrified.

No matter how many times he'd imagined something like this happening, no matter how prepared he thought he was, now that it is actually happening, his knees have turned to water, and he can barely breathe.

Sporadic gunfire begins, followed by the dreadful hammering of machine-gun fire.

The Schiffers huddle together on the narrow settee holding their hands over their ears and heads. *Frau* Schiffer is crying. There's nothing they can do.

Numbly, Max sits down at the table. He feels utterly helpless. He drops his head into his hands, his elbows on the table, and sinks into the horror of what's happening. In one of the brief moments between rounds of gunfire, he hears *Frau* Schiffer's soft sobs. Shaking his head to ward off the sense of doom engulfing him, he begins to turn the dial on the radio, his fingers trembling.

Nothing but static comes from the standard stations. He can't find the BBC or the renegade German station he listens to. He twists the dial in the finest increments, searching for news of any sort. A Swiss station is broadcasting music. There's nothing from Czechoslovakia. The shortwave holds more promise of course, but the signal is almost non-existent.

The gunfire lessens, or perhaps it's farther away from the Schiffers' apartment, but instead, every so often, there's a louder explosion, a deep, rumbling boom that shakes everything to its core. *Frau* Schiffer jumps at the sound each time it begins. Tears trickle slowly down *Herr* Schiffer's face.

Max takes a deep breath and tries to stay focused on the radio. After a good twenty minutes of fiddling—with a brief break to bring the Schiffers some chicory coffee and bread that he finds in their corner kitchen—he finally connects with another shortwave operator.

"The *Heimwehr* and the police are raiding workers housing blocks all over the city, working together," the other operator reports. "They say they're looking for weapons supposedly hidden there."

"My god," says Max.

The other operator continues, "When they're refused entry to the complexes, they shoot their way in." Then the connection is lost.

Running footsteps pass the door again, this time from the other direction. Max opens it a crack to see a dozen men wielding guns running toward the front of the complex. The shooting is booming and closer now. A loud voice, probably amplified by a megaphone, calls out, "Stay away from all windows and walls! Get out of your apartments! Gather in the courtyards unless you have a weapon!"

Max and the old couple grab their coats and shuffle along the hall with the crowd of other tenants as it moves slowly toward the center of the complex. There are so many people jammed into the hallway that they move forward only sporadically.

"I knew it was coming to this," a man near Max says. "I knew it, I knew it. Our own damn government is attacking us."

Just then the greatest of all the booms shakes the whole building. The group freezes. For a few minutes, they stand silent and trembling as similar booms shake them again and again.

When they finally abate, the group begins to creep forward again.

"Coming through, coming through!" Men carrying sheets of plywood are pushing through the crowd, forcing everyone against the wall. From his cramped position, Max can see, not fifty feet away, in a hallway adjoining the one he's in, a gaping hole in the side of the building being rapidly patched with the wood. Through the hole, he can see the barrel of a huge gun. He quickly turns his eyes away—only to meet those of the others around him, each of them as terrified as he.

The crowd moves forward again until they're pushed against each other, even more tightly this time, and a group of injured people, bleeding, moaning, crying with pain, are carried or stumble on their own toward the front of the group. The people from the corridor with the bombed out wall are joining the exodus. Forward movement becomes even slower.

Only rigidly standing still with his eyes tightly closed brings Max the slightest feeling of relief. If the crowd stops for more than a few seconds, he tries to force himself to derive comfort from feeling the other bodies pressing against his. Comrades, he tries to remember. But then the crowd pushes him forward, and he is thrown back into the mix of panic and resignation all around him. He steps forward once, twice, three times, and he realizes he hasn't been breathing. For how long?

When, after an eternity, the group reaches the central courtyard and the crowd thins, a man directs Max to where he can help build barricades using galvanized steel trashcans. He walks toward the work area, passing one of the large dining rooms. Isn't that Gisi's friend Elsa leaning over someone lying on a table? It looks like her—then he remembers that she's a nurse. From a little closer, he can see that the man Elsa is tending has lost an arm. It's lying on the ground next to the table. He turns away again; it's too much for him. He retches. Dozens of other wounded people, old people, children, men and women, many shrieking with pain, are being carried in from the courtyard to be laid on the tables, waiting for someone like Elsa to come and help them. Blood is everywhere.

❦

Gunfire and shelling continue on all sides of the complex until late at night.

❦

Workers' complexes all over the city are all being attacked simultaneously. The chaos is so great and the workers are so demoralized that few heed the call for a General Strike. It's called off within hours.

❦

At some of the municipal housing complexes, *Schutzbund* units wait hours for armaments to be delivered, but none come. The men who know where the arms are hidden have been arrested or killed.

❦

At another of the workers' complexes, Engel-hof, the tenants frantically dig holes in all the courtyards, women tearing up the beautiful gardens with their hands while men use the few spades they have to search for their hidden cache of arms. In the end, they don't find it, and the building is taken by the *Heimwehr*.

Gisi stays inside the apartment with her family for three days. She doesn't know where Max or any of the others are. Day and night, they hear the sound of shooting coming from all directions. The panes on the windows and glasses on the shelf tinkle every time a cannon is fired.

Helene, *Herr* Berger, and Gisi barely say a word to each other. There's nothing they can think of to say. Gisi and her mother cook silently and eat vacantly. The old man doesn't eat at all. He tries to tune the radio but his fingers are shaking so much he can't locate the stations. Days and nights blend as they sleep at odd hours, listening, listening, and feeling the booms of the heavy artillery.

At Reumannhof, another of the complexes, steel-helmeted police break through the front gates on the afternoon of first day's fighting and use truncheons to beat the men defending their buildings. When women and children appear at the windows crying, the police shout, "Get back from the windows or we'll shoot!" When a single gun shot is heard, it isn't clear where it came from—the police? a resident?— because at the very same moment, the *Heimwehr* and army troops appear and machine-gun fire opens.

The police and the *Heimwehr* ruthlessly storm that great complex filled with men, women, and children—and all the others like it all over the city—fighting their way through bitter resistance from building to building, corridor to corridor, floor to floor.

279

Red Vienna

Reumannhof is the first of the complexes to fall.

※⊱⊰※

The war spreads all over Austria.

※⊱⊰※

Sitting in a cozy cafe near the lake in Basel with a cup of coffee and a pastry, Emil learns about the civil war in Austria from the morning newspaper. He rushes home and frantically tries to reach his parents and Gisi, but no telephone service is available.

※⊱⊰※

Some of the worst shelling happens at the complex called Ottokring. When it too is finally taken, the body of the Socialist councillor from the area is found hanging in a window facing the courtyard. He chose to end his life there, in full sight of his constituents.

※⊱⊰※

At a complex called Liebknecht-Hof, a Red Cross ambulance drives up to the gates and is allowed in by the *Schutzbund* guard. Inside the courtyard, its doors fly open, a dozen steel-helmeted police with rifles and machine guns spring out and open fire. Though they're successfully driven out by the defenders at first, the battle is just beginning.

280

Austerlitz-Hof is taken late on the first day of fighting. Armored cars and tanks crash through the gates and soldiers attack the tenants, who are armed only with rifles and pistols, until the tenants' ammunition runs out. After the surrender, all the occupants, among them Anna and Hugo, are imprisoned in the meeting rooms or in their apartments.

On the Lauerberg, a street in a working class neighborhood, the *Schutzbund* sets up a defensive position by building strong barricades and digging trenches across the fields between two blocks of workers' houses and arming it with two thousand men. Five battalions of the Austrian army plus the *Heimwehr* and the police attack it. Poorly clothed, poorly shod, hungry and thirsty, the two thousand men defend their homes for three bitter cold February days and nights before they to surrender to the government forces.

Leo and Toni don't meet for lunch. When they hear what's happening, they turn around and go straight home.

Later, Leo and Felix make several attempts to leave their family's apartment to get food, but they're stopped by bayonet-wielding soldiers at the corners of their block. There's barely enough food in the apartment for two people, much less six. By the third day, Leo is so hungry he's about to nibble on one of their precious candles when Felix gives him a look he will remember for the rest of his life.

⊕⊣{3⊰}⊱⊢⊕

Gert goes to her family's apartment in Leopoldstadt, so Toni is left alone in their apartment, trembling and crying, for three days. She runs out of food the second day and the water is cut off on the third when a grenade hits a water main. A group of neighbors in the building bring whatever food they have left to the apartment of the owner, who lives on the ground floor, and together they make a thin soup to share. Toni is so hungry that she finds herself wondering what the neighbors who didn't contribute saved for themselves, and she imagines ways of breaking into their apartments.

⊕⊣{3⊰}⊱⊢⊕

"For heaven's sake," mutters *Frau* Schiffer, who is by then too weak to leave her bed. "Why do they waste their ammunition? They should just wait until we all die of hunger or thirst!"

⊕⊣{3⊰}⊱⊢⊕

Many of the tenants of Karl-Marx Hof hide in the sewers underneath the complex for the three days while above them the *Heimwehr* uses Howitzers and trench mortars to attack their buildings. Three times the Government moves into the complex believing they have won, and three times, the defenders emerge from the sewers to fight again. Hundreds die. Karl-Marx-Hof holds out until its main tower falls to artillery fire on the third day and, then, finally, the SDAP capitulates.

❧❧❧

On Thursday morning following the surrender of Karl-Marx-Hof, a military car drives slowly from one complex to the next, stopping at the main gate of each. A good-looking, elderly but still erect officer steps out of the car followed by a trumpeter. They walk to the center of the main courtyard in an orderly procession. The old officer is Prince Alois General Schönburg-Haretenstein, Austria's Minister of War. When the two reach the very center of the complex, the trumpeter plays a few notes, and the workers and their wives come out and gather around to see what is happening.

At each stop, the old man stands unguarded in their midst, reading aloud a proclamation offering amnesty to the leaders if they hand in their arms by noon. In a fatherly way, he then translates the official words into Viennese dialect, and says how much he admires the courage of the men. But the fight is over, he says to them gently. "You must accept your defeat and surrender now. Or you will pay with your lives."

❧❧❧

When it's over, one of the *Schutzbund* commanders tells a reporter proudly that, throughout the fighting, there was not a single incidence of looting. This is confirmed by a government official, who also points out that it might have been better for the defenders if the *Schutzbund* had not been such gentlemen. A little bit of looting, he says, might have helped their cause—not only by providing much-needed food, but also by distracting the police. Instead, the full force of the police and army was concentrated on the *Schutzbund* defense.

***

Otto Bauer and Julius Deutsch escape to Czechoslovakia. Fifteen of the Social Democratic leaders who didn't escape are hanged or shot after summary proceedings over the following few days.

The Social Democratic Workers Party and its affiliated trade unions are dissolved.

In Vienna, the SDAP counts two thousand men, women, and children dead, and over five thousand wounded.

Chapter 50

The Morning After

February 18, 1934
Brigittenau
Max's apartment

At four in the morning on February 18, Max, stinking, hungry, and thirsty, furtively unlocks the door to his family's apartment. He slips in and immediately locks it behind him. He'd climbed out of the sewer at Karl-Marx-Hof just two hours earlier, and made his way home flattened against the walls of buildings, deep in the shadows, through the darkest alleys and streets of the city.

Leaving his mud-caked boots in the hall, he skirts past his sleeping father and goes into the kitchen where he throws some bits of coal onto the embers in the stove, and drinks down every drop of the boiled water left in the pot. Then he refills the pot and sets it on top of the stove again.

He shivers as he takes off his clothes and puts on his threadbare bathrobe. It would be a good thing if he could throw those clothes away, but it's out of the question. Instead, he pulls the big galvanized tub out from under the sink and begins to fill it, pot by pot, with water heated on the stove. As he waits for the water to heat, he eats whatever he can find, some dry bread and most of a can of pickled herring. An hour later, when the tub is full enough, he steps in, sighing deeply as the steaming water surrounds him and slowly warms him. He washes himself thoroughly and then lies back and relaxes until the water is almost cold. Later, dried off in the heat of the fire and wearing his nightshirt, he adds another pot of boiling water to the washtub and drops his filthy clothes into it.

It's after six in the morning when he lies down on the settee. He sleeps for the next twelve hours, barely stirring when his father comes into the room and pulls a blanket over him.

❦❧❦❧

After covering his son, Seppe quietly leaves to go to his cafe, where he finds Dolf and Fredl sitting in a booth in the back room.

"Quick, sit," says Dolf.

"It's safe?" asks Seppe.

"I haven't seen anything to make me think it's not. But who knows anymore?" says Fredl. "They're picking up more of us every day. We take a risk being here, but being at home might be an even bigger risk. Who knows anything anymore."

"Max is back," Seppe tells them.

"Thank god!" says Dolf. "Did he tell you where he was?"

"He's still sleeping."

"At least he's home. The news is all very bad."

"Yes, Dollfuss is telling the world that the housing complexes were built as fortresses to store weapons for an armed takeover, and that they stopped it from happening just in time," Fredl says.

"And they're also putting out that we were in league with the Soviets," finishes Dolf. "The headline on the *Fatherland Front* says 'Armed Insurrection Averted.'"

Fredl says, "They claim only two hundred died, but I've heard it's in the thousands."

"And they're hanging more as we speak," Seppe says.

❦

When he wakes up and finds himself alone, Max gets up, eats the last of the herring, dresses, and creeps down the stairs into the shop. The rooms are unchanged, though he feels he is seeing them for the first time, an eerie feeling. In the back room, as if in a trance, he breaks up some twigs and starts a fire in the coal stove. When the fire catches and the small sticks of wood begin to glow, he adds a few pieces of coal and turns on the radio very softly. Thank god there's still electricity, he thinks.

He's trying to find a signal when he hears someone rapping on the front door. His heart stops. Is the fighting still going on? Did someone smell his coal fire? Is it the police rounding people up? Had someone seen him coming home and reported it? Would they take him now? Will he die after all? He closes his eyes as the horror of the past three days overwhelms him.

A whistling sound on the radio brings him back to the present. He turns it off. The knocking is still going on. It's erratic, urgent in spurts with long gaps in between. Max sits still, slumped in his chair, listening, not moving a muscle. In the pauses between the starting and stopping of the rapping, a deep silence falls, broken only by the occasional crackling of the kindling in the stove.

Then Max thinks he hears a woman's voice calling his name softly. Can it be? It's so faint he isn't sure he'd actually heard it. But there it is again, accompanied by round of gentle rapping at the door. Very cautiously, holding his breath, he

287

peeks around the workshop door to see if he can tell who it is. The voice calls out his name again, a little louder. He breathes out, recognizing it. It's Gisi.

He runs through the shop, unlocks the door clumsily, and lets her in.

The relief and gratitude they feel at seeing each other again is incalculable.

They hug for a long time, their bodies trembling, and then sit down to share stories of the past three days. Both of them cry again and again, but the fire takes, and Max adds a little more coal. With the door to the main part of the shop closed, the small workshop warms up quickly and soon they are sitting side by side watching the glowing coals through the stove's dirty window, their legs touching, sipping comforting cups of chicory coffee.

Their respite is short-lived. Less than an hour later, Max and Gisi both freeze at the sound of more knocking at the door, this time much more forceful than the last. Max creeps to the front of the shop again, crouching under the little window, slowly raises himself up against the wall to see through the frosted pane obliquely. From that vantage point he can make out the shape of the caller. It's Anna.

After another round of tears, she tells her story and shares what news of the others she's been able to gather.

"The worst moment for me was when I finally came out of the apartment," she tells them. "I stood on the balcony and looked down into the courtyard. They were laying out the bodies. It was terrifying, the blood, the torn and broken bodies." She covers her face with her hand. "There must have been forty or fifty of them lying there in neat rows."

"So many just in Austerlitz-Hof!" Gisi cries in horror.

Anna is crying again. "My school friend Klara was there,"

she sobs. "And her husband. I saw them laid out there in the courtyard, side by side. Klara was covered in blood."

"*Ach*! And the children?" asks Gisi, not wanting to know.

"All three of them, lying in a row beside Klara. The oldest was only four years old. I'd been to his birthday party a few weeks ago. And the baby! She'd just learned to crawl. She wasn't even a year old."

"Oh no. It can't be!" Gisi puts her head in her hands.

"And there are so many more at Karl-Marx-Hof," Max says. "And in all the housing complexes."

"Dead?" cries Anna.

"Yes, and more injured. Who knows how many."

"*Schrecklich, schrecklich*! People we know!" says Gisi. "Our people!"

"And many whom we don't know. So many." Anna takes out her handkerchief, filthy and wet, and tries to dry her eyes, but her tears won't stop flowing. Then she is sobbing hard again, gasping, howling into her handkerchief to muffle the sound, and Gisi joins her.

Finally Anna pulls herself together again. She says, "Both Luitpold and Papanek got out, from what I hear. Apparently they're safe in Brno, Czechoslovakia, with Bauer and Deutsch. And Leo and Felix are with their family. They got word to Hugo somehow and he told me last night when we were released from our apartments. He was one of the lucky ones, too. He made it out of the *Rathaus* where he'd been for a meeting the day it began and spent the last three days at home at Austerlitz-hof—but this morning he took a chance and went to Toni and Gert's to see what happened there. Who knows if he ever got to at their place or if he'll ever come home again."

"But what about Peter?" asks Gisi.

"Thank god, he's with a family who lived down the hall from Hugo's place. The family was never active in the party, so he should be okay there," she pauses, "for the moment anyway." She goes on. "Hundreds, maybe thousands, of our people have been imprisoned—including Mayor Seitz, Rosa Jochmann, and the head teacher at my school. I don't know who else among our friends, but I'm sure some of those who survived that no one's heard from yet have been picked up. Maybe Franz. No one seems to have seen him."

"I haven't heard anything about him either," says Max. "But we didn't hear much in the sewer. Let's hope he's fine."

Anna picks up her cup and turns it in her hand. The ersatz coffee Gisi poured for her is long gone. "They hung Münichreiter and Georg Weissel this morning. Without a trial—though dozens of trials are said to be scheduled. It's all happening so fast that it's impossible to keep up. The party itself is being accused of planning a treasonous coup—that's the excuse they're giving for attacking us." She looks at her brother. "You really should go into hiding, Max. I'm sure your name is on a list."

"I know, but where can I go?" asks Max. "If my name is on a list, I won't be able to travel out of the city, much less the country. I probably should join the others in Brno, but how can I get there?"

"That's true," she says after some thought. "You're probably best off here for the time being, not answering the front door, and being ready to leave by the back door anytime. Pack your suitcase."

Gisi sighs. "Oh god. We're not just defeated—we're completely decimated. Where is there any hope now?"

CHAPTER 51

ONE GOOD THING

the same evening
the Baum apartment

It's after ten o'clock at night but neither Gisi nor Anna has left Max's place to go home. Around supper time the three of them go up to join Max and Anna's father in the apartment. Anna puts some lentils on to boil, and they sit around the kitchen table wrapped in blankets and their coats listening to the radio. A little while later they share a bite of dried sausage, some bread, and the lentil soup that Anna prepared.

The government reports continue to play down the immensity of the attacks on the municipal housing complexes and to blame not only the *Schutzbund* for firing the first shots but also the political wing of the SDAP for planning the whole catastrophe, which they are now calling a civil war.

Gisi rocks back and forth in her chair, unable to relax. Seppe moves away from the table and sits by the coal stove, drawing on his empty pipe and then knocking it on the stove again and again.

Max turns the dial on the radio endlessly, leaving the official reports unfinished before he looks for something else to listen to. They find some small comfort when he tunes into a Tchaikovsky symphony that probably comes from somewhere in the east, but when it's over the station goes off the air.

After trying for hours, Max is finally able to pick up the German-language BBC broadcast on the shortwave. A live interview with George Gedye, a long-time central European foreign correspondent who's in Vienna reporting, is about to start.

After introducing him, the BBC interviewer asks Mr. Gedye for his thoughts on the events of the last few days. The voice of the simultaneous translator rises above the English.

Max turns up the volume and Gisi, Anna, and Seppe pull their chairs closer to the radio. The foreign correspondent pauses for what seems like an unusually long time before responding to the interviewer, as if he's trying to find the right words. Finally he speaks.

"This is how it is for me. About six years ago, a retired Austrian General whom I knew well said to me, 'George, one day we are going to stop that business in Vienna by fair means or foul. Parquet floors and shower-baths for workers, indeed—you might as well put Persian carpets in a pigsty and feed the sow caviar.'

"How absurd!" cries Anna. "People like that will never understand!"

"It's incredibly offensive," says Max, but with less indignation than he would usually feel. He's too tired to be indignant.

"Shh!" says Seppe.

The reporter continues his story, "Well, that 'business in Vienna' is being stopped now, and the means do not seem to me to be particularly fair."

"How is that, Mr. Gedye?" asks the interviewer.

Gedye pauses again and then says, "It isn't really the

slaughter that made such an indelible impression on my mind, though it was terrible beyond words. I've seen slaughter more than once before, though."

Gisi shudders.

"What was worse, what I could never forget through those three nights of horror, was that I was forced to be present at the ruthless destruction—by unintelligent, unimaginative selfishness—of a great and world-recognized example of what could be done by devoted idealists and scientific reformers to give the great masses of my fellow-beings something of the good things of life that I demand for myself: clean homes, sunshine, pure air, a glimpse of green from at least some of their windows, decent sanitation and simple opportunities for personal cleanliness, a corner of safety from traffic for the children to play in, medical attention in cases of emergency."

"What one would wish for everyone," comments the interviewer. "A beautiful vision."

"And all this was offered not as charity, for which the recipient would be expected to show humble and respectful gratitude, but rather as something which it was the recognized duty of the community to provide, even at the cost of a little less superabundant luxury and inconsumable wealth for the small class of the very rich."

Tears rolls down the cheeks of all four of the listeners.

Gedye continues, "And now these fair dream-cities, with their promise for the whole world, which had grown up out of the jungle of slums, dirt, and dependence, are being trampled back into the jungle again by beasts who would not tolerate their existence."

"Turn it off," Anna says. "I can't listen." Max switches off the broadcast.

The room is silent for several minutes.

"Oh, I just remembered something!" cries Gisi suddenly. "There's one more thing I forgot to tell you. One thing happened that's actually good."

"By all means, tell us. Please!" says Max. "We all need to hear one good thing."

"Though I can't imagine any good at all that could possibly come out of this disaster," Anna adds dryly.

Gisi, eager to share, ignores her. "It's a small thing," she says, "but nevertheless—you know how it seemed like every time the cannons went off it made the whole city shake?"

Everyone nods. They'd all felt it. It isn't a feeling that anyone who'd experienced it is ever likely to forget.

"Well," Gisi goes on, "When I was at home, moments after one of the biggest and most frightening of those booms—it must have been very close by—it was so incredibly loud—I noticed that something was different about the room we were in. At first I couldn't tell what it was—I just knew something was different. Then I noticed the old clock. The pendulum was swinging ever so slightly. I got up from that chair I must have been sitting in without moving for at least the last three hours, and I went over to the clock and opened the glass door. The pendulum *was* swinging, very gently, so I gave it a little push to keep it going. Then I moved one of the hands of the clock just a little bit. The clock started to tick! And believe it or not, it's been going ever since then."

"No!" says Anna. "I don't believe it!"

"But it's true! I used my grandfather's pocket watch to set the clock to the right time—and this is the part you'll really never believe—it seems to be chiming on time now!"

"Well, I'll be damned," says Max. "In the midst of chaos, a small miracle."

Gisi smiles at him through her tears.

The End

Red Vienna is the first of the three volumes in the series, *Two Suitcases*. An excerpt from the beginning of *Underground*, the second volume, follows.

Underground

CHAPTER 1

BRNO

Two days later, just a week after the brutal attack on Social Democratic Party of Austria, the SDAP, in February, 1934, Max and Hugo, young party activists and secular Jews, lie squeezed under a false bottom of a truck filled with sacks of debris heading to a dump in Czechoslovakia. They arrive in Brno dusty, thirsty, and very stiff, but safe. The following day, their friend Leo arrives under the same truck bed.

During the first few days and weeks after the attack, hundreds of Social Democrats in Vienna emerge from their hiding places in basements, attics, sewers, secret rooms, to witness the widespread looting of their homes and property. Many thousands are still in prison, charged with high treason. The remains of the housing complexes, the sports clubs, schools, gardens, and union offices have all been confiscated by the Fascists. Social Democrats are still being shot on the street by the police.

"In the name of restoring order," says *Herr* Berger bitterly to his daughter Helene and granddaughter Gisi, who sit side-by-side near the window of their small apartment, sewing in the fading light. Catholic by birth, none of the three is particularly known for their political beliefs, so their lives continue relatively unchanged on the surface. Nearly everyone in their working class neighborhood is a Social Democrat, and no one is turning anyone else in. But Gisi, twenty-one and a student in medical school, will never be the same. The horror of knowing so many people who were brutally murdered by her own country's government is fresh. Images of the bombed out housing complexes where she'd spent so many happy hours haunt her. She barely leaves the apartment and worries that she won't have the courage to attend classes when they begin again.

"What's odd," her mother comments as she rethreads her needle, "is how quiet the Nazis are now. All the bombings seem to have stopped."

"That's true," her grandfather says. "I haven't heard of a single telephone box blown up since the attacks. The current violence is still targeting SDAP activists, and it's coming from our own Fascist government. But there's so much censorship. It's possible that it's not being reported."

"Or that they're collaborating with the Fascists," Gisi says.

Her mother asks, "Who's collaborating with the Fascists? What do you mean?"

"That the Fascist government made a deal with the Nazis to stop the bombings for the time being so that no one is distracted from the glory of the SDAP's defeat."

"Could well be," said her grandfather. "Nothing surprises me anymore."

Brno, Czechoslovakia

Underground

February 24

Leo presses the last of the type into the galley and holds it up to read back what he's about to print. Under the *Arbiter Zeitung* banner is the headline, "After the Fight." It's the first issue of the Socialist newspaper to be printed in Brno to be smuggled back into Vienna.

With pride, he reads the editorial on the front page:

> First, our thoughts go to our martyrs. Let us promise they have not died in vain. The liberation of the working class—the dream for which they lived and died—must still be won. The victory of economic justice must be the legacy of their deaths—that is the sacred task that we consecrate to survivors.
>
> Our thoughts also go to our prisoners who are languishing in the jails of the Dollfuss/Fey government, defenseless and captive, abused by the Heimwehr criminals. The courts have sentenced them to 10, 15, and 20 years in prison. But it will be much, much less long! Dollfuss and Fey themselves are going to stand in our Revolutionary Courts. Our immediate goal is to free our prisoners as soon as possible.

"We aren't beaten yet!" Leo says as he sets the press in motion.

www.ingramcontent.com/pod-product-compliance
Lightning Source LLC
Chambersburg PA
CBHW060429030726
47495CB00003B/794